English Homework Blues

It took the poetry specialist twenty minutes to locate anything on Gavin Gunhold. Finally, she led Raymond and Sean to a small cubicle and handed them a file folder marked "Canadian Poetry: Gunhold, Gavin."

The two boys found themselves staring at the obituary page of *The Toronto Telegram*, July 23, 1949. At the top of the sheet of yellowed newsprint was a small headline that read:

GAVIN GUNHOLD, 1899–1949

Raymond emitted a short gasp, as though he'd been hit full force in the stomach by a battering ram. "That's it. They finally got Jardine. Gunned down in the research wing of the New York Public Library." He turned to Sean. "He's dead, Delancey! Dead! *And he only wrote one poem!*"

A SEMESTER IN THE LIFE OF A GARBAGE BAG

Other books by GORDON KORMAN

A SEMESTER IN THE LIFE OF A GARBAGE BAG

Gordon Korman

SCHOLASTIC INC.
New York Toronto London Auckland Sydney

ISBN 0-590-44429-8

Copyright © 1987 by Gordon Korman Enterprises, Inc. All rights reserved. Published by Scholastic Inc. POINT is a registered trademark of Scholastic Inc.

12 11 10 9 8 7 6 5 4 3 2 1   0 1 2 3 4 5/9

*For anyone who has ever turned his eyes
skyward in grievous complaint.*

*And for Jean Feiwel and Brenda Bowen,
who made sure I didn't have to.*

One

Although Sean Delancey had not yet met Raymond Jardine, Raymond had been scouting him for some weeks now. Raymond, new to the school, was in Sean's English class, but their first official meeting didn't come until Mr. Kerr designated them partners for the semester's major project.

"Modern poetry is the true reflection of twentieth-century society," Mr. Kerr announced to the students, who were certain it was not. "When we study modern poetry, we are really, in a way, studying ourselves."

Raymond looked Sean squarely in the eye. "Delancey, S., student number 5112, junior, height: 5' 11", weight: 160 pounds, hair: blond, eyes: blue, grade point average: 3.2. Extracurricular activities: varsity basketball.''

Sean looked from Raymond to Mr. Kerr and back to Raymond again. ''Huh?''

Raymond produced a sheet of paper from his English book. ''On September nineteenth, you signed up for the Nassau County high school program in Greece next summer. Eight weeks on Theamelpos, the most beautiful island in the Aegean.''

''So?''

''So, that's *my* trip — Jardine's only alternative to another summer working in my uncle's fish gutting plant in Secaucus. Think about it. A paradise in the Aegean versus fish guts in New Jersey. Now do you understand?''

''This project will make up sixty percent of your final grade,'' proclaimed Mr. Kerr genially.

Sean's head was spinning. ''Wait a minute! What's with you? You think they're taking only one guy to Theamelpos?''

''Maximum six per school,'' Raymond retorted. ''Listen, I was the first guy to sign up for this trip. I destroyed all the notices telling about the program. They put up new notices, and I tore them down every time. I even stole the poster of Theamelpos from the travel agent in the mall. I don't know how you found out about it.''

''My mother teaches in Massapequa,'' Sean admitted almost apologetically.

Raymond looked up to the ceiling. ''His mother teaches in Massapequa,'' he repeated. ''Nice. So that's why, on September nineteenth, Jardine came to school in a perfectly good mood to find that

Delancey, S., had signed up for *my* trip. And you obviously have a big mouth, because by the end of the day, there were three more names on that list. Now there are seven of us, and maybe more on the way, going for those six spots, thanks to Delancey, S., and his mother in Massapequa. Those aren't good odds when you've got an uncle in the fish business."

Sean wasn't sure if he should chew Raymond out or say, "I'm sorry." "Listen. We're missing the assignment! Did he just say something about footnotes?"

"The bottom line is competition," Raymond went on, as though Sean had not spoken. "I didn't ask for it, but I've got it. That's why I keep complete files on every name on that sign-up sheet. I want to know exactly what I'm up against." He glanced at the paper in front of him. "This is a really bad picture of you. Did you have the mumps or something?"

Sean could bear it no longer. "What's your problem, huh? How can you take a summer trip that's supposed to be fun and turn it into a life-and-death strategy war?"

"Because I have to try twice as hard as everyone else," Raymond said readily. "You see, I have no luck — none at all, zero, zip, zilch — and as soon as I saw that seventh name go up on the list, I knew my back was against the wall because, given half a chance, the heavens will open up and dump crud all over Jardine."

"What good are those files going to do you? If they don't pick you for the trip, all the spying in the world won't help."

3

"Ah, yes. But these records are the equivalent of what the staff will look at when they're making the selection." He began to riffle through the sheets. "For example, grades. The only one of us running a D average in one of his courses is — let's see — Jardine in — uh — English." He looked disgusted. "And I just got for a partner the guy who started the run on Theamelpos in the first place. He gets great grades across the board, except for — get this — English, which won't hurt him, but will probably be enough to bury Jardine."

Mr. Kerr was finishing up his list of instructions. "The due date will be the end of the semester. No late papers accepted. Any questions?"

"How long should the finished project be?" asked a girl in the front row.

"At least twenty-five to thirty pages," the teacher replied. "Typed, of course."

"Do you at least type?" Raymond asked Sean.

"Three-and-a-half words a minute," Sean replied defiantly.

Once again, Raymond looked at the ceiling. "He doesn't type."

Q. David Hyatt was looking at the school. This was nothing unusual. Each day he would stop his new Cadillac at the edge of the school property and spend a pleasant ten or fifteen minutes just looking.

Actually, DeWitt High was a not-very-new, squalid-looking red brick building. The only thing that made it different from any school anywhere was that the Department of Energy had selected DeWitt as the field-test site for the Solar/Air Current Generating System, or SACGEN.

4

Hyatt's eyes traveled to the apparatus on the roof, a large and complicated affair that looked like nothing more than a battered hat surrounded by cylinders, squares, oblongs, and half circles, all of dull metal and glass. True, it was ugly, but to Hyatt it was the ninth wonder of the world, the eighth being the fact that he was principal of the school selected to be host to such a masterpiece. His chest swelled with pride.

An anonymous letter, probably from one of the students, had arrived at his house the day before, saying that SACGEN looked as if a giant garbage truck had parked in the sky over DeWitt High and dumped its load on the roof of the school. What appalling ignorance! SACGEN, with its solar energy panels and wind collectors, was powering the entire building from nothing more than the sun and air currents of southern Long Island. No wonder he had rushed right out to the Cadillac dealer as soon as they had begun construction. No wonder he had spent the hundred dollars to have his license plates changed to SACGEN. The principal of the school entrusted with the only working SACGEN in the world had an image to maintain.

Parking the car, Mr. Hyatt walked along the driveway to the school's front entrance. Once again, he paused. He felt a certain warm tingle every time he saw the light on in the foyer. This was coming from the sun and the wind, not from any electric company.

Suddenly the foyer lights went out, along with every other light in the building. The loving smile on the principal's face disappeared as quickly as if he, too, had been hooked up to SACGEN.

5

Oh, well. Revolutionary new inventions always had a few bugs to iron out at the last minute. No problem.

"The SACGEN system is working perfectly. This is only a test," the public address system had announced just before the entire school was plunged into darkness.

There was a loud chorus of boos, hisses, and jeers in English class and every other room in the school. It had taken the students at DeWitt only three or four days to figure out what the entire Department of Energy and Q. David Hyatt refused to accept — SACGEN didn't work. Oh, yes, the solar panels collected, and the wind rotors turned, and it did power the school. But it broke down constantly, wreaking havoc on the building's electrical system. SACGEN itself, apparently, had never been shown the schematic diagrams that proved beyond a shadow of a doubt that it worked perfectly. It insisted on being a thirty-three-million-dollar lemon.

"We're in the dark again," observed Mr. Kerr's voice from the front of the room. "I don't suppose anyone would be interested in continuing by flashlight."

His response was a sympathetic murmur.

A strange sound drew Sean's attention back to Raymond. He squinted in amazement. His new partner was drumming out ancient tribal rhythms on his desk. As if this weren't enough, he was intoning a low ritual chant in a made-up nonsense language, the only recognizable word of which was "Theamelpos." It kept coming up every second sentence or so, whined out in a strange accent.

The sound of a textbook slamming shut signified that Mr. Kerr had had enough. "Forget it," the teacher announced. "We'll try again tomorrow."

The halls were brighter, because of the large school windows, and Sean mingled with students from other classes, which were gradually being let out as teacher after teacher threw in the towel to the "test." His plan was to put as much distance as humanly possible between himself and Raymond Jardine.

"There he is!" Randy Fowler jogged up, Chris McDermott in tow. "The man, the myth, the legend, *the star!*"

Chris began running in circles, moving his hand as though dribbling a basketball. "Five seconds left, they get the ball to Delancey, four — three, he puts it up, two — one, *it's in!* Sean Delancey has won the game on a beautiful twenty-foot shot!"

Sean smiled modestly. "It was only eighteen feet."

"In that case," said Chris, "I take back my congratulations."

The halls were buzzing with the news of last night's basketball game with Freeport High. Sean had played his usual strong game, capping the performance with a game-winning basket just as the last second died.

Playing the hero was greatly improving Sean's spirits. *This* was what high school was all about — not getting forced into stupid English projects with Raymond Jardine! Pausing to shake a few more hands, he idly hoped that Mindy O'Toole, his ex-girl friend, knew about the game. Three days earlier, Mindy had dumped him because their relationship was fading, whatever that meant.

"Hi."

Sean wheeled to find his younger sister, Nikki, hurrying to join him.

"What's going on, Sean? You didn't tell me there was going to be a SACGEN test today." Nikki was a freshman, and seemed to think upperclassmen were informed about such issues as SACGEN tests. "I killed Mom's quilted pot holder. The sewing machines all went apewire."

Sean didn't feel like talking to her. There were still a lot of people around who hadn't congratulated him yet. "I'm a junior, Nik. When they need permission for a SACGEN test, they go to the seniors. We're only consulted on public executions and acid rain. Besides, that wasn't any test. The windmill died like it always does."

"Aw, come on, Sean. I'm serious. That was going to be Mom's Christmas present. Now it won't be ready until Mother's Day."

"Well, if you really step up production, and the windmill behaves itself, you might be able to give it to her for Groundhog Day."

"It's not funny, you know, Sean! Sean?"

Her brother was not paying attention. In the rapidly filling hallway, he had caught sight of Raymond in a sheltered alcove, lying flat on his back, staring up into his files, shuffling pages and studying intently.

"Probably plotting who has to die so he can go to Theamelpos," Sean muttered through clenched teeth.

His sister looked at him quizzically. "What?"

"Nothing. Let's go grab a soda or something."

Nikki nudged his arm. "Hey, Sean, there's someone waving at you."

Sean turned and followed her gaze until his eyes fell on Raymond, who had put down his notes and was beckoning and grinning.

"Who's that?" she asked.

Sean turned away quickly. "Nobody."

"But why is he waving at you?"

"He must be looking for somebody else." His brow knit. Why was Raymond smiling at him? At Sean, whom he had just accused of putting Theamelpos in jeopardy? Weird!

As they headed for the cafeteria, Nikki was still looking back at where Raymond lay, once again absorbed in his notes. "Are you sure you don't know him? I'm almost positive he was waving at you."

"Give me a break, Nik!"

Sean left school on the run that day, darting for the bus stop at top speed. He had come back from computer class to find a note taped to the door of his locker: *Catch you later. Jardine.* The mere thought of spending more time with Raymond than absolutely necessary had given his feet wings. But even this was not enough to put him on the early bus, which pulled out, leaving him standing there fuming. His computer teacher, Mr. Lai, waved at him from his seat at the back window.

Frowning, he began to saunter back toward the school building, intent on buying a Coke to pass the twenty-minute wait between buses. The local transit stank, but it was better than waiting for the school bus for two reasons: First, he'd have to hang out with Nikki and her obnoxious friends as they talked their brains out, trying to get in those last few opinions before they could get home and phone each other; second, he'd stand an increased chance of running into Raymond Jardine, a meeting much to be avoided. As he walked, he came across a battered ancient Honda motor scooter leaning against the school's chain-link fence. The red paint was so badly pockmarked with rust that Sean had to squint to make out the name scratched into the mudguard — *JARDINE*. Sean wheeled in his tracks and headed back to the bus stop. From nine o'clock to ten minutes of ten every day until Christmas, he was going to be faced with Raymond. The rest of his life was going to be Jardine-free time.

Dinner at the Delancey house was an event unmatched anywhere else in the world, Sean reflected as he toyed with his veal cutlet. It had been this way ever since Gramp had come to live with them two months before. Gramp was Mr. Delancey's father, a spry eighty-eight, and had been dragged under protest from his beloved old apartment in Brooklyn because he was "too old" to live by himself. Sean knew that if liveliness was any indication, Gramp was the youngest person in the household.

"So, Pop," said Mr. Delancey conversationally, "what did you do with yourself today?"

Gramp chewed thoughtfully. "Well, let me see. The President needed some advice on foreign policy, so I was on the phone most of the morning. And Raquel Welch dropped over for lunch. Then we had some Indian trouble in the backyard. So I had to go on the warpath. After that, I climbed Mount Everest, swam the English Channel, and came back by pogo stick through the Adirondacks just in time to whip up a cure for the common cold right here in your kitchen." He paused. "On second thought, that must have been somebody else. *I* sat around all day and listened to the grass grow."

Sean's mother tried to chuckle. "Aw, come on, Pop. Where would you be if not with us?"

"In Brooklyn," the old man said stoutly, "where I belong. I don't like grass. You never know where you stand with grass. I'll take a good sidewalk any day."

"A broken-down old building in a neighborhood teeming with street gangs and hoods," said Mrs. Delancey derisively.

"Lovely boys," her father-in-law corrected her. "They were like my own children." He glared at his son. "Better, even. Who do you think painted my apartment, and shopped for me when I was laid up with gout? And bright, too. If I ever got locked out of the house, or lost my car keys, they could get inside in a snap."

Mr. Delancey rolled his eyes. "Now, Pop, you know your building was being torn down."

The old man shook his head. "I guess when you've been on Long Island for a few years, you forget little details like the fact that there's more than one apartment building in Brooklyn."

Nikki looked into her plate. "Why are the potatoes black?"

"Don't blame me," her father said quickly. "Blame Mr. Schnitzenberger next door."

"Why?"

"He illegally gained access to the house, snuck into the kitchen, and set fire to our potatoes," said Gramp seriously.

"Come on, Pop," said Mr. Delancey. "It was the wireless remote radio-activated oven control we bought last week, Nik. You know — so Mom can set up the oven in the morning and turn it on from anywhere within forty-six miles of the house."

"What happened?" Sean asked.

"Mr. Schnitzenberger's garage door opener works on the same frequency," Mrs. Delancey explained. "The potatoes cooked for over seven hours."

"The nerve of that guy!" Gramp exclaimed, pounding on the table in anger. "Ten years ago, when he bought his garage door opener, he should have predicted this! Some neighbor!"

"Pop, *please*," said Mrs. Delancey.

"Mom's home by four o'clock anyway," Sean pointed out. "Why do we need remote control?"

"We live in an age where everyday people can be *pioneers*!" said Mr. Delancey grandly, launching into his usual speech explaining why he and his wife poured their money into every new invention on the market. "Think of the technological advancements that are made every year! In this modern era. . . ."

Mentally, Sean tuned him out. It was a great speech, but it sounded too much like Q. David Hyatt haranguing the students on the wonders of SACGEN. Besides, it was hard for Sean to be inspired when the images of past examples of the "modern era" were still fresh in his mind. It had only been two weeks since his mother's revolutionary new iron had burned through his pants, the ironing board, the floor, and most of the asbestos casing on the furnace in the basement. Before that had come the robotized light-bulb changer, which had covered the floor with so much broken glass that Mr. Delancey had been forced to call into service the turbo-charged vacuum cleaner to suck up the glass along with half of the house, including fifteen hundred dollars worth of wall-to-wall broadloom. But the *pièce de résistance* had come last year with the extreme voltage air purification modulator. Sean could still remember the humiliation he'd endured when the device had belched out an enormous toxic blue cloud over the Delancey house.

Some families had a treasured heirloom — a piece of furniture or jewelry handed down through the generations. At the Delancey house, the most prized possession was an argon-neon laser, which sat on a pedestal in the living room, projecting a tiny red dot on the bookcase. It was the current flagship of the household.

"Take the SACGEN unit in your school, for example," said Mrs. Delancey. "Where would we be without projects like SACGEN?" She was a dyed-in-the-wool SACGEN supporter, reading voraciously on the subject, and collecting pamphlets, posters, and Department of Energy bulletins. It was a source of great pride to her that her children attended DeWitt.

Sean thought otherwise. If it got around that his mother was a windmill fan, all the jump shots in the world couldn't save him. "I know where we wouldn't be," he said. "In the dark. Mom, I've told you a million times, SACGEN doesn't work. Ask Nik."

"I certainly don't think the Department of Energy would say how successful it is if it weren't so," said Mrs. Delancey sternly.

Gramp was up at the refrigerator. "The kids are at that school every day, Tina. Why would they lie?" Suddenly, he clutched at his heart. "We're out of prune juice!" He staggered back against the dishwasher.

"Pop, that's not funny," Mrs. Delancey admonished. "A man of your age shouldn't joke about things like that."

"Who's joking?" he returned bad-naturedly. He walked over to his daughter-in-law's shopping list, pulled a thick marker out of the pen holder, and wrote PRUNE JUICE in three-inch letters, filling up the rest of the sheet.

Grandfather Delancey said the words "prune juice" with a reverence and respect matched only by his pronunciation of the name "Brooklyn." For him it was the elixir of life, and a glass a day gave him the right to eat all the foods his doctor, "that medical robot," said were bad for him. He wasn't one of those grandparents who lived in the past, or couldn't seem to adjust to the modern world. But he refused to wear anything polyester, and insisted on smoking cheap cigars, called Scrulnick's. These were made only in Brooklyn, and gave off an odor halfway between smoldering hemp and sewer gas. He tolerated modern hairstyles, but firmly believed that people who wore them were robots. And he held firm to his conviction that a robot was the worst thing anybody could be. The ncarest definition Sean could think of for Gramp's use of robot was "normal." Gramp got along with Sean best of any of the family members, but that didn't mean much. Gramp called Sean "the all-American robot."

"Look at you!" Sean could remember Gramp once saying. "Varsity basketball, good grades, but not too good — oh, no. Then you'd be an egghead. And Mr. Popularity. You're perfect. How do you stand it?"

Sean had smiled painfully. "I get by."

It was a typical evening at the Delancey house. Mrs. Delancey finished marking ninth-grade papers and sat down with her husband to leaf through *Techno-Living* magazine. Nikki took possession of the phone. Gramp lit up a Scrulnick's, settled into the TV room, and turned on his favorite station, the Weather Channel. Sean joined him because, with his sister tying up the line, there would be no late messages of congratulations for his game-winning jump shot coming through.

Sean looked at the screen with distaste. "How can you stand to watch this stuff?"

Gramp's eyes never left the set. "I like it."

Sean snorted. "Des Moines — partly cloudy. Why would anybody care whether or not it's partly cloudy in Des Moines unless they were *in* Des Moines, in which case they could *see* it?" Resignedly, he stretched out on the sofa and shifted his mind into neutral. His relaxation lasted five seconds.

From outside there was the sound of a very feeble outboard motor revving and shutting itself off. Outboard? But they were five miles from the water. The only other thing that could sound like that would be an old — motor scooter? Before Sean could react, he heard the doorbell ring, and soon his mother's voice calling, "Sean, your friend Raymond is here."

Sean froze as he had a sudden vision of the note taped to his locker: *Catch you later. Jardine.* Apparently, this was later, and he was caught. For an instant, he actually considered hiding under the sofa until his new partner went away. But then the door of the TV room opened, and Raymond was upon him.

Gramp jumped up in sudden recognition. "Hey! You're the kid with the motor scooter who always runs out of gas in front of the deli!"

Raymond snapped his fingers. "You're the old guy who's always getting thrown out of the deli because of those smelly cigars! What are you doing here?"

"He lives here," said Sean coldly. "He's my grandfather."

"Yeah? No kidding! I've always wanted to meet you. I love the way you throw your bagel right through the ring salami into the Little League team portrait just before you stomp out." He grabbed Gramp's outstretched hand and shook it vigorously. "Jardine. It's an honor."

Gramp beamed. "You always kick the gas tank, and then you look up and talk to the sky. I kept wondering what you were saying."

Raymond shrugged modestly. "Oh, I just talk to *them* — you know, up there, telling them thanks for the leaky gas tank. I appreciate it. I needed the exercise anyway. That kind of thing." He took in his surroundings. "Hey, wow. The Weather Channel. And my favorite program, the *Evening Forecast.*"

Then, before Sean's shocked gaze, Raymond and Gramp sat down in front of the TV and launched into a long, involved, knowledgeable conversation all about weather. Finally, Sean could bear it no longer.

"Could I just interrupt for a second?" He looked Raymond straight in the eye. "Why are you here?"

Raymond leaned back. "Well, we have to discuss what we're going to do for our poetry assignment."

Sean stared at him. "Tonight?"

"Yeah, tonight. This project is going to be the key grade to get us to Theamelpos this summer. We've got to pull off something big."

"We? Us?" said Sean sarcastically. "I thought all you cared about was getting *yourself* to Theamelpos."

"Well, yeah," said Raymond. "But with you doing better than me in every subject across the board, it looks like if I go, you go. Now, I figure if we get an A on this project, I can pull a B for the course, and if my other grades don't go toilet on me, and everyone else has a weak semester, Jardine just might squeak by in the number six spot. And like I said, you'll be up there ahead of me. So you see, we're in this together."

Gramp shook his head. "I can't believe that my grandson is in the same class with the guy who always runs out of gas in front of the deli!" He stood up. "Well, I've got to go fill out my monthly mail order to Scrulnick's. Nice meeting you, Jardine."

"Good-night, Gramp," said Sean.

"Yeah, nice meeting you, Gramp," Raymond added.

Sean looked daggers at Raymond. What was so big about running out of gas in front of a deli? How did that make Raymond an honorary grandson? He breathed deeply. "Now listen, I'm not sure I go for this 'you and me in this together' thing. You gave me a pretty hard time in class today."

Raymond was mystified. "How?"

"You were talking like I'd jammed a knife in your back by signing up for the Greece trip — like I did something terrible."

"It *was* terrible; terrible for Jardine. Don't take it personally. You get this way when you have *no* luck."

Sean was unforgiving. "I still think you came on pretty strong."

Raymond looked at the ceiling. "That's right. Give Jardine a personality conflict with his partner. Thank you."

Sean relented. "We don't have a personality conflict," he mumbled. "We'll work on the project. I want to go to Theamelpos just as much as you do."

"Until you've spent a couple of days in a fish gutting plant, you can't know how much Jardine wants to go to Theamelpos. Now, here's my plan. Since neither of us knows beans about English, we have to do something unusual. If we pick some big-time poet, Kerr will be able to compare our paper with other ones on the same guy and, let's face it, ours is going to be lousier. So we have to dig up some Joe Blow poet nobody's ever heard of. We do a halfway decent job, and Kerr gives us an A for effort and originality. Simple."

Sean sat forward on the couch. "Why don't we pick a nice, safe, respected poet, do our best, and take whatever Kerr gives us instead of figuring the angles?"

Raymond shook his head. "If we're going to get to Theamelpos, we're going to have to scratch and claw. Trust me. You don't get any breaks when you're partners with Jardine."

"Don't you think you're overdoing it a little with this luck thing?" Sean asked in annoyance. "Did you ever consider that your luck is no better or worse than anyone else's and the real problem is your attitude?"

Raymond was patient. "Have you ever seen the commercial for garbage bags where they test the strength of the bag by seeing how many pounds of pressure they can put on it before it breaks?"

"Yeah? So?"

"So that's Jardine — a garbage bag hooked up to a hydraulic press, doing his best not to fall apart in spite of the guy who keeps turning the knob up."

While Sean was attempting to digest this, the door of the TV room opened, and Nikki peered in. "Sean, I'm having some ice cream — " She stopped short when she caught sight of Raymond. "Oh, hi. Want some ice cream?"

"No," said Sean.

"Sure," said Raymond.

They adjourned to the kitchen. Sean was still trying to figure out Raymond's garbage bag philosophy while Nikki played social director. Nothing more was said on the subject of school or Theamelpos until Raymond announced that he'd better get going.

"We'll pick our topic in class tomorrow," he said, slipping into his leather jacket, which read JARDINE in nail studs across the back. "Remember, think Mr. Nobody. And think of that picture of the beach on Theamelpos, with the entire female population of Sweden frolicking in the sun."

Sean asked the question that had been on his mind ever since their first meeting in English class. "What's so big about Theamelpos, huh? I mean, sure, it's a beautiful beach with great weather and tons of girls. But you don't have to go all the way to Greece for that. What's wrong with Cape Cod or the Carolinas or something?"

Raymond's eyes assumed a far-off, dreamy look, and for a moment Sean was afraid he would start chanting again. "Ah, Theamelpos," he breathed. "The warm breeze, sand beneath my feet — why, certainly, Jolanda, I'd be delighted to have this dance — "

"Raymond, what are you doing?"

"Shhh. Jardine is in a blissful state." Suddenly, he was back to normal. "There's luck on Theamelpos, Delancey. Magical luck. And I can't think of anyone who could use a little magical luck more than Jardine."

"Oh, come on, Raymond!" Sean exploded. "Give me a break. . . ."

Raymond was already out the door, heading down the front walk. "Seriously, Delancey," he called over his shoulder. "I've done a lot of research on this." He disappeared around the corner.

No sooner had the door shut than Nikki opened

up with both barrels. "I could just kill you!"

"Why?"

"In the hall today you told me you didn't know him!"

"It was wishful thinking," Sean said defensively. "So what?"

"So what? He's just the coolest guy in the whole school, that's all! I'll never forget the first time I saw him way back at the beginning of September. He kicked his locker so hard that the whole hall echoed, and then he looked up at the ceiling and said, 'That's right. Give Jardine a locker that won't open.' I almost died!"

Sean grew solemn. "Nik, stay away from that guy. He's crazy."

"He has so much — you know — charisma. When I tell Marilyn and Carita that I met him, they'll die!"

"Nik, this is serious stuff here! We're talking about a guy who thinks he's a garbage bag!"

"He's wonderful!" said Nikki without reservation.

"Watch your mouth." The day had been ruined by Raymond; why not the evening, too? As for the night — the mere prospect of an entire semester of Jardine would take care of the night. Magical luck! Hmmph!

Idly, he picked up a copy of *Techno-Living* magazine, which was open to the Techno-People section.

Larry Steinberg was an unemployed dockworker from Brooklyn until he traveled to Greece. There he met future Swedish supermodel Inge Dergmyr while both were vacationing on the island of Theamelpos. The two were married there and returned to Stockholm to find Dergmyr's father had sold his modest farm for a small fortune to a real estate developer. Steinberg and his new father-in-law invested the nest egg in a bankrupt brassiere factory from which they built up the biggest microchip business in Scandinavia. It was around this time that wife Inge's modeling career began to take off. Comments Steinberg, "Life is totally fantastic. . . ."

Sean threw the magazine onto the floor as though he'd just discovered it was cursed. Was there no safe haven from Raymond Jardine?

Two

Howard Newman deftly shuffled the cards and looked out at his three opponents around the table in the corner of the school corridor. "Okay. Seven-card stud, the card after the last jack is wild — unless it's red, in which case deuces are wild. If no jacks pop up, then a one-eyed jack facedown is wild, but a two-eyed jack is nothing. Got it?"

"Deal," said Sean as the two other players murmured their assent. Sean was no big poker enthusiast, but after a sleepless night of trying to figure out Raymond's garbage bag theory while haunted by the magical luck of Theamelpos, he was ready for anything that would divert his mind.

Sean and Howard had once been best friends,

23

back when Howard had been forced to repeat kindergarten as a classic underachiever. The friendship had ended a year after that when Howard had taught Sean to play poker and had proceeded to win all of his toys. Things were cool between them still, except that Sean now knew that Howard's uncanny skill with cards came from the fact that he cheated like crazy.

Expertly, Howard dealt each player two cards facedown, and opened for ten toothpicks. He was in an especially good mood that day, because *Popular Science* was sending a team of photographers over to do a feature layout on SACGEN. With this in mind, Howard had snuck out during the night and festooned the solar and wind collectors on the roof of the school with pink and white floral toilet paper. At this very moment, he knew that eleven Department of Energy engineers and an almost hysterical Q. David Hyatt were scrambling around the roof trying to unwind his little present. He dealt another round of cards.

"I hid out in the parking lot to get a good look at Q-Dave's face when he saw it. Man, it was pretty. I've never seen anybody so trashed out. Raise twenty."

Sean threw a stack of toothpicks into the pot. "Won't they just take it all down before the photographers come?"

Howard dealt again. "It's not coming down so fast. I've got twelve rolls up there. Stuck on with library paste."

"I can't understand why Q-Dave loves that stupid windmill so much," mused Randy, counting out his toothpicks.

"Oh, I can," said Howard. "I mean, I *hate* it so much. So just picture someone who's the opposite of me." He glanced to the window where a small sheet of pink paper floated gently to the ground. "You're doing fine, boys. Keep ripping."

Out of twenty-two hundred students who didn't think too much of SACGEN, Howard Newman was easily the best hater in the place. He had virtually dedicated his life to insulting SACGEN. It had been Howard who had given SACGEN its popular nickname during the first blackout of the year, which occurred at the opening assembly. As soon as the lights went out, Howard's voice boomed, "Way to go, Q-Dave! You bought us a bum windmill!"

In fact, Howard had been holding his running poker game in the third-floor washroom, which had fallen to the wreckers when the entire center of the school had been gutted to make room for the SACGEN core. As far as he was concerned, he had been unlawfully evicted, and had lost his folding cot and upwards of ninety thousand toothpicks. He had taken his game out into the hall, and was cheating his way back from bankruptcy because, as he put it, "When I get enough toothpicks, I'm going to trade them in for a nuclear warhead, and drop it on the windmill."

"Four queens," announced Howard, raking in the pot with both arms. "It's mine."

Just then, Mr. Hyatt's voice sounded over the p.a. system. "Your attention, please. Would the person or persons responsible for defacing the SACGEN superstructure please report to the office immediately."

"That's yours, too," said Sean.

25

Howard shook his head. "This is exactly why Q-Dave is never going to move up in the world. He's not too bright. Does he expect me to go down to the office and say, 'Hey, Q-Dave, here I am. I'm the guy who t.p.'d your windmill'? Now, if he was smart, he'd say something like, 'Someone has found twelve rolls of toilet paper on the roof. Would the owner please come to the office and claim them.' Then he'd have me."

Sean pocketed his toothpicks and stood up. "I've got a class."

"So do we," said Howard, dealing another hand. "Sit down."

Sean thought it over. It was only one English class — not even a lecture. They were supposed to consult with their partners on a project topic. He shuddered. That meant Raymond, fifty minutes, uninterrupted. He tossed his toothpicks back onto the table and sat down again. "Deal the cards." There was plenty of time to pick a topic tomorrow. This way he would have twenty-four more hours to resign himself to the idea of working with Raymond Jardine, and all it would cost him was a couple of hundred toothpicks.

As it turned out, he got the worst of both worlds, because Howard continued to be unbeatable at poker, and Raymond showed up anyway.

"This is impressive," Raymond announced, a painful smile on his face. "And here was Jardine thinking you were going to waste your time doing a poetry assignment. What a relief."

"Howard, Randy, Chris," said Sean quickly, "this is Raymond Jardine." He added, "My English partner." God forbid anyone should think he and Raymond were friends. An ugly rumor like that could kill a guy's image.

Greetings were exchanged all around.

"I'm the guy who put the toilet paper on the windmill last night," Howard informed Raymond.

"Right — uh — thanks. Come on, Delancey. We've got to go hit the library."

Sean was incensed. "I'm in the middle of a hand! What was the bet? Thirty-five?"

Howard raised it to fifty.

Raymond picked up Sean's hole cards and snorted. "You think you're going to beat him with three lousy queens? He's already got two aces showing, probably one in the hole, and the one in his sock makes four."

Howard blew up. "Hey, will you let the guy play, huh?"

"I fold," said Sean, tossing his cards into the center of the table. Randy and Chris did the same.

Howard slapped his forehead and looked daggers at Raymond. "Man, you just cost me a hundred and fifty toothpicks!"

"I'll make it up to you," Raymond promised. He patted his pockets experimentally. "Hmmm. Fresh out of toothpicks. Would you accept maybe a good-sized roll of dental floss instead?"

"Raymond — " said Sean warningly.

Howard stood up. "My game is off limits to you!"

"Are you sure?" asked Raymond innocently. "It's lightly waxed, shred-resistant — "

"*Out!*"

"I'll see you guys later," said Sean quickly, grabbing his toothpicks and hustling Raymond away from the game.

When they were out of earshot, Sean turned on his partner. "Nice going. Do you always make friends so charmingly?"

Raymond shrugged. "The guy cheats."

"Of course he cheats. And everybody knows it. The point is, Howard Newman is the easiest guy in the world to get along with. All you have to do is play poker and hate the windmill. He liked everybody — until you came along with your dental floss."

Raymond shook his head, indicating that he had no time for such small talk. "Never mind that. The worst thing that could have happened has just happened. Cementhead has signed up for Theamelpos."

"Cementhead? Who's that?"

"You know — the guy with a big cement block for a head, who wears shirts with no sleeves even when it's freezing. Steve Cementhead."

Sean was outraged. "His name is Steve Semenski, and he's one of my best friends. He's a good guy."

"If he was a good guy," said Raymond, "he'd stay away from Jardine's trip." From his clipboard he produced a sheet of paper and held it out to Sean. "Look at his record. It's enough to make you cry."

SEMENSKI, S., 5669, Junior
Height: 5' 10" Weight: 160 lbs.
Hair: brown   Eyes: brown

Extracurricular activities: varsity football, basketball, baseball, volleyball, track & field,

water polo, wrestling. (Who is this creep?)
Comments: Forget it! He's going to Theamelpos unless someone accidentally uses his
head to put up a skyscraper.

Sean reddened further. He and Steve had become friends in eighth grade, when the two had
formed a secret society, which had turned out to
be not so secret, since practically everybody had
known about it. Actually, the whole thing had
started as a dare to see who would have the guts
to sneak into the girls' locker room during gym
class and steal Karen Whitehead's underwear.
Gradually, a few others had been admitted to the
society, but since Karen Whitehead was the biggest
and meanest girl in the entire eighth grade, it had
been almost summer vacation before Steve had
finally accomplished the mission. This explained
why the secret society had lasted all through the
year, and was probably the main reason why Sean
and Steve were so close.

"*You* are a vicious person!" he accused Raymond. "What has Steve Semenski ever done to
you, huh? Here you are cutting the guy up when
you know nothing about him! Steve *is* on all the
teams, but he never gets to play. He's just good
enough to be the last guy who makes it before the
cut. He plays substitute for every team we've got,
but he never so much as breaks a sweat."

"That's even worse," said Raymond. "He gets a
record that makes him look like an Olympic de-
cathlon champion, and he doesn't even have to do
anything to earn it. He's never going to get injured,
he's never going to get kicked off a team for lousy

play, and he's never going to neglect one sport for another, because he doesn't play anything. This guy must have been born with a serious horseshoe up his diaper! Now I know why I have no luck. They gave it all to Cementhead! How's Jardine supposed to compete with a guy like that?"

Sean held his head. "Look, you compete with our poetry assignment, remember? Come on. Let's go to the library."

Raymond was not so easily consoled. "I'm starting to think that a poetry assignment isn't going to be enough to pull this off." He looked up at the ceiling. "Who's going to sign up next — Superman? Delancey, we need some of that extracurricular garbage on our side, too. Like it or not, we've got to get involved."

Sean frowned. "You're my English partner. Don't make me your partner at anything else."

The library was a nightmare. He and Raymond sat at a long worktable, surrounded by mountains of books, desperately skimming for a topic for their project. To make matters worse, Raymond was being difficult. He was still dead-set on the idea of pulling some obscure poet out of nowhere, bringing him to Mr. Kerr's attention with their brilliant analysis, and chuckling about it all the way to Theamelpos.

"Too famous, Delancey," Raymond said for about the fifteenth time. "Look at the universities he taught at. Look at the prizes they gave him. He's practically the Cementhead of poetry. What we're looking for is the Jardine of poetry."

"Quit calling him Cementhead," Sean growled.

"Now look. We've got to get thirty pages out of this. I haven't seen anything I could do thirty words on! Not even three!"

Raymond looked over at the book opened in front of Sean. "How about 'This really stinks'?"

"Come on! At least we can do research on some of the famous guys!"

"We've got till Friday to pick a topic. Keep looking."

Sean's mood was not helped by the fact that Mindy O'Toole was sitting right across the table. When he said hello, her return greeting sounded as though she were talking to the gas man who had come to read the meter.

"How's it going?" Sean asked her.

"*Fan*-tastic," she replied, and returned to her work, shutting him out completely.

Mindy was also in Mr. Kerr's class, and was in the library searching for a topic with her partner, Danny Eckerman. Actually, Danny was sitting passively by, munching on an apple, while Mindy slaved diligently over a volume of modern poetry. Danny was presently enjoying his second term as student body president, and was far more concerned with discussing the school's upcoming Halloween party than rendering any assistance to poor Mindy.

"Halloween is the ultimate party night," said the president, "and I give awesome Halloween parties. Remember that blowout we had last year?"

Sean, who had been there for a total of forty-five seconds en route to a different party, said, "How could I forget? It was amazing."

"An event like that practically plans itself," Danny

went on, "but there are always a lot of little details to look after, and I'm pretty busy these days. I need a couple of helpers."

Before Sean could issue a certificate of ineligibility, Raymond was out from behind a stack of books, throwing his hat into the ring. "No, you don't. You've got two helpers — me and Delancey." He stuck out his hand. "Jardine. Pleased to meet you."

Smiling with all thirty-two teeth, Danny shook Raymond's hand and then Sean's. "I love this school," the president declared emotionally. "There's always someone ready to lend a hand." From his pocket he produced a handwritten list and passed it over to Sean. "I jotted down a few basic ideas for you to take a look at. They should be helpful."

Sean could hardly contain his rage until they left the library en route to second period. Then he turned to Raymond with a vengeance. "How could you be so stupid?"

Raymond was mystified. "What do you mean? This is a real break for us. Think how great it'll look on our records — 'Student Social Activities Planning Committee.' And all we have to do is show up once or twice and help El Presidente put up streamers or something."

Sean shoved the list under his nose. "Check this out, Mr. Streamer-Putter-Upper! 'Food, drinks, music, lighting, games, contests, prizes, advertising, decorations — ' Get the picture? When you volunteer to 'help' Danny Eckerman, it means you have to do it for him! He *never* does *anything*! He's the laziest guy in the school! You saw how he had poor Mindy doing all his work for him. I'll bet she even wrote this list. See? This is *her* handwriting!''

Raymond examined the paper. "Hmmm. Doesn't leave much for him to do, does it?''

"See? And look! Our posters have to say 'Danny Eckerman invites you to a Halloween Extravaganza'! I could kill myself! We've got a thirty-page poetry assignment with no topic, and now we've got to put on the social event of the season!''

Raymond looked up at the ceiling. "Cementhead doesn't even have to play.'' He shrugged. "Oh, well. We need the Brownie points. When we're on Theamelpos, it'll all seem worth it.''

SACGEN behaved itself for the people from *Popular Science*. So for that one day, the students were given respite from the usual breakdowns and inconveniences. This was largely because the Department of Energy sent in fourteen engineers instead of the usual two. It was their policy anytime visitors were expected to see to it that their pet project's every mood was lovingly catered to. For this reason SACGEN, which was a complete turkey for the students who had to deal with it daily, had a perfect performance record in front of observers, and was fast earning a reputation in the industry as the energy source of the future.

Howard Newman was pleased to note that there was still one undiscovered small strand of toilet paper waving feebly but proudly from the back of an angled solar collector on the roof. He took out a subscription to *Popular Science* that very day.

The next day, Sean knew it was business as usual when he arrived at school to find the lights dim and flickering and a strange *ping* sound echoing through the hall every ten seconds or so.

There was only one other student by the east-side entrance. Raymond was in the process of removing the school's notice advertising the Theamelpos trip and replacing it with one that read:

COOKING WITH CABBAGE
A SYMPOSIUM

Raymond looked at it critically, nodded with satisfaction, then ripped the Theamelpos ad into sixty-four pieces and spread them among three garbage cans. He was chanting again, too, a vague Latin-American rumba melody in time with the *ping*. It was all gibberish except for "Theamelpos," which was sprinkled here and there amidst the nonsense. He wasn't exactly dancing, but there was a certain spring in his step, and his movements were all to the beat of his music.

"That's dishonest, you know," Sean said behind him.

Raymond nodded absently. "Uh-huh."

"Well, it is, you know. Never mind the notice you ripped up. What if some poor jerk really wants to sign up for" — he squinted at the new paper — "Cooking with Cabbage?"

"Oh, no sweat," said Raymond seriously. "I admit a couple of people enrolled when I tried it with Knuckle-Cracking, but there wasn't any fuss when it didn't come off. I was on the right track with Seminar on SACGEN, until Q-Dave signed up. But this is perfect. It won't even get a nibble. Any brilliant poetry topic inspiration come to you?"

"I'm too preoccupied with Halloween," Sean said sourly.

Raymond nodded sadly. "My uncle called last night — you know, the fish guts czar of New Jersey. He asked me what I was going to be doing next summer." He shuddered. "I said I was going to be seventy-five hundred miles southeast of Secaucus, flaked out on a beach, catching a rap with Miss Stockholm. He just laughed and told me I was getting a thirty-five-cent raise." He reached down to pick up his clipboard, which was leaning against the wall, and began to walk. Sean followed.

It was ten to nine, and the halls were bustling with students putting in those last few minutes of hanging out before first period. Raymond pointed to a tall dark-haired girl waiting in front of the physics lab.

"See her? She was the first one on the Theamelpos list after you. Amelia Vanderhoof. The day she signed up — poof — the first of those six spots — gone. Q-Dave and the teachers all love her."

Sean felt his lips forming into a smile as he distinctly remembered telling Amelia about this great trip that had just been proposed. "Cut it out, Raymond. Amelia's a friend of mine. She's really nice. Kind of a goody-goody. . . ." He waved at Amelia, who smiled and waved back.

"Good for her; *terrible* for Jardine. She's got a record Albert Schweitzer couldn't match. And the thing that bugs me is that she'll get *nothing* out of that trip, when it would be such a rich and rewarding experience for Jardine!" He waved the clipboard under Sean's nose. "Read about her! Read about her and weep!"

VANDERHOOF, A., 3992, Senior
Height: 5' 11" Weight: 119 lbs.
Hair: dark brown
Eyes: twin dots of India ink
Grade point average: 3.95 (I may throw up.)

Comments: *Definitely* going. Will probably put a damper on trip for everyone else. The most boring person alive.

Sean looked up to find Amelia standing in front of him, and quickly jammed the clipboard into Raymond's chest so hard that it almost winded him.

"Hi, Sean. Nice shot last Monday."

"Thanks, Amelia." Sean paused. "Uh — this is Raymond, my English partner." He was relieved to note that Raymond was polite and friendly, not to mention careful to keep his clipboard well concealed.

"So where did you live before here?" asked Amelia after Raymond had mentioned that he was new to this school.

"Oh, we didn't move," Raymond explained. "The town moved."

"Pardon?"

"My house used to be in Seaford, but the town boundaries were changed, so suddenly we're in DeWitt."

"That's really interesting," said Amelia blandly. "Oh! Time for class. Bye." She headed off.

"You never told me all that stuff about your house and the town lines," said Sean as he and

Raymond settled themselves in English class. "I figured you just moved here."

Raymond looked pained. "It's not one of Jardine's favorite things to think about. You know what was affected by the rezoning? Two gas stations, a 7-Eleven, a flower shop, a Mexican food place, and one house. One house! Jardine. I live two blocks from Seaford High, but I can't go there anymore because I woke up one morning a resident of DeWitt."

Sean rolled his eyes. "Did you like it better at Seaford High?"

Raymond shrugged. "The lights worked there. But in the end, it doesn't matter where Jardine is. *They* find him." He cast a significant glance at the ceiling. "Did you catch the late news last night? There was this great piece on that sewer cleaner who went to Theamelpos and came home to find that he'd won the lottery. Eight-point-three million smackers."

Sean scowled and tried to concentrate on the front of the room where Mr. Kerr was in a terrible snit. Ashley Bach, a transfer student newly arrived from Staten Island, had been placed in his class, thereby throwing off the partner system. As the twenty-seventh student, she had no one to work with on the term's major assignment.

"Why couldn't you have come before?" lamented the teacher. "Where am I going to put you?"

Ashley looked mystified. "Can't one of the groups have three of us?"

Mr. Kerr winced. "But that's so sloppy. If you'd come Monday, I could have made nine groups of

37

three. Or if there were two of you, an extra pair —
or seven groups of four! Wouldn't that be something!"

Ashley shuffled uncomfortably. "Sorry, sir."

"Oh, I guess it isn't your fault. Go over there
and work with" — he consulted his class list —
"Delancey and Jardine. It has no balance, but I
suppose it's the simplest solution."

Sean let his breath out, and suddenly realized
that he had been holding it. He heard Raymond
do the same. Ashley Bach was easily the most
beautiful girl in the school and quite possibly the
whole world.

"I thought you said you had no luck," Sean
whispered to Raymond.

"This must have been *your* luck," Raymond
whispered back.

The two watched mesmerized as Ashley gathered up her books and made her way over to the
vacant seat beside Sean. She smiled at them, and
Sean was positive that he saw a few soft strands
of her auburn hair stir in the breeze as she passed
the ventilation duct.

"Hi. I'm Ashley. I hope you guys don't mind me
joining your group." The expression in her green
eyes was open and friendly.

"Hi," Sean greeted her, craning his neck to con-
firm that Mindy had noticed that this vision had
been assigned to *his* group. "Welcome to DeWitt.
I think you're going to like it here. I'm Sean Delancey, and I play on the basketball team. I'm a
guard, and — " He gawked. "Raymond, would you
cut that out?"

Raymond had made a noose out of a piece of

string, and was pretending to hang himself as Sean spoke. Ashley turned to Raymond, but by that time, he had the noose off his neck and out of sight.

"Cut what out?" he asked innocently. To Ashley, he added, "I'm Raymond Jardine. Welcome aboard."

"Do you play on a varsity team, too?" she asked.

"No. I'm a free agent."

Sean groaned. "Raymond here has no luck," he informed Ashley. "None at all. Zero, zip, zilch. That's only until the summer, of course. Then he's taking a trip to the luck place — "

"*My pen's out of ink!*" Raymond howled suddenly, sitting bolt upright in his chair.

Mr. Kerr glared at the back of the room. "Is there something wrong?"

"Uh — no, sir," stammered Sean.

Ashley was digging around in her purse. "I think I've got an extra pen in here somewhere."

"Oh, that's okay," Raymond told her. "Mine writes again. It must have been a temporary defect. Thanks anyway."

Ashley was still fumbling through the many possessions in her purse, a look of consternation on her face. Then she was on her feet, heading for the door. "I left my makeup mirror in the washroom," she told a shocked Mr. Kerr. "I'll be back in a sec."

Sean grabbed Raymond by the shoulder. "The next time you let out a bellow like that in the middle of class," he hissed, "be prepared to die! Got it?"

"What was I supposed to do?" Raymond challenged. "Let you tell another person about Theamelpos? Haven't you done enough?"

"Maybe if you weren't acting like such an idiot, I wouldn't have to have said anything!"

The two partners were sitting nose to nose, glaring defiantly at each other, and a rough-and-tumble fight seemed inevitable, when Sean noticed that Mr. Kerr had stopped the lesson and was looking straight at them.

"Would you two kindly leave the room?" the teacher requested with icy politeness. "I'll send someone to bring you back when we study war poetry!"

So it was that when Ashley returned to English class, her makeup mirror tucked safely in the zipper pocket of her purse, she found her two partners standing in the hall in disgrace, involved in a heated argument.

"What's with you guys?" she asked, interposing her shapely body between them. "You shouldn't be fighting. Don't you see? If the three of us get along, we could have an *awesome* time in class together!"

This made Sean stop and think. "How awesome?"

"*Awesome* awesome!"

"Well," said Raymond cautiously, "Delancey and I, we're really serious students, so we don't want to spend too much time having — uh — fun in class. Right, Delancey?"

Sean was about to agree when the green eyes fell on him, and he was lost. "Well, we have to show Ashley a good time. She's new, and — "

"Yes," Raymond agreed painfully, "but it's *urgent* that we come up with a *top-notch* project for the poetry assignment. Right?" He glared at Sean.

40

"Well, yeah, but — "

"Right!" Raymond concluded positively. "So, Ashley, what do you know about poetry?"

"Nothing," she replied in sweet surprise. "I'm a model."

"Oh, God," said Raymond.

Sean beamed in admiration.

Ashley touched a hand to her mouth. "Oh! I forgot! I'm not kicked out of class like you guys. What a drag! We were just starting to get along. See you later. And remember: no fighting."

Sean watched her walk down the hall and disappear into Mr. Kerr's room. When he turned back again, Raymond was staring at the ceiling.

"That's right. Keep dumping your boulders and your boiling oil and your nuclear warheads down on Jardine. He can take it. He likes it."

Sean looked mystified. "What are you complaining about? She's incredible!"

"Yeah, but this chick is like a death sentence to our English project. Face it, Delancey, we needed a bookworm and they sent us a calendar girl. How could it be worse? We'll be graded harder because there are three of us now; she's going to be zero help except to interfere with everybody's concentration; Kerr's going to hate her if she carries out her plan to have an "awesome" time in his class; and the bottom line is Jardine is going to wind up with another summer of fish guts in New Jersey!" He moaned in real pain. "Yesterday everything was okay. Not great, but for Jardine that's the best that can be expected. Today — our new partner has arrived. I might as well get on the bus for Secaucus right away and save myself some trouble."

"Come on," said Sean. "I'm sure we can teach her to be helpful."

"Tell me about it. We'd have an easier time teaching Moby Dick to tap-dance."

"Listen," said Sean in growing irritation, "we're going to do the work with or without her, and we're not going to let her distract us. We're grown — teenagers, and surely we've got the strength to function despite the fact that Ashley happens to be good-looking. We're going to be so nice to Mr. Kerr that he'll forget about today and begin to love us. And never again are we going to fight in front of Ashley, which includes not hanging yourself while I'm trying to talk!" His voice rose in volume. "I promise to do everything in my power to get you to Theamelpos! And I'm making this promise for no other reason than *to shut you up!* Okay?"

Raymond brightened. "You're a real pal, Delancey. Jardine needed that boost. And we're going to work three times as hard as everyone else. We're going to get to Theamelpos no matter how many curves and spitballs they throw at Jardine. You and me, on the beach, catching rays. . . ."

The DeWitt cafeteria was a cramped affair, because almost half the space had been converted into solar energy storage batteries for SACGEN. With these batteries right next door, the temperature in the dining room always hovered in the mid to high eighties. This was ten degrees cooler than the temperature in the food line.

Thompson Food Services had sent out an inspector in mid-September to find out why sales of coffee, tea, hot chocolate, and soup stood at zero.

The man suffered heat prostration after a day in the kitchen, and was transferred to the Anchorage office some weeks later at his own request.

For a nickname for the new cafeteria, the students had looked to Howard Newman. He did not disappoint them. At an emergency assembly, after Mr. Hyatt had assured everyone the temperature would be under the eighty mark by January, February the latest, Howard had piped up, "Way to go, Q-Dave! We really needed a windmill right next to Miami Beach!" And Miami Beach it became.

Thus the students would sweat their way through lunch in varying stages of undress, captained by the intrepid Howard, at his beachfront poker location. The players would appear daily, dressed in swimming trunks and armed with towels and sunglasses. The house supplied complimentary #18 sunblock for their noses. Like the game in the hall, the toothpicks were flying in all directions and ultimately, most of them would settle in the mountain in front of Howard.

Sean was about to tie into his lunch that day when a tray was placed on the table opposite his, and he looked up into the sea-green eyes of Ashley Bach.

"Hi, Sean. Do you mind I if join you?"

Calm down, Sean told himself. She was new. She needed someone to have lunch with. She was not — repeat, *not* — hitting on him. Then again, there was the possibility that someone had told her who the hero of Monday night's basketball game was, who had pumped in that beautiful eighteen-footer. Hmmm. This situation called for casual suaveness and, if it turned out that Ashley was a sucker for a good jump shot, there was Contingency Plan B. According to Contingency Plan B, he would go for it and blow off the poetry assignment and his promise to Raymond, who could spend the rest of his life in Secaucus for all Sean cared.

"Sure, Ashley, sit down. How was the rest of your morning?"

"Bor-ing," she sang out. "I wish you and Raymond were in my other classes." She fiddled with her collar. "Why is it so hot in here?"

Sean shrugged. "The windmill." He had been planning to say something else, but she was looking directly at him, and his mind went momentarily blank. Suddenly he realized he was staring, and he flushed beet red and diverted his concentration to his hamburger. It was an eighth of an inch from his mouth when she said, "Hey! You're not going to *eat* that, are you?"

"Uh — yeah. It's my lunch."

She was all concern. "That's not food! That's poison! It'll ruin your health or, worse yet, you'll get fat!"

"But — "

"Look at that lunch! A hamburger! French fries! And a large soda! I'll bet it isn't even diet."

"Well — uh — no," Sean admitted. He glanced at her tray. Everything was green but the cottage cheese and the bowl of granola. It looked like an aerial photograph of the Amazon rain forest.

"Now let's see," said Ashley, beginning to count on her fingers. "Spinach, 38 calories; plus lettuce, 35; makes — 67; plus 106 for the granola — 148. Plus skim milk, 90 — oh, wow, I must be close to 200."

44

Sean took a tiny nip out of his hamburger and chewed inconspicuously. Ashley looked at him in reproach and began to pick delicately at the Amazon rain forest.

"Hi, guys." Raymond placed his tray on the table and sat down beside Sean. "This day is shaping up into a real lemon. Miss Ritchie just gave us the due date on our Political Science project. Next Monday. Guess who hasn't started yet? If you said Jardine, you're right." He looked down at his tray with great relish. "I *need* this delicious double-chocolate milkshake — my favorite flavor. It just might prove that it was worth my while getting out of bed this morning." Eagerly, Raymond sucked on the straw hard enough to pull a softball through a hundred and fifty feet of vacuum cleaner hose. Then he looked up at the ceiling. "Strawberry," he said with resignation.

Ashley shook her head. "You, too, with the terrible lunch! Do you want to poison yourself?"

"You got poison?" asked Raymond brightly.

This started Ashley laughing so hard that she had to leave the table to fix her makeup.

"I don't think we should tell any more jokes in front of Ashley," Raymond decided. "She's a laugher. If this ever happens in front of Kerr, we can kiss Theamelpos good-bye."

"Who died and left you Chief Decision-Maker?" Sean asked. "I'll do what I like."

"I noticed," Raymond snapped back. "Where do you get off, Mr. Let's-Ignore-the-Fact-Ashley's-Good-Looking, having an intimate lunch with her with love in your eyes?"

"It just so happens," said Sean, "that I was already here when she sat down. And what if it works out that she likes me, huh? Am I supposed to throw it away? I wouldn't expect you to hold off if it was you she was after." This was a lie. Sean knew that if Ashley and Raymond ever became a couple, he would feed himself to SACGEN or, at the very least, cry.

Raymond read his mind. "You don't have to worry. Girls like Ashley don't happen to Jardine. Fish guts happen to Jardine. I'll be satisfied if nobody gets Ashley. That way I won't be missing out on anything, so there won't be anyone to be jealous of."

When Sean caught sight of Ashley making her way back to the table, he emptied the remainder of his French fries into his mouth, cramming the rest of his burger in there, too.

Raymond was not interested in trying this tactic himself. "You want to choke, Delancey, that's your business. She can see me eating *live toads* for all I care. She'll have to accept our religious differences — she's a model, and I'm Jardine."

Ashley sat down. "Oh, you guys are so funny! Now, I'm definitely going to have to do something about the food you eat. I'm great at nutrition stuff."

Silently, Raymond mouthed the words "live toads."

Sean glared at him.

Three

The DeWitt gymnasium rang with cheers as star guard Sean Delancey sank yet another outside jump shot. Late in the third quarter, the home team held a commanding twenty-point lead over the visitors from nearby Bellmore.

It was one of those games where Sean couldn't seem to do anything wrong — his best game so far, partly because of his superb play, and partly because Ashley Bach was there to witness it. Mindy was, too, he noted with satisfaction.

Suddenly there was a discordant note in the symphony of crowd noise running through Sean's mind, an all-too-familiar voice calling, "Attaway, Delancey!" He wheeled. There was Raymond, standing at the gym entrance, waving and applauding.

"Oof!" Distracted by his English partner's presence, Sean didn't see the pass, which hit him in the pit of the stomach, winding him momentarily. Recovering, he grabbed the ball and dribbled toward the basket. Seeing none of his teammates open, he pulled up to shoot, but just as he was releasing the ball, Raymond's voice reached him again.

"Shooooot!"

The ball hit the rim with a resounding *boing!* and fell right into the hands of the visiting center.

Then Raymond once more: "That wasn't a very good shot, Delancey!"

The rest of the game was like a nightmare for Sean. Cheered, whistled, and chanted on by Raymond, he blew every single shot he attempted, frequently missing the rim and backboard altogether. By end of the quarter, the visitors had narrowed the gap to six points. Raymond kept up a steady stream of chatter as Coach Stryker dressed down his players.

"Sean! What happened to you? All of a sudden you're stone cold!"

Sean wiped his forehead with a towel. "I'll get back in it, Coach."

"It's your concentration! You're distracted! Pay attention!"

Sean started off the fourth quarter by missing two foul shots. Five minutes later, when the visiting team caught up and took the lead, he was back on the bench, sitting out the rest of the game, looking miserable.

"Everything you threw up was a brick!" snapped

the coach. "You were building a house!"

"Sorry, Coach," mumbled Sean, positioning himself on the bench at an angle where he wouldn't have to look at Ashley or Mindy in the rapidly thinning bleachers.

"We'll get 'em next time, Delancey!" exclaimed Raymond.

After the clock had run out and Coach Stryker had finished the postmortem in the locker room, Sean went to find Raymond and ban him from all future games, but his English partner had already left. So much the better. Sean probably would have gone for his throat, which was unfair. Raymond hadn't been out on the court putting up lousy shots. Raymond hadn't single-handedly stunk out the gym. All he'd done was attend — the right of any registered student. Sean sighed. Raymond's "no luck" apparently meant no luck for anyone he was associated with, too.

He headed out to the transit stop at the end of the school driveway. Heroes ride on the shoulders of their adoring fans; slobs have to wait for the bus.

The trip home did nothing to improve his mood. Dragging his feet, he dropped his gym bag in the kitchen, went to the TV room, and gawked.

The pungent smell of Scrulnick's hung in the air like a heavy fog. Gramp was following the progress of Hurricane Kevin up the east coast on the Weather Channel, with none other than Raymond Jardine at his side.

"This is the best stuff on TV," Gramp said positively. "Kevin's a hurricane you can really get behind and root for."

"You should see this, Delancey," said Raymond

with equal enthusiasm. "He kicked butt in Florida, but then he got downgraded to a tropical storm, and everyone figured he was in the toilet. But we had faith. Sure enough, he worked himself back to a hurricane and did a number on the Carolinas."

Gramp slapped his knee and put an arm around Raymond. "That's real-life drama. Who knows how far he can go? Maybe all the way to Canada!" Gramp's big ambition was for a hurricane to make it up the coast to level Long Island so he could go back to Brooklyn.

Sean counted to ten. "What can I do for you?" he asked Raymond.

"I came over to cheer you up. I figured you'd be pretty bummed out after all those shots you missed."

"I don't need cheering up," said Sean, tight-lipped.

"Sure you do," said Gramp. "Sit down. Maybe they'll show films of some of the damage."

"Yeah, come on, Delancey," Raymond added. "Plus we can work on a topic for the poetry assignment. We don't have much time, you know."

Sean glared at him. "I've already suggested a hundred topics."

"Yes, but we need one good enough to get Jardine where he's going," said Raymond patiently. "There are Nordic beauties who'll be disappointed if I don't show up this summer."

As Sean was racking his brain for something nasty to say, the door flew open, and Mr. Delancey stormed into the room, the picture of indignation.

"Don't blame me!" he exclaimed, throwing himself into an armchair. "It's not my fault, so don't blame me!"

"What happened?" asked Sean.

"The new electronic insect trap," his father replied, shaking his head.

"It doesn't work?" asked Raymond.

"Of course it works!" snapped Mr. Delancey, highly insulted. "Do you think they'd write it up in *Techno-Living* if it didn't work?" He shuddered. "It attracts insects like a charm. In fact, they're lining up from far and wide to die in it. Our kitchen looks like a bug sanctuary. Ants, grasshoppers, crickets, caterpillars — you name it. Your mother found some kind of beetle that, according to the encyclopedia, isn't supposed to live north of the equator!"

"It serves you right for buying such a dumb thing!" Sean exclaimed.

"Dumb thing?!" his father cried. "This is a technological masterpiece. It's been turned off for half an hour, and they're still swarming in like there's no tomorrow. Just don't blame me!"

"Who bought it?" asked Raymond.

"Me."

"But Dad," Sean persisted, "we've never had a problem with bugs before, and now we do, thanks to your technological masterpiece."

"That's not true. Nik saw an ant in the kitchen just last week. The poor girl was very upset."

"This is a blessing in disguise," Gramp prophesied. "We'll open up an insect zoo. We'll be rich! Who wouldn't part with a few bucks to see an equatorial beetle infesting a Long Island radar range?"

"I can see the sign," Raymond added. " 'Do Not Feed the Praying Mantises.' "

Sean looked at Raymond. "Isn't it about time you were going?"

After Raymond's departure, Sean checked on the insect situation in the kitchen. His mother had restarted the trap to kill some of the bugs already there, but that only served to attract new visitors. Sean suggested ant powder but was rejected outright. It wasn't technological enough.

Later, as he was making his way upstairs to his room, Nikki's door opened, and he was hauled bodily inside.

"Hey, Nik, what's the big idea?"

"You and Raymond Jardine were eating lunch with a girl at Miami Beach," Nikki began.

"You've been spying on me!" Sean accused.

"Not me. But Betty, who my friend Carita knows because she took a kitten the last time Carita's cat had a litter — not her friend, but her friend's friend saw the three of you, and it got back to me through the grapevine. The girl — is she with Raymond?"

Sean's head was spinning. Nikki was a freshman. When had she had time to set up a communications network? "Yeah, she was with Raymond," he said finally. "She was with me, too. We were having lunch together. So?"

"No, no!" Nikki was impatient. "Is she *with* him? Is she his girl friend?"

"Of course not," said Sean. Then, a little less positively, "Did she look like she was — interested in him?"

Nikki sighed. "Who wouldn't be?"

Sean cleared his throat carefully. "What makes

you so sure she wasn't 'with' me?"

"Oh, come on, Sean. I mean, no offense, but a girl like that — you know — a girl that pretty wouldn't — well, you know — "

Sean was enraged. "I'm on the *varsity* basketball team!"

"Yeah, yeah, Sean, I know — "

"A starter! The best player!"

She smiled placatingly. "Sure, Sean. You're right."

"I'm going to break all your records," he said tersely.

It was coming down to the wire for the submission of a topic for the poetry assignment, and Raymond and Sean worked in the library through English class and lunch period, and then long after school was over. It was at five o'clock Thursday afternoon, when the chief custodian unceremoniously threw them out of the building, that Sean decided it was time to panic.

"Come on, Raymond! Let's just pick any old poet and do him! Kerr wants our topic nine o'clock tomorrow morning!"

Raymond was adamant. "If we can't find the right poet, we may as well do no project at all. I see no point in passing eleventh-grade English if I can't go to Theamelpos."

Thus, the next morning at six-thirty, the two partners met outside the school, snuck into the library when the chief custodian wasn't looking, and locked themselves into the audiovisual room with every volume of modern poetry the library had. Raymond had even thought to bring a flashlight in case of SACGEN failure. As it turned out,

53

his batteries were stone dead, but fortunately, SAC-GEN provided them with a dim glow right up until first period. It took almost that long.

Sean had long since ceased to function. He sat crumpled in a chair, bathed in sweat, glancing at his watch, and pulling at his collar. You're going to flunk, he told himself. Everybody was going to know that the star of the basketball team flunked. They'd probably kick him off the team, too, all because this *idiot* was making him flunk. He looked narrowly at Raymond, who was still scanning books at five to nine, and decided that Sean might flunk, but Raymond was going to die!

Countdown: T minus four minutes and counting: three-fifty-nine, fifty-eight, fifty-seven —

"Here it is," said Raymond suddenly. "I say we do this guy."

"What? *What?*"

"This poet. Gavin Gunhold. Here, read it. See what you think."

"Not necessary!" Sean exclaimed. "I trust you! Here, let's get this to class!" He grabbed the book and darted out the door.

Raymond followed, calling, "Hey, mellow out. We've still got more than two minutes."

With Raymond in his wake, Sean barreled through the hall, clutching the book to his heart like a football player heading for the end zone. They arrived at English just as Mr. Kerr was about to shut the door, and fell into their seats beside Ashley.

"We've got our topic!" Sean whispered in triumph.

Ashley was filing her nails. "Topic?"

"The poetry assignment," Raymond supplied

patiently. "We've found the poet we're going to work on."

"Oh. That's nice."

Mr. Kerr began calling on the groups one at a time to present their topics for approval, which gave Sean's heart time to resume a steady rhythm as he became accustomed to the idea that no, he wasn't going to flunk after all. Then and only then did it occur to him to open the book and read the only poetry that had touched the soul of Raymond Jardine.

"Registration Day" by Gavin Gunhold (1899–   )
Toronto Review of Poetry, 1947

> *On registration day at taxidermy school*
> *I distinctly saw the eyes of the stuffed moose*
> *Move.*

Sean sat forward in his chair as though he had been hit across the back of the head with a shovel. This was it? This? Of all the poetry in the English-speaking world, Raymond had chosen *this*? Sixteen words of — of — how would you describe it?

Raymond was positively glowing with accomplishment. It made Sean want to wipe the grin off his partner's face with a sixty-millimeter howitzer.

"Isn't it perfect?" Raymond whispered ecstatically. "That Gavin Gunhold is some poet! I can hardly wait to start reading his other stuff!"

For spite, Sean handed the poem to Ashley. When she saw what Raymond had done, she'd never forgive him.

As Ashley read, both boys regarded her intently,

their eyes following the movement of her beautiful lips. Finally, she looked up and said, "Wow. That's awesome."

Sean's brow knit. "It made sense to you?"

"Of course not. But it's really heavy."

Just as Sean was weighing the pros and cons of a tantrum, Mr. Kerr called for Delancey, Jardine, and Bach.

"Gavin Gunhold is a nonconformist Canadian poet," Raymond explained to the teacher. "He's not very famous in America, but Ashley, Sean, and I find his work really interesting and enjoyable, and we're looking forward to studying him in depth." He made no move to show the teacher "Registration Day," and kept the book in plain sight but shut.

To Sean's amazement, Mr. Kerr smiled broadly. "I must say I'm delighted, and very impressed. In choosing a more obscure poet, you're showing a desire to *explore* and, as a teacher, I find that very gratifying. But you realize that your path will be more difficult. Are you sure there's enough material for such a major study?"

"Oh, yes," said Raymond. "He's been writing since the forties."

"Well, that's wonderful, then," Mr. Kerr pronounced heartily. "Carry on. And enjoy yourselves."

Sean walked back to his seat in a daze. Well, how about that! Raymond was right! Pick the last poet anyone would ever think of paying attention to, and everything else falls into place. As for "Registration Day," maybe it wasn't so bad after all. If the *Toronto Review of Poetry* thought it was good enough to publish, who was Sean Delancey to say no? He looked at his partner with a newfound respect — a cautious respect.

Even Ashley was impressed, commenting, "Wow, you guys are smart," before returning to her nails, the poetry assignment completely out of her thoughts.

"So what's our next move?" Sean asked Raymond on the way to Miami Beach at lunch that day. "I guess we should read up on Gavin Gunhold and pick which of his poems we're going to do, huh?"

Raymond had other ideas. "We've got half a semester to worry about that kind of stuff. Our problem now is to pull off that Halloween party."

Sean groaned. The agony and triumph of topic selection had completely driven Halloween from his mind. Now, less than two hours after deciding maybe Raymond wasn't such a bad guy after all, Sean remembered the most recent reason he wanted to strangle his partner. "You know, this project isn't going to be easy, and Kerr is expecting a lot from us. I wish you hadn't opened your big fat mouth to Eckerman!"

Raymond was shocked. "Are you crazy? Do you have any idea how good Student Social Activities Organizing Committee is going to look on our records when the staff decides who's going to Theamelpos and who's going to Secaucus? This party is important. It's our first step toward appearing like well-rounded dudes. Which, of course, we aren't, but who's going to know?"

"You see, Raymond. . . ." Sean paused. "I never

go to these school dances. I like house parties better. Sure, I might drop in for a few minutes on my way to someplace else — you know, just to put in an appearance. But how can I plan what I've hardly ever seen?"

Raymond frowned. "Seriously?"

"Yeah!"

"But what happened to the all-American, Mr. Popularity, Varsity Big Man on Campus?"

"He didn't go to school parties."

Raymond looked at the ceiling. "That's right. Give Jardine a hermit for a social planner. Go heavy on the dull. Nice touch."

Sean bristled. "Let's get this straight here. I don't go in for the school stuff because I've got too many other parties to go to that are a lot better. So shut up about dull. You're no one to judge — "

"I'm not judging — I'm dying! We're in trouble, man! How was I supposed to know there was another eight-ball in the world? Dances? Who goes to dances when you're Jardine? It's everybody else I always figured has a rich social life!"

Sean clenched his teeth and fists at the same time. "If you listened to any mouth but your own, you'd have heard me say that I *have* a rich social life. The only hermit is you."

"I've got an excuse. I'm Jardine. Let's not lose sight of the issue here, Delancey. We are standing on the threshold of a *really lousy* party. We need help."

"Who's going to help us? Eckerman? He's never planned a party in his life! Who do you know who knows anything about parties?"

They entered Miami Beach, each flinching slightly

from the oppressive heat, as though they had just come through an airlock into a blast furnace. There, waiting for them outside the cafeteria line, stood Ashley Bach. And suddenly they were standing still, grinning at each other.

"Are you thinking what I'm thinking?" asked Sean, vaguely disconcerted that a great person like himself could be sharing thoughts with Raymond.

Raymond nodded, terribly pleased. "Eureka. Doth I see before me a party goddess?"

"Hi," said Ashley brightly. "I'm glad I caught you guys. Go get a table and sit down. I'm picking out lunch today."

Oh, no, thought Sean, having a sudden vision of the Amazon rain forest.

"Terrific," said Raymond. "I could use a change."

Sean raised pleading eyes to Raymond, who looked back sternly. Ashley trotted off into the food line, and the two boys selected a table.

"Aw, Raymond," Sean was whining, "why did you have to encourage her? You know what kind of food she's going to bring us — all that stupid healthy model stuff. Look at her over there in the salad section. We're going to get nothing but sprouts, and roots, and leaves, and grass."

"If she'll bail us out on this party, I'll eat her whole front lawn," Raymond promised devoutly. "Today we bite the bullet, gag down the granola, and from now on, we just make sure we get to Miami Beach before she does. One lunch of garbage to pull our party up out of the toilet — fair enough."

"You're not planning to dump it all on Ashley the way Eckerman dumped it all on us, are you?"

Sean asked. This, he reasoned, was out of concern for another human being rather than the fact that he was dying to date Ashley.

"Of course not," said Raymond. "We just need advice. If she wants to help us beyond that, that's up to her."

They sat, anticipating the unpleasantness that was to come in the form of lunch, and watching the excitement at the beachfront poker game. There was much cheering and shouting going on, because Howard actually seemed to be losing a few hands that day. Nearby, Steve Semenski and some of his friends were tray-surfing, another activity developed by Howard. The surfer stood balanced on a cafeteria tray atop a long dining table, while two others hoisted the end of the table over their shoulders, sending him careening down the "wave," executing hot-dog maneuvers. It was one hundred percent against school rules, but naturally, the teachers never came anywhere near Miami Beach. It was too hot.

As usual, Steve was the biggest show-off among the surfers, strutting around in loud bathing trunks and a sleeveless muscle shirt. He immediately caught the jaundiced eye of Raymond.

"Look at him! Cementhead! Doesn't it make you want to cut his head off and stick it in the sand on Easter Island?"

Sean was annoyed. "Listen! His name is Steve, and he's a good friend of mine. So quit calling him Cementhead."

Ashley appeared, her tray holding an expanse of green. "Now you guys are going to learn what real good eating is all about."

What followed was a nutritional nightmare for Sean as 217 calories (Ashley's calculations) made their way down his throat and lodged themselves along his digestive tract. It was exceedingly painful to be so hungry, and to be faced with a plate of food, and yet have absolutely nothing to eat. He would have traded his parents' argon-neon laser, his grandfather's supply of Scrulnick's, and thrown in Nikki for a single bag of potato chips. He could see that Raymond, too, despite his resolve, was suffering, and it brought him some small comfort. The only other positive thing that Sean could see coming out of this experience was the fact that Ashley was watching them eat with loving pride.

Due to the crunching, conversation was limited, and the Halloween party didn't get mentioned until the last spoonful of bran had scratched its way down their throats. Ashley's ears perked up at the mere mention of the word "party."

"You guys are incredible! You're the most happening guys in the school! I *love* Halloween parties! Can I help you with it?"

Raymond pretended to consider this. "I guess so," he said finally. "Got any ideas?"

"Of course! The most important thing at a party is the music. We'll hire my friend from the city. He's a great deejay. He's got a giant sound system and an amazing light show. And he'll emcee the trampoline contest."

Sean, who had been nonchalantly searching for stray chip crumbs on the table, suddenly snapped to attention. "Trampoline contest?"

"Yeah! It's all the rage in the city. The prize goes to the person with the best costume who can do

61

the most stuff on the trampoline. It's so fun! Plus, we'll need to make sure all the kids know about the party. I take art, and I bet I can get my whole class to paint us up some great posters. Oh, parties are my favorite things! We'll need soda, and pizza, and chips, and peanuts, and create-your-own banana split. . . ."

Sean checked to make sure his tongue wasn't hanging out on the table. It was cruel to list such a menu in front of someone who had just finished an Ashley Special. Raymond, too, appeared a tad peckish, but nothing could mitigate his air of triumph as Ashley described the Halloween party of everyone's dreams, detail by detail. When she finished outlining her plans, Raymond actually applauded, and Sean joined in, too, saying, "Gee, Ashley, you're going to be a great — uh — help."

"*Surf's up!*" came a bellow from across Miami Beach.

Everyone turned. There was Steve, poised and waving, perched on a tray on the longest dining table on the beach, manfully awaiting the Big Wave.

"Hang ten!" chorused the many spectators.

Two stalwart surfers hoisted the end of the table, and Steve slid down at breakneck speed toward the floor. Just before point of impact, his bare feet kicked the tray backward high into the air. It spiraled down, and Steve caught it deftly with one finger, to tumultuous cheers from his audience. It was well known that Steve was the best surfer in Miami Beach.

"Hey, Howard," called Steve. "What did you think of that one?"

Howard, who had discontinued his poker game

in an attempt to stem his losing streak, adjusted his sunglasses and rolled over onto his back. "I'm working on my tan."

Ashley, who had been watching the surfing with great interest, sighed dreamily. "Who is that absolutely gorgeous guy?"

Sean stiffened. "Who?"

"The one who just surfed. The one in the black muscle shirt."

Sean goggled. "You mean *Cementhead*?"

Raymond looked up at the ceiling and mouthed the words, "She likes Cementhead."

Ashley leaned across the table, her sea-green eyes animated. "You know him?"

"No!" chorused Raymond and Sean.

By fifth period, Sean's hunger pangs had changed into a great numbness in his stomach. By sixth, the numbness was a queasiness with a touch of heartburn. And by seventh, he was in the corner stall of the second floor washroom, feeling not very well at all. He cursed Ashley, not only for the killer lunch, but also for turning her beautiful eyes away from the ever-so-worthy Sean Delancey to cast them upon the ever-so-cementheaded Steve Semenski. He hadn't been so jealous since eighth grade, when Steve had proved he had the guts to sneak into the locker room and steal Karen Whitehead's underwear.

He heard the washroom door open, and then a few footsteps on the tile floor. There was the squeak of a worn-out tap, and the sudden rush of water from air-bound pipes.

"That's right," came a voice. "Give Jardine a

booby-trapped sink. Soak him good. He wasn't comfortable in those dry clothes anyway."

"Pssst! Raymond — is that you?"

"Hi, Delancey. Nice day for a stomach-pumping, isn't it? I take it lunch has done a number on you, too."

Sean groaned. "I'm dying."

Raymond entered the next stall. "You're lucky. I think I'm going to pull through."

There was an awkward pause, and finally Sean ventured, "I've been thinking about Ashley and Steve."

"Another one of Jardine's favorite subjects."

"What are we going to do about it?"

"Do? There's nothing we can do except hope and pray that they never get together." He thought it over for a moment. "Or we could kill Cementhead — or Ashley — or ourselves. Take your pick."

"So you don't think we should tell Steve that she likes him," said Sean hopefully.

"I don't know the purpose of life, Delancey, but I've already ruled out the possibility that Jardine was put on this Earth to make things more pleasant for Cementhead."

"He wouldn't be good for her anyway," Sean decided.

"Right. He'd string her along all year, and then blow off to Theamelpos in Jardine's spot, leaving both her and Jardine brokenhearted. She won't even be able to talk to me about how cruel life is, because I'll be in Secaucus experiencing it first-hand."

At that moment, the lights died without warning, and a strange rattling sound rose in the building.

Sean groaned. "Oh, no! Not the windmill! Not *now*!"

Suddenly, the electricity came on again, and Mr. Hyatt announced, "There is no cause for alarm. The malfunction has been corrected. . . ."

In the background, the p.a. carried the half-demented voice of Engineer Sopwith shrieking, *"For God's sake, DO something!"*

Then the lights went off again, and only the rattling remained. As Sean was preparing himself mentally to wait out the blackout, he heard a new sound. In the next stall, Raymond was drumming and chanting a sort of souped-up fox-trot in time with the SACGEN noises. And there it was again, so religiously repeated amid the strange sounds — "Theamelpos . . . Theamelpos . . . Theamelpos. . . ."

Four

The red motor scooter putt-putted down Sean's street, with Raymond hunched over the handlebars, Sean hanging on for dear life, and six dogs of varying mixed breeds in hot pursuit. The sound was a combination of the scooter's feeble motor, and full-throated bays, barks, and yaps as they turned into the Delancey driveway in a wide, ungraceful arc, stopped, and dismounted, ready to do battle with their canine pursuers.

Sean, who had been avoiding dogs ever since his aunt's deranged Chihuahua had taken a chunk out of his leg (hampering his jump shot for almost a month), smiled weakly at the pack. "Nice doggies."

Raymond was disgusted. "That's not how you talk to dogs. *Beat it! Scram! Get out of here! Go guard a prison camp!*" The dogs scattered. "That's how you talk to dogs."

The partners had spent that Saturday afternoon at the DeWitt Public Library. Determined to get a good head start on the poetry assignment, Sean had resigned himself to a few extra hours of Raymond. He had searched the library for information on Gavin Gunhold, but unfortunately, the files had absolutely nothing on the Canadian poet.

"Don't sweat it," was Raymond's opinion. "To get info on a total nobody like Gunhold, we're going to have to go to the big library in New York."

And Sean agreed. So, to pass the time while Raymond worked on his political science project, due Monday, Sean wrote up an analysis of "Registration Day." Briefly, the narrator represented the human race, and the stuffed moose with moving eyes was nature abused and exploited by man. It took twenty minutes, and filled three quarters of a page. From there Raymond directed him to the periodical section to study articles about people whose lives had blossomed after a trip to Theamelpos.

Raymond, meanwhile, was handling his new project very much like the old one. Faced with an in-depth analysis of the political system of the country of his choice, he had scoured the globe in search of a nation so insignificant and small that "How much fancy politics could there be for me to not understand?" Of the two-hour library visit one hour and fifty-seven minutes were spent searching for this wondrous country; the remaining three were spent rejoicing when he found it.

"This place is perfect! They have a king, period. That's the whole government. If the king wants something, that's it. I love it! None of this representation of the people, no elected officials, no courts, no Bill of Rights to get Jardine all mixed up. Just King Phidor, long may he reign. What a break! I can write it up tomorrow night in half an hour."

Sean was looking forward to borrowing the car and dropping in on Steve, and maybe Randy or Chris. But as he started to say his good-byes to Raymond, the front door flew open, and out shot Nikki like a Polaris missile. In enthusiastic detail, she described the chocolate cake that Raymond simply had to have a piece of, and led him into the house. As an afterthought, she mentioned that Sean could have some, too, if he felt like it.

When Sean got to the kitchen, a cozy domestic scene was being enacted, and his worst fears were realized. Marilyn and Carita, Nikki's two best friends, fabled for their ability to talk a farm auctioneer into the ground, were seated at the table, fussing over Raymond.

Raymond seemed entirely oblivious to their adoration. "Hey, Delancey," he mumbled, his mouth full. "Have a seat. The cake's great."

Stiffly, Sean sat down and cut himself a small piece of cake as the giggling bubbled up around him.

"And you call yourself a hurricane!" came a bellow from the TV room. *"You couldn't even make it as scattered showers! You're a bush league bum!"* The door was kicked open, and out stormed Gramp, his head engulfed in a cloud of Scrulnick's smoke.

Silence fell at the kitchen table as he approached, cut himself an enormous slab of cake, and sat down, sulking.

"Kevin?" Raymond asked him sympathetically.

Gramp nodded grimly. "Kevin. He's dead, fizzled out into the Atlantic. I tell you, Jardine, you give your heart and soul to a storm, follow it through thick and thin, and *this* is how it repays you. I haven't been this depressed since the Dodgers broke up."

"The Dodgers moved, Gramp," said Sean. "To California."

"The real Dodgers broke up," the old man insisted stubbornly, "and some crook started up another team in Los Angeles with the same name and the same players."

Raymond nodded. "My father always says that. He's still a member of the Brooklyn Dodgers Booster Club."

Gramp slapped the table approvingly. "You and me, Jardine, we're the only sensible ones around here."

"So, girls," Raymond said to Nikki and her friends, "are you all psyched up for the big Halloween party? Meet the organizers, two superinvolved members of the school community!" He put his arm around Sean's shoulders, only to have it slapped away.

"Fan-tastic!" Nikki exclaimed. "And I'll bet you know everything there is to know about throwing a great party."

"We try," said Raymond modestly, whereupon all three girls pledged to be there, sporting costumes so inventive and brilliant that Raymond would not be able to believe it.

Gramp looked at Sean oddly. "I thought you said only stooges and goody-goodies worked on those school parties."

"Yeah, well, I sort of got roped into it."

The old man shrugged. "It wouldn't hurt for Mr. All-American Robot to get up off his throne and see what life is like down here in the trenches."

There was an insistent kicking at the front door. Nikki ran to answer it, and returned a moment later with her father, who was struggling with a huge, awkward package. He set it down on the kitchen floor with a thud, and announced, "Guess what I bought!"

"What?" asked Sean.

"Guess," his father persisted.

Gramp regarded the bulky parcel. "A house?" he ventured innocently.

"No!" Impatiently, Mr. Delancey ripped off the wrapping paper to reveal a large metal box covered with dials, switches, and meters. "It does the dishes!" Five pairs of eyes traveled to the family dishwasher. "Oh, yeah, I know we have a dishwasher. This is better. It uses ultrasound." Eagerly, he gathered up the cake-smeared plates and loaded them into the front chamber of the device. Then he plugged it in, flipped the ON switch, and counted off ten seconds. When he opened the door again, there was nothing there but a neat pile of fine powder on the acrylic floor of the chamber.

"It works!" cried Gramp. "They're spotless!"

Marilyn and Carita were beset by a terrible case of the giggles. Mr. Delancey stared dumbly into his machine. "Don't blame me," he said finally.

Suddenly, Raymond announced, "Well, I guess

I'd better be going. Nice to see everyone. Take care, Gramp."

"Don't be a stranger, Jardine."

Sean walked his partner to the door.

"I wanted to stick around for the tantrum," said Raymond, slipping into his jacket, "but I figured it wouldn't be polite."

Sean bristled. "Hey!"

"No offense, Delancey. I mean, every family's got its share of — well, not exactly nuts, but — "

Sean was furious. "I know a family on the Seaford-DeWitt town line that's got a *real* problem! This guy thinks he's a garbage bag!"

"That's my point," said Raymond good-naturedly. "*Every* family. See you Monday." He walked out, leaving Sean clawing at the screen door.

On Monday morning, the New York *Daily News* published a long article on SACGEN and, naturally, Howard Newman purchased the paper to "read up on the enemy and find his weak spots." Thus was the morning poker game interrupted, and Sean sat with three others, listening to Howard read aloud, and occasionally insert his own comments.

" 'Despite SACGEN's unblemished record, students at DeWitt High School are inexplicably resentful of the project.' See? They know about me. 'It is referred to disparagingly as The Windmill, and no opportunity is lost for putting it down in typical teen fashion.' Hear that, guys? We're typical teens. 'Says Principal Q. David Hyatt' — that's Q-Dave — 'If SACGEN were any kind of nuisance or inconvenience, this attitude would be understandable. But with SACGEN working perfectly, this can only be interpreted as an immature rebellion against all forms of authority.' Oooh, heavy stuff, Q-Dave.''

Everyone laughed except Sean. ''Now, this isn't fair!'' he declared hotly. ''They're making us look like idiots to everyone who reads newspapers, because they refuse to admit SACGEN won't work! Something should be done about this!''

''I t.p.'d the windmill, but it didn't help,'' said Howard thoughtfully. ''Maybe I should grease the control room floor.''

Randy Fowler shook his head. ''If we phone the paper and tell them about the blackouts and breakdowns, they'll figure we're making it up just to do rebellion against formations of authority, or whatever it said.''

''Well, this is really lousy,'' said Sean. ''They crack on us for being immature, and here's Q-Dave telling lies in the newspaper. 'Working perfectly'!''

''There's more,'' said Howard. '' 'Hyatt adds: ''We are confident that the students will outgrow their thoughtless reaction and come to look at their education in the shadow of this technological marvel as an honor and a privilege.'' ' Now this — '' he slapped the paper '' — *this* is why Q-Dave is stuck in a dead-end job. He's a nice boy, but he just hasn't got the brains to make it. He knows nothing about people. I'm not going to accept the windmill as *anything* until it's a shoeboxful of radioactive dust. And if that's immature, well, then, goo-goo, ga-ga.'' He laughed at his own joke, but his smile faded as Raymond walked up to the group. ''Oh, no. You again.''

Raymond ignored him and beamed at Sean. ''Here

it is. Isn't it a beaut?'' He thrust out a white folder, which bore the title "The Political System of the Kingdom of Pefkakia,'' by Raymond Jardine.

Sean goggled and turned pale. "Oh, Raymond! Not Pefkakia!''

Raymond looked puzzled. "What's wrong, Delancey? I thought it was pretty good.''

"But — but — '' Bereft of speech, Sean grabbed Howard's newspaper and pushed the front page under Raymond's nose. The banner headline blazoned:

PEFKAKIA ROCKED BY MILITARY COUP
CROWDS CHEER AS KING PHIDOR BEHEADED
IN PUBLIC SQUARE

Raymond grimaced. "I don't suppose that there's another country called Pefkakia that just so happens to have a king named Phidor.''

"Oh, Raymond!'' was all Sean could say.

Raymond looked up at the ceiling. "That's right. Bull's-eye. Keep lobbing those poison darts in there at Jardine. Jardine's finished his project? Good! Let the revolution begin!'' He looked pleadingly at the postage-stamp-sized photo of King Phidor during better days. "Your majesty — what happened? Where did we go wrong? But what do *you* care? You're lucky! You're dead! It's Jardine who's left to face the music!''

Randy looked at Raymond. "You did a politics project on a government that got overthrown on the due date? Man, did anybody ever tell you you've got no luck?''

"I suspected it," said Raymond ironically.

"But what are you going to do?" asked Sean.

Silently, Raymond produced a pen and, to the title "The Political System of the Kingdom of Pefkakia," he added "(Until Yesterday)." He shrugged. "I guess it wouldn't be so bad, except that I put that the system works great, and that King Phidor is beloved by all the people. What a drag."

It was a rough week for SACGEN — three defective solar collectors, a wind tunnel malfunction, a leaky battery that ate half the floor, seven broken rotor blades, a transformer fire, and a stink bomb in the control room (courtesy of Howard).

"Would the person responsible for placing ill-smelling material in SACGEN Control Central please report to the office at once," came Mr. Hyatt's voice over the p.a. system.

"There he goes again!" said Howard incredulously. "The boy's got no future! *Think*, Q-Dave!"

In addition to these breakdowns, SACGEN also decided that it no longer intended to heat the DeWitt pool. Sean discovered this during Monday's swimming class when he dove into the fifty-six-degree water in one heart-stopping shock. As the week progressed, however, the water temperature dropped further, at a rate of two degrees per day so that, by Wednesday and Thursday, Monday's freeze-out seemed as if it had been a sauna bath.

Engineers Sopwith and Johnson worked around the clock, but could only report that, in their opinion, everything was functioning perfectly. So Mr. Hyatt informed Coach Stryker that the pool was just as it should be, whereupon the coach offered to push the principal into the water for a first-hand fact-gathering session. In the ensuing scuffle, a compromise was reached. The water would stay cold, but Hyatt would put in a requisition for thirty bedsheet-sized Turkish towels for the students to shiver in between dips.

Concerned with the school's rapidly growing hostility toward SACGEN, Mr. Hyatt called a special assembly so that Engineer Sopwith could present an updated report on progress. He was laughed off the platform when SACGEN seized up a scant three minutes into his speech, plunging the building into darkness. Though the power failure only lasted sixty seconds, by the time the lights came on again, the auditorium was empty.

Undaunted, the principal printed up a glowing notice to send home to the parents, and each student was given a copy. That was the day of Howard's famous schoolwide paper airplane races out of the third floor east study hall window. The town of DeWitt registered a formal complaint on behalf of its street cleaners, but Howard reported the contest an unparalleled success as several hundred notices were flung into the wind before his very eyes. The winner of the contest was Steve Semenski, whose airplane managed to plunge down the open sunroof of a Maserati doing about eighty-five on the nearby highway.

"Born with a horseshoe up his diaper," confirmed Raymond, whose own entry had been doing nicely until a sudden draft had sucked it down a sewer.

"That's his name!" Ashley whispered to Sean. "Steve. What a great name!"

Not half as great as his other name, Sean thought as he watched Steve take victory bows, resplendent in his PROPERTY OF THE DALLAS COWBOYS TRAINING CAMP T-shirt with the sleeves cut off. As a friend, he should really say something to Steve, but Sean had already told Ashley that they didn't know each other. He was hoping that Steve would find another girl friend soon. Ashley, seeing him unavailable, would look to the men closest to her, Raymond and Sean. She would pick the one with the best jump shot who didn't think of himself as a garbage bag. Aloud, he said, "Can we go to the art room and see those Halloween party posters now?"

"Maybe I should go over and congratulate Steve," Ashley mused thoughtfully.

"Well — uh — you know how impatient Raymond can get."

She looked surprised. "He can?"

Sean nodded. "He may not look it, but he can turn into a madman," he whispered confidentially. "And he's very anxious to get those posters up on the walls."

The art wing was on the first floor near the main offices. Ashley sat Raymond and Sean down at a table and pulled a stack of posters from a low shelf.

"I think you're going to like these," she said, placing the stack on the table. "The whole class spent Monday and Tuesday painting them up."

Raymond and Sean lifted up the top poster and stared.

ARSE PRESENTS
SUPER HALLOWEEN PARTY
FOOD, DRINKS, GREAT MUSIC
HALLOWEEN TRAMPOLINE COSTUME CONTEST
FOR THE MYSTERY PRIZE
DON'T MISS IT!

She smiled proudly. "What do you think?"

"Nice," said Sean, wondering why Raymond had suddenly gone so silent and so pale.

Finally, Raymond found his voice. "But Ashley, why does it say" — he pointed to the top line — "*that?*"

"That? That's us. Our initials — Ashley, Raymond, Sean, and Eckerman — I couldn't remember his first name."

"I get it," said Sean.

Raymond was positively white. "The other kids who worked on them — they didn't — say anything about the posters? The wording maybe?"

"The whole class really liked them," said Ashley. "I think everyone's favorite part was the initials thing. They thought it was clever."

Raymond looked up at the ceiling. "Oh, it was."

After Ashley had gone, Sean turned to Raymond. "What's eating you?"

"The initials — the word!"

Sean stared at the posters. "What word? I don't know it."

"Sure you do! You're sitting on it!"

Light dawned on Sean. "Oh, now I remember. Gramp sometimes says that. It means — "

"Yeah! And we have to get it out of there!"

Sean flipped through the stack. The posters were identical, and apparently, the artists had all given special attention to those first four letters, using bright colors, stripes, and polka dots. One enterprising soul had even highlighted it with sparkles.

Sean's eyes darted from Raymond's morose face to the poster he was staring at with horror and loathing. Sean snickered.

"Don't laugh, Delancey," said Raymond, clearly in agony. "This isn't funny."

"I think I'm going to laugh, Raymond."

"A terrible thing has just happened to Jardine. Don't laugh."

Sean thought he was going to burst. "I've got to laugh, Raymond! I'm starting to laugh!" He put his head down on the table and roared with mirth. "I'm sorry! It's *so* funny!"

Raymond cast him a withering glare. "Okay, laugh. You can laugh even harder when the teachers ask Eckerman who put up the posters with the *word*, and he tells them Jardine. And they say, 'Jardine? Isn't that the guy who formerly had a chance to go to Theamelpos, until now?' Man, is that going to be funny!"

Sean managed to get himself under control. "Oh, come on, Raymond. She meant well. And the posters are great. So what's one little word?"

"Nothing, after we paint it over. Now — what can we put instead?" He leaned over the table and pulled several jars of poster paint and some brushes off a shelf.

"Raymond, you can't. Ashley's really proud of the initials thing. You'll hurt her feelings."

Raymond dipped a brush into the background

color and looked at the poster critically. "Jardine's heart bleeds for Ashley's feelings."

"Well, at least we can do something like this." Sean grabbed the brush and painted over the "E." Then he took a fresh brush and, in red, drew another "E" at the beginning of the word. "See? We keep the initials, we change the word, and we tell Ashley we had to do it because Eckerman insists on his initial being first."

"Yes, but now it says EARS," said Raymond.

"It does? Hmmm. Kind of stupid, huh? Well, at least it's better than what it said before."

Raymond sighed heavily. "EARS it is. It might even get us the sympathy vote for Theamelpos — you know, 'Let's send the EARS guys. They're so stupid they deserve a break.' And it just occurred to me that, since Ashley's doing ninety percent of the work for this party, it's a good idea to keep her happy."

"That's a terrible attitude," said Sean. "Ashley's a good friend of ours."

Raymond pulled the second poster from the pile and began working on it. "Good friends of Jardine don't fall in love with Cementhead."

Sean glared at him, but deep in his heart he agreed.

The next Monday, Sean arrived at school to find Raymond taking down his old Cooking with Cabbage poster and replacing it with one that read:

COOKING WITH CABBAGE CANCELED
DUE TO LARYNGITIS CONTRACTED BY
GUEST CHEF MONIKA VON KALBEN

Sean smiled sardonically. "A lot of people are going to be heartbroken over this."

"Forty-six names," said Raymond in disbelief. "I stopped by the guidance office just to check the sign-up sheet for my fake cabbage symposium, and there were forty-six names on there. Forty-six. Springsteen wouldn't get that kind of turnout from this school. What's the matter with these people? And guess who, too? Ashley was on it, and Amelia Vanderhoof, Miss Ritchie, *your* sister, Cementhead. . . . Why does Cementhead want to know about cabbages? They don't come in barbells."

"Come on, don't call him Cementhead."

Mindy O'Toole came rushing down the hall, peering in doorways. She spotted them and ran over. "Hi, I've been looking all over for you guys. You're helping Danny with the Halloween party, right?"

"No," said Raymond. "We're *doing* the party while Danny sits on his derriere."

Mindy looked at Sean strangely for a moment, then continued, "Well, Danny wants to know why it says EARS on all his posters."

"We don't know anything about *his* posters," Raymond said icily. "If he's asking about *our* posters, tell him it's none of his business why they say EARS. Tell him he should be grateful they don't say NOSE, as in 'punch in the.' "

"They were supposed to say 'Danny Eckerman Invites You,' you know."

"We thought it over," said Raymond, "and we decided that EARS was more appropriate."

"Well, I'll tell Danny, but he's not going to like it."

"He doesn't have to like it," said Raymond. "It's not his party. If it wasn't open to the whole school, he wouldn't be invited. And you can tell him one more thing: Jardine is not pleased with him."

She turned to Sean. "What's going on? Why's he talking like that?"

Sean was really enjoying the look of dismay on Mindy's face. "I don't have the slightest idea."

Mindy looked confused and ran off.

"Wow!" exclaimed Sean. "What is this — clamp-down week?"

"This," Raymond replied, "is aggravation. Allow me to tell you what else Jardine saw in the guid-ance office this morning. Two more names on the Theamelpos list — the Sap family."

"You mean the Sapersteins? They're not a fam-ily. They just happen to have the same name."

"I figured that out," said Raymond, pulling a sheet of paper out of his clipboard. "I raided their files, which, incidentally, were right next to each other."

SAPERSTEIN, MARK/MARLENE,
3567/3568, Seniors
Description: Just look for two people joined
at the lips.
Grade point average: Mark — 2.65/
Marlene — 3.5

Extracurricular activities: each other. Have been engaged since kindergarten. Also pres-ident and vice-president of the Dental Hy-giene Club.
Comments: will set up cozy little dental

practice, preferably with *no* snapshots from Theamelpos mounted on the wall. Only hope is that if she makes it, he doesn't, she won't go without him, leaving spot open for Jardine.

Sean looked up from the paper. "Your mind works in some very strange ways."

"I don't like it," said Raymond. "Vanderhoof gets the first spot, Cementhead nails down the second. If the Sap family makes it, that leaves only two spots for us. Which means all it takes is one bozo with a flashy record to come along to send Jardine for another summer of fish guts."

"Calm down, idiot," said Sean patiently. "You're forgetting the party, which, thanks to Ashley, is going to be fantastic. She's already got the music, the lights, the food, and the drinks. It's going to be a big success and make us look really good."

Raymond slapped his forehead. "I forgot to tell you! Another nice little tidbit, sent special delivery from *them*" — he glanced at the ceiling — "to Jardine. Last week I visited every store in the mall to ask them to donate a prize for the party in exchange for a plug in the school newspaper. Well, they must have found out we don't have a school newspaper, because, so far, the only thing we've got for the super mystery prize is a tire gauge from Nick's Auto Shop. Retail value: $2.95. Man, if I got myself dressed up like an egg salad sandwich, and spent my night bouncing up and down on a trampoline so well that I beat out all the other bouncing egg salad sandwiches, I'd kill the burger who tried to slip me a tire gauge!"

Sean was appalled. "We'll look like idiots if you can't get something better than that! Is there a chance anything decent'll come up?"

Raymond was skeptical. "The only thing that's going to come up is Jardine's number when he has to present the super mystery prize. For anything else, he's not holding his breath." He sighed. "Anyway, I've got a meeting with Miss Ritchie. She wants to see me about my Pefkakia project. Like it's my fault King Phidor bit the big one."

"Well, you've got to admit it was worse luck for Phidor than it was for you," said Sean with a grin.

"I'm not too sure about that," said Raymond. "Before the revolution, Phidor was a king; Jardine was, is, and always will be just Jardine."

Five

Ashley Bach was a genius at organization, especially when what she was organizing was her favorite thing in the entire world, a party. Showing the style of a consummate professional, she took charge of the Halloween extravaganza and, with a combination of her friendly charm with people and her Manhattan contacts, lined up an October 31 designed to bring the house down.

Raymond and Sean were pathetically grateful. Their own contribution to the affair still stood at a tire gauge, if one did not count nerves. Raymond's anxiety came from the fact that he judged this party to be yet another river to cross on the road to

Theamelpos. Sean wasn't quite sure why he was so uneasy — possibly because he'd never spent much time at school parties, and didn't particularly want to spend any at this one, either. Certainly, walking around in public dressed in Gramp's World War I Doughboy uniform was ample reason for a few butterflies in the stomach. Not to mention the fact that, if something went wrong tonight, it was Sean's public image on the line.

The party was scheduled for eight o'clock, but Sean came to school right after dinner to help set up the DeWitt gym. He needn't have bothered. Ashley had her art class there already, hanging streamers, blowing up balloons, and setting up the food and drink tables. He felt a twinge of guilt as he regarded the papier-mâché pumpkins, witches, skeletons, and countless other decorations that had been produced by this group, which had apparently forgiven Ashley the doctoring of the original posters and pledged to follow her anywhere. His mind kept coming back to himself and Raymond, and their measly little tire gauge.

Ashley was at the far corner of the gym, helping Zeke Decibel set up a sound system that would have blown the roof off of Madison Square Garden. Zeke (whose real name was Reginald Ipswich, but who preferred the pseudonym because it had more flow) boasted a show with flash bombs, bubbles, mist, and over sixty colored lights. The lights were already in place, attached to two enormous arcs that had been fastened to the lower horizontal beams of the gym ceiling.

Spying Sean, Ashley dragged him over to Zeke,

introduced him, and whispered, "We were lucky to get him on a big party night like this. He has mist!"

By seven o'clock, all was in readiness after Sean and a few of the art students had pulled out the school's trampoline and positioned it in the beam of Zeke Decibel's biggest spotlight. All manner of chips and soda sat waiting on the buffet tables, with the pizza and create-your-own-banana-split fixings residing in the nearby home ec room. By this time, the first of the students had begun to trickle in, and the workers were retiring to washrooms to change into their costumes.

When Sean saw Ashley, it was all he could do to keep from going into cardiac arrest. She was done up as a devil, in a red leotard, with sheer red stockings, and red spike heels. She had a forked tail and matching horns, and in her hand she carried a red pitchfork. She was, in Sean's eyes, arresting, devastating, fabulous, stunning, and totally great. Had he not spent the last two weeks listening to her list the virtues of Steve Semenski, he would have proposed marriage on the spot.

As he looked around at some of the other students, he decided that his own costume was boring and unimaginative, not to mention moth-eaten. Of the early arrivals alone, there were already a few standouts. One boy was dressed in a full scuba suit, complete with oxygen tank and shark repellent. Two girls had gotten together and built a two-person cardboard replica of a Boeing 747. They had come with their boyfriends, who were dressed up as a horse. There was also a Marie Antoinette in a hoop skirt so huge and a wig so tall that, by land or air, no one could get within shouting distance of her. Behind her was a boy costumed as a ball of string. Apparently, a lot of people had taken great care with the selection of their outfits. Sean knew that Nikki and her two best friends hadn't spoken to each other in over a week so as to maintain security while they worked on their own creations. Even he didn't know what his sister would be wearing that night.

Sean hefted his small duffel bag and headed for a nearby washroom to change. No sooner was he inside than the door of the center stall swung open, and out stepped a thirties-style gangster in a loud pinstriped suit and a white hat with a black band. The costume was so striking that it took Sean a few seconds to realize who it was.

"Raymond! You look good!"

"Don't be sarcastic, Delancey. I feel ridiculous enough as it is."

"No, seriously. For a minute I thought it was Al Capone himself coming out of that stall."

Raymond snorted. "I'll bet Al Capone never dropped his machine gun in the toilet." He opened up the black violin case he was carrying to reveal a glistening wet plastic toy tommy gun. "I borrowed this from the kid across the street — which is, of course, in the next town. He said, 'Jardine, if you wreck my gun, I'll kick your butt.' I'd better get to Theamelpos fast. That kid can get nasty."

Sean changed into his Army outfit and stood in front of Raymond for inspection. "What do you think?" he asked defiantly.

"I think it's fairly decent when you consider maybe they didn't have mothballs in 1918."

"Give me a break, huh?"

"Nothing personal. I mean, it's a little big, too, but who cares if your shoulders sag during a mustard gas attack?" He fiddled with Sean's helmet; muttered, "Hmmm. Lucky these things come with chin-straps"; and adjusted his own white tie, which stood out against his black shirt like forked lightning on a moonless night. "Let's go, Delancey. We're the hosts."

"Have you got the prize?" Sean asked.

"Yeah, it's in my pocket. You know, it may not be worth big bucks, but it's a handy gadget. It told me that my back tire needed some air."

Sean was appalled. "You *used* it? Raymond, it's a prize! Somebody's going to get a *used* prize!"

Raymond shrugged. "And if it was new, he'd be impressed?"

Sean bit his lip and followed Raymond out to the party.

The gym was gradually filling up, although the party was not to begin officially for twenty minutes yet. The staff supervisors had arrived, and were standing in a group, talking, laughing, and glancing ravenously at the buffet tables. Sean was surprised at the turnout, and toyed with the idea that he might get a lot of credit for pulling off such a well-attended party. A festive atmosphere prevailed as friends engaged in good-natured laughing at each other's costumes.

People continued to arrive in a steady stream right up until eight, by which time the gym was mobbed. It seemed that many students had misinterpreted the EARS logo, as there were quite a few rabbit suits in the throng, and one boy had actually dressed himself in gigantic, foot-high cauliflower ears.

At five after eight, a group of Ashley's art classmates brought out the pizza and the ice cream, and when the five staff supervisors fell on it like wolves, Ashley gave Zeke Decibel the thumbs-up signal. Zeke grabbed his microphone and let out a bloodcurdling scream. The music started up full-blast, and colored lights blazed in all directions. A string of flash bombs went off, one so close in front of Sean that he staggered backward into the arms of Ashley (which pleased him enormously). Thousands of bubbles filled the air, and as the partygoers rushed to the dance floor, a layer of mist formed at their feet and began rising. A roar of appreciation went up.

Ashley grabbed Raymond and Sean by the arms and hauled them out to join the dancing. The music was far too loud for anyone to hear Sean say, "No, thanks. I don't dance." His attitude was, If you're not Baryshnikov, dancing can only make you look silly. But he was doing pretty well until Raymond, really getting into the swing of things, bonked him over the head with his violin case, knocking the World War I helmet into the pouch of a girl wearing a kangaroo suit. Ashley found the resulting melee hilariously funny, and Sean was positive that her smile lit up the mist, which was now up to waist level.

"*Hey, everbody!*" bellowed a foghorn voice that very nearly drowned out the music. "*Make way for the windmill!*" Into the crowd charged Howard Newman, dressed up to fulfill his life's purpose — making a mockery of SACGEN. Somehow he had managed to come up with a windmill costume, incorporating a Styrofoam wrap extending from shoulders to knees, and painted to look like an old stone mill. A huge windmill blade was attached to his forehead by a heavy rubber band, and he twirled this with flailing arms. His stone body was pierced with two knives and an arrow, and perforated with bullet holes. He wore a noose around his neck, and on his back he had spray-painted in huge letters NUKE ME. Applauding, the dancers formed a circle around Howard, and Zeke Decibel obligingly threw him a spotlight. Even the teachers interrupted their eating for a few cheers.

When Sean and Raymond finally managed to communicate to Ashley that they were exhausted and had to take a break, they scrambled away from the dancing and found themselves staring into the used-car-salesman eyes of Danny Eckerman. Either Danny wasn't wearing a costume or, Sean guessed, he was going as himself, since there was no way the subject matter could be improved upon.

"Raymond," said the president, managing to sound earnest even though he had to shout to be heard, "Mindy tells me that you feel I haven't been pulling my weight for this party."

"That depends on how much you weigh," said Raymond shortly. "For example, if you weigh zero, then you're pulling your weight perfectly."

"Well, I just want you to know that I've got no hard feelings over how you guys flubbed the posters," Danny went on. "And I intend to give you and Sean full credit in my speech."

"Except that you're not making a speech," Raymond finished for him.

"But I always speak."

"Well, you see," Raymond explained pleasantly, "this time you decided that since you did absolutely nothing for this party, you have absolutely nothing to say. Right, Delancey?"

Sean was not listening. Through the mist and flashing lights he had caught sight of a girl dressed as a Dallas Cowboys cheerleader. As his eyes followed her on the strobe-lit dance floor, it suddenly hit him like three hundred pounds of wet cement that he was looking at Nicolette Delancey. Purposefully, he pushed his way through the crush and insinuated himself between her and the werewolf she was dancing with.

"Nikki!" he hissed. "Where do you get off wearing an outfit like that?"

"Why? What's wrong with it?"

"What's wrong with it?! It's — it's — if Mom saw you like this, she'd kill you!"

Nikki laughed. "Mom picked it out for me."

"Well — what about Dad?"

"He liked it, too. It's Gramp who reacted just like my *modern* brother. Oh! There's Raymond! I've got to go tell him how great he looks!" She darted away, abandoning both her brother and her werewolf.

Mortified, Sean slunk off into the mist. To take his mind off his sister, he danced with Amelia Vanderhoof, who had come as a very tall, very skinny Queen Victoria.

Under the magical direction of Zeke Decibel and his mist, the party was shaping into a great success. It had everything — excitement: the dancing at fever pitch, the music incredible as twenty-five hundred watts of sound electrified the air; love interest: the Sapersteins, dressed as they were every year, as teeth (she an incisor, he a molar), cooing at each other in a foggy corner; conflict: Nikki, trying to break up the fight between her two best friends, Marilyn and Carita, who had independently come up with identical black cat costumes, each one positive that the other had stolen her idea; humor: the Boeing 747 and their boyfriends, the horse, finding dancing extremely difficult; political statement: Howard kneeling on the dance floor, inviting all others to "hoof the windmill in the behind"; machismo: Steve Semenski, arriving fashionably late in a suit of gleaming armor (sleeveless, of course).

"Look at him!" muttered Raymond in disgust. "Cementhead!"

This time Sean didn't even snap at his partner. He was not at all pleased that he kept seeing Ashley glancing in Steve's direction as she danced. "I didn't know there was such a thing as sleeveless armor."

"There isn't," Raymond scowled. "He probably spent all afternoon cutting the sleeves off with a can opener. But you'll notice he's wearing the gauntlets. That's to make it easier to scratch away any weeds that grow up through cracks in the cement!"

As the song that was playing ended, an oppressive silence fell, and Raymond and Sean looked at the deejay's booth to find Mindy O'Toole standing at the microphone, with Danny Eckerman right behind her.

"Attention, everybody. Before we go back to the dancing and the fun, let's have a warm round of applause for the person who made this party possible, our student body president, Danny Eckerman!''

Sean looked to see Raymond's reaction, but Raymond was no longer beside him. What the students then saw happened so fast that many of them weren't sure what to make of it. As Danny stepped up to the microphone to speak, a gangster carrying a violin case snatched a helium balloon from midair and fiddled with the knot. Then he put down his case and, with his free hand, grabbed the president's head, shoved the balloon in his mouth, and pressed hard, forcing all the helium inside. Danny staggered backward, then spat out the empty balloon and shouted, *''What did you do that for?''* in a high-pitched munchkin voice somewhere in the range of D above high C.

All at once, the shocked students broke into laughter, and the music started up again.

Raymond reappeared at Sean's side. "Anything happen while I was away?''

Sean had to laugh. "It was the best speech Danny ever made.''

It was a great party. Even Sean Delancey, who thought school social events were boring, was forced to admit that he would have been having a good time had he not had so many things on his mind, like who Raymond might offend next, Nikki's costume, and Ashley's burning looks in Steve's direction.

The dancing continued steadily until ten-thirty, when the spotlight shone on the trampoline in the gym corner, and it was time for the contest to begin. Zeke Decibel put on some "funky Halloweenin'

Careenin' Trampolinin' '' music as background, the four safety spotters moved into place, and the contestants lined up to take their turns. Raymond and Sean were the judges, and Ashley stood with them, radiant with the success of her efforts.

"This is an awesome party!" she said reverently. "Look at Steve's costume! Isn't it the cutest?" She got no reply.

There were thirty-three entrants, each one of whom was allotted ninety seconds in which to strut his/her stuff while Zeke convulsed the audience with his hilarious patter. There was cheering, laughing, screaming, and chanting as the contestants, most of them hampered by bulky costumes, bounced comically through their routines. By this time, even the staff was paying attention and joining in the goings-on, having totally ravaged the buffet tables. Some of the jumpers put on great shows; others spent their ninety seconds scrambling not to fall off the trampoline; still others couldn't even manage that. Steve Semenski in particular took a spill that would have flattened a rhinoceros, only to leap athletically back onto the trampoline to finish his routine in spectacular fashion. The ball of string attempted the same maneuver, but he was starting to unravel, and had to withdraw. Marie Antoinette was another scratch, as she was unable to see the trampoline beneath her enormous skirt. The contest was such an unparalleled success that, by the time the last entry came up, there were only twenty minutes left before school rules were to close the whole business down at midnight.

A bit of a dispute was in progress over whether

the Boeing 747 would be able to enter, since that would be placing two people on the trampoline at once. However, the front end of the aircraft complained she couldn't bounce without the back end, and vice versa, and soon both girls were in a spirited argument with Raymond, who figured if they killed themselves while he was judge, this could jeopardize his chances of going to Theamelpos. Zeke Decibel put an end to it all by declaring, "Boeing 747, this is the control tower! You are cleared for take-off!"

As the airplane began to bounce gingerly on the trampoline, there came a strange flickering from Zeke Decibel's two giant arcs of lights. The music slowed, and sped up again, warbling in time with the waxing and waning of the lights. Everyone looked around.

"It's me!" screamed Howard. "The windmill! I'm lousy! I don't work! I'm screwing up again!"

The flickering was much worse now, and the room went from complete darkness to blinding light in erratic intervals, as the lights were fed pulses of three times as much power as they were meant to handle. Zeke Decibel ripped his stereo needle from the record it was chewing, but the lack of music only revealed another sound — a loud grinding throughout the school that the students all recognized as SACGEN's little way of saying, "I Quit." The big spotlight sparked, sizzled, and began smoking. Zeke pulled and twisted madly at his control panel, but to no avail.

"Do something!" he shouted to the student standing nearest him. With a free hand, he pushed his ladder out from the deejay's booth toward the boy. "Get up to the light bars and pull the plug!"

The boy scrambled up the ladder and stood il-
luminated like an angel in a halo of sparks as
SACGEN spat out one final gigantic power surge.
Then both light bars went up in smoke and the
gym went dark. Unfortunately, the school's fire
alarm was not hooked up to SACGEN, so a wild
ringing split the air. This set off the automatic sprinkler system, and a heavy spray rained down on the
screaming crowd.

Total chaos reigned. The Boeing 747 made an
unscheduled landing on its two pilots' heads as the
partygoers stampeded for the door. Normally, the
exodus would have been fairly quick, but the bulky
costumes made movement awkward, and the students were falling and bumping into each other in
the dark. The water coming down from the ceiling
drenched everything, causing cardboard and papier-mâché to come apart, and making the hard-
wood floor as slippery as a skating rink. Raymond
had the soggy baggage compartment hatch of the
747 broken over his head as the pilots evacuated
the disabled craft. Sean was stuck in the gym door-
way, jammed between Marie Antoinette and the
ball of string. The bottleneck created a pushing
scene worthy of the Sack of Rome, until finally the
pressure from the back ranks proved too much,
and the students literally exploded out of the gym
and into the night in a matter of seconds.

Raymond was one of the last to burst through
the breach, his suit sodden, his white fedora flattened on his head. He sloshed out of the crush to
some free space, fumbled open his violin case, pulled
out the machine gun, held the barrel to his temple,

and squeezed the trigger. There was a weak rat-a-tat sound for a moment, then nothing. Water oozed out. Raymond looked up at the sky accusingly.

Howard stood in the center of the swarm of students, howling, "Windmill failure! Windmill failure! *Windmill failure!*" Gleefully, he tore his costume to shreds and threw himself dramatically to the ground, coughing and gasping, a dead windmill.

At that moment, the DeWitt Fire Department came roaring up the drive, sirens blaring. Each carrying a massive hose, two firemen burst into the gym, sprayed everything, and then stopped to peer into the gloom, activating high-powered flashlights.

"Hey!" one of them cried suddenly. "There's someone still in here! On a bar at the ceiling!"

"It's some kind of animal," said the other fireman.

"No, it isn't," came a feeble voice from above. "I'm wearing a bear suit."

Quickly, one fireman ran for a ladder while the other stayed with the stranded partygoer. Outside, the word spread quickly, and a crowd gathered at the gym door.

Overcome with guilt, Sean grabbed Raymond, who was still talking to the sky. "Now are you satisfied? Huh? We had to have a party to get you to Theamelpos, and now some poor guy's life is in danger!"

"They'd have had the party with us or without us," Raymond reasoned.

"Yeah, but if it was without us, this wouldn't have been my fault!"

"It *isn't* your fault, Delancey."

"Yes, it is! It's my fault! And it's your fault that it's my fault!"

"He's down!" shouted someone from the front as the group broke into applause and cheers.

Sean allowed his heart to beat again. Disaster or no disaster, at least the party would have no death toll.

"See?" said Raymond triumphantly. "It's *nobody's* fault."

"Listen," said Sean wearily. "It's after midnight, and there's nothing anybody can do about anything anymore. Let's just give someone the prize, and go home."

Raymond nodded. "Good idea. And there's only one person who deserves this fabulous prize." He reached into his pocket and pulled out the tire gauge. "Cementhead."

"Aw, Raymond, why do you have to stir things up? Just give it to Randy. Or the werewolf. He was pretty good."

"No way," said Raymond firmly. "Jardine is going to get some satisfaction out of this lousy night by seeing the look on Cementhead's face when I hand him this beautiful piece of automotive equipment."

Sean sighed. "Oh, all right. But remember, you can't call him Cementhead. You have to say, 'The winner is Steve Semenski.' "

Ashley, who had overheard this last bit, came up to them, eyes shining. "I've just thought of how we can improve the prize! Throw in a night on the town with a New York City model!"

"But Ashley," Sean protested, "where are we going to get a New York City model?"

"Me, silly!" said Ashley. *"I'm* a New York City model!" She moved her head closer and continued in a confidential tone, "That way you don't have to give a lousy prize, and I get to go out with Steve!" She gave them the thumbs-up signal, and joined the crowd to await the announcement, leaving Raymond and Sean staring at each other in true pain.

" 'Give it to Cementhead!" Sean mimicked savagely. "Nice going, *stupid!*"

His face a thundercloud, Raymond stepped forward to address the swarm of ex-partygoers. "The judges have reached a decision for the trampoline contest. The winner of the Special Mystery Prize of a tire gauge in addition to a night on the town with a genuine New York City model is Ce — Ce — the winner is Ce — the winner is — "

Suddenly, Sean jumped in front of him, eyes wild. "The guy who was stuck up at the top of the gym ceiling for — for his incredible portrayal of a bear on the flying trapeze in the rain! Congratulations, uh — man!"

Ashley's face drained of all color. *"Sean!"*

Raymond looked deeply moved. "Delancey, I love you."

Six

" '. . . When the DeWitt Fire Department arrived on the scene,' " Sean read aloud from the next day's *Newsday*, " 'they found no fire, but one student, Sheldon Entwistle, stranded atop the disc jockey's lighting bar, suspended twenty-five feet above the floor.' "

"Our grand-prize winner," said Raymond, nodding wisely.

The two were sitting side by side on the Long Island Railroad, bound for New York City, intent on hitting the big Forty-Second Street library to research Gavin Gunhold for their poetry assignment.

Sean slapped his knee. "I still can't believe Ashley bought that load of garbage you fed her about how it was morally right to give the prize to Entwistle."

"I had to. She looked like she was about to rip out your liver. It was the least Jardine could do after that service you performed for mankind — stopping me from setting up Ashley and Cementhead."

"Don't call him Cementhead," Sean said mildly. He laughed. "Before she left, she told me that, in her opinion, we're the most sensitive and considerate guys she's ever met."

Raymond shook his head. "Terrible judge of character, our Ashley. But I couldn't very well tell her that we would rather be dissected than hand her over to Cementhead on a silver platter. And you've got to admit that that Entwistle guy deserved a break, even if it came just because you're in love with Ashley."

"Hey!" Sean snapped indignantly. "I'm not in love with Ashley! I'm just sort of . . ." he paused, "in *like* with her."

Raymond shifted in his seat. "You don't have to explain anything. I feel the same way you do."

Sean's face was red. "Well, you've got it just as bad as I do, so don't talk!"

"Let's not take it personally, Delancey. Jardine is just pointing out the facts."

"There are tons of girls I could go out with if I wanted to," said Sean.

"But they aren't Ashley," Raymond returned cheerfully.

Frowning, Sean turned his attenion back to *Newsday*. " 'According to Engineer Claude Sopwith of the Department of Energy, the incident had nothing to do with the Solar/Air Current Generating System in use at DeWitt. Said Principal Q. David Hyatt, "That nonsense must have come from the students, who have some immature desire to blot the record of the SACGEN project."

" 'In fact, those allegations came from Mr. Zeke Decibel, disc jockey for the party, who claimed his equipment was overloaded by a series of power surges. Engineer Sopwith dismissed this as "utter claptrap."

" ' "The thirty-three-million-dollar SACGEN project has been heralded as an unparalleled success for the Department of Energy. His [Decibel's] equipment was at fault," added Sopwith.' "

Sean threw down the paper in disgust. "I can't believe it! Those people absolutely refuse to admit that their precious windmill doesn't work! They're blaming Decibel for something that happens every day at school!"

"Shhh, Delancey. Let them blame Decibel. Let them blame the Kremlin, private industry, fluoridated water, sunspots, or Mother Teresa. Just so long as they don't blame Jardine. Be grateful. We were the organizers of that party."

"But Raymond, it's such a snow-job! If we were real men, we'd waltz in there on Monday and tell Q-Dave what we think of it!"

"But we're not real men; we're real mice," Raymond reminded him. "And we hope to be having our cheese on Theamelpos this summer. That's the beauty of it. They have to cover up for the windmill, so they can't come after us for practically wrecking the place with our party."

Sean made a face. "Every time I think of SAC-

GEN, I think of all those stupid gadgets my father buys. I can't handle it. I've got a big windmill at school to deal with, and fifty little ones at home."

Raymond nodded sympathetically. "Still," he said, "good old SACGEN. It made the difference between two Theamelpos candidates with a successful social activity on their records, and two disgraced schnooks with a room reserved in their names at the Secaucus Hilton."

Sean made a face. "Yeah, I guess so," he mumbled. "But it's not fair."

Raymond shrugged. "You can't make life fair. But if you get to Theamelpos, you can make it worth living."

Soon the Manhattan skyline appeared on the horizon, and Sean watched it grow as Raymond sat back in a trancelike state, intoning calypso music about Theamelpos to the rhythm of the train wheels.

It took the poetry specialist twenty minutes to locate anything on Gavin Gunhold. Finally, she led Raymond and Sean to a small cubicle and handed them a file folder marked "Canadian Poetry: Gunhold, Gavin."

Raymond rubbed his hands in anticipation. "I can't wait to read some more of his stuff. 'Registration Day' is the best poem I ever saw!"

Sean looked nervous. He had already noted that the file folder seemed woefully thin. He set up his steno pad, arranged a stack of file cards in front of him, and took out two ballpoint pens (just in case one ran out of ink). Then he opened the Gunhold folder.

The two boys found themselves staring at the obituary page of *The Toronto Telegram*, July 23, 1949. At the top of the sheet of yellowed newsprint was a small headline that read:

GAVIN GUNHOLD, 1899–1949

Gavin Gunhold, service station attendant and poet, was killed tragically yesterday waiting in line in the Canadian Imperial Bank of Commerce when the Queen Street trolley car jumped the track and crashed through the bank's front window. Gunhold, three months overdue on his rent, was in the bank to cash the fifteen-dollar check he had received for the publication of his first and only poem, "Registration Day," by the recently bankrupt *Toronto Review of Poetry*.

Raymond emitted a short gasp, as though he'd been hit full-force in the stomach by a battering ram. He slumped back in his chair, face turned straight up. "That's it. They finally got Jardine. Gunned down in the research wing of the New York Public Library." He turned to Sean. "He's dead, Delancey! Dead! *And he only wrote one poem!*"

Frantically, Sean riffled through the folder. There was a copy of "Registration Day," and six blank sheets of paper with NOTES printed at the top.

Raymond continued to lament. "It's over. I may as well throw away my Swedish phrase book and start learning to speak fish. This is the end. Good-bye, Theamelpos. Good-bye, beautiful beaches. Good-bye, Mediterranean sun. Good-bye, Nordic beauties. Good-bye lifetime of wonderful luck. Hello,

New Jersey. Secaucus — prepare to receive Jardine! He's beaten! There's no fight left in him! A broken man with a broken dream!" He turned his face to the ceiling. "You hear that? Jardine surrenders! You win! You're the better chess players! Thirty-eight years ago, you sent a trolley car into a bank — in *Canada* — just to wipe out Jardine's chances of going to Theamelpos! Well, you did it! Congratulations! You destroyed me! I wave the white flag! I throw in the towel! *I quit!*"

The poetry specialist stuck her head into the cubicle. "*Shhhh!*" she admonished. Then, as an afterthought, "Shh."

Raymond turned to Sean, his face open and sincere. "When you work in a fish gutting plant, your life is in suspended animation. You are no longer a participant in the world, because you smell like fish guts. Families of cats follow you around on the street. You hail a taxi, and the driver takes a whiff and speeds away. Department stores won't let you try on clothes unless you promise to buy them. And can you blame anybody? I mean, when the President is checking the guest list for a White House dinner, he doesn't say, 'Make sure you invite at least one guy who smells like fish guts.' " He sighed with indescribable melancholy, gurgled something that sounded like "Arrxbblgh!" and slumped forward so far that his head was very nearly touching the floor.

"We'll change our topic!" said Sean suddenly. "Kerr won't get mad because — uh — we'll figure out an explanation for why it took two weeks. Like — we won't tell him we're changing our topic. We'll just do it, and say that we told him, but he forgot to write it down. No, I've got it — we'll tell him the truth! We picked the topic three minutes before the deadline, and didn't follow up on it for two weeks because of our Halloween party. No, ditch that. We'll say that the book said there were lots of other Gunhold poems, and the book was wrong, and it's not our fault, and the two weeks were spent — uh — sick. No, that's no good. We were in class. Come on, Raymond! Don't just hang there! We're really up the creek! Think!"

Raymond lifted his head another inch and a half to shrug miserably. Shakespeare himself could not have come up with a more perfect image of tragedy and despair. It was at that moment that it dawned on Sean that Raymond was out of this game, totally incapacitated, sitting on the bench, an empty shell. Delancey had the ball now, under his own basket, down by a point, a second left to play. This was no time to pass, dribble, or even think. This was the time to heave the ball across the court and hope for the best.

"We'll write more poems," he said abruptly.

Raymond sat bolt upright. "What?"

"We can't change our topic, we don't have enough stuff to analyze, so we write new stuff and say it's Gunhold's."

"New stuff?" Raymond echoed, hope stirring in his heart.

"Yes!" Sean continued, bearing down. "I've got news for you, Raymond. 'Registration Day' is a *stupid* poem written by a gas station attendant. We're qualified to pump gas, so we can write poems just as lousy as that one."

"More poems," Raymond repeated, a little more positively.

"That's right!" said Sean decisively. "More poems."

"More poems," said Raymond again, the color returning to his face. His eyes took on a lively gleam. "More poems!" Suddenly, he leaped up, hauled Sean out of his chair, spun him around a couple of times, and sent him reeling dizzily into the wall of the cubicle. *"More poems!"* He looked up at the ceiling, gesturing wildly. "Did you hear that? We've got more poems coming! Forget what I said before! Jardine is still in this thing!"

"Oh, shut up, Raymond!" said Sean in annoyance. "Save the celebration. We've got a lot of stupid, unnecessary hard work ahead of us, and it's all your fault. 'Oh, Gavin Gunhold is such a terrific poet!' " he mimicked savagely. " 'I can hardly wait to read the rest of his stuff. He's been writing since the nineteen-forties.' Or he would have been, except that there was a trolley car with his name on it! If you'd listened to me and picked somebody *normal*, we'd be half finished by now! But no! We had to do it *your* way! So not only do we have to come up with thirty pages of analysis, but first we have to write the poetry! I could kill you, Raymond!"

"That's a little strong, Delancey. But because of all we've been through together, I'm going to let it pass. That was some real clutch thinking you did back there, and Jardine is grateful." He shook his head as though to clear it. "Whew! What a close one! I thought I was in Secaucus for sure. But we're going to try five times as hard as everyone else and pull this off somehow. Trust me."

Raymond and Sean caught the two-fifty-six back to the Island and reported to Sean's house for their very first case of writer's block. *Deciding* to write poetry, they found, was a lot easier than actually doing it. And it wasn't any help to have to listen to the shouts of delight as Mr. and Mrs. Delancey experimented with the argon-neon laser, using aerosol spray to illuminate the invisible beam.

Sean crumpled up yet another piece of paper, and tossed it into the overflowing basket. "My apologies to the late Mr. Gunhold," he said savagely. "It takes just as much effort to write stupid poetry as the good stuff."

"Well, why don't we try some of that heart-warming garbage?" Raymond suggested. "You know — tweeting birds in the meadow, hosts of golden daffodils — that stuff."

"Because Gavin Gunhold wouldn't write about that."

"I should hope not; a man in his condition! He should be getting a lot of rest. So then why don't we try a style like all those downer poems. You know, 'Death, death, oh, welcome death.' Huh? How about it?"

"Raymond, no! We're trying to sound like the guy who wrote about taxidermy school. It's impossible to guess how his mind worked. I'll bet you in the entire history of the English language, he's the only writer that even *mentions* a taxidermy school. Face it, Raymond. He may have been the best service station attendant in Canada, but as a poet, he was weird. For all we know, he got his ideas by taking a dictionary, throwing it open at random, and writing about the first word he saw. That's the only explanation I can think of for taxidermy school."

Raymond snapped his fingers. "Delancey, you're a genius!" He ran over to Sean's bookcase and pulled out an enormous volume entitled *The Encyclopedia Dictionary for Growing Young Minds*. He paused as he read the title. "Hmmm. Grown any young minds lately? Okay. To business." He plopped the dictionary down on Sean's desk, threw it open about a third of the way, closed his eyes, and stuck his finger in the center of the page. "Well, Delancey, what'd I get?"

Sean regarded the pointing finger. "Fruit fly," he reported. "Now there's a subject to stir the heart of any poet."

Raymond scanned the entry. "I don't know. There's drama here. Listen, if you're a fruit fly, your whole life takes place in three lousy weeks. That's tragic. Wait! I'm having an inspiration: 'Due to the tragically short life span of the average fruit fly — ' "

" 'College is not really an option,' " Sean finished in disgust.

"Great!" cried Raymond. "I love it!" He sat himself down in front of Sean's old manual typewriter and began to peck away slowly with his two index fingers.

"Aw, come on, Raymond, quit it. This is stupid. Kerr's going to kill us if we try to feed him poems about fruit flies in college! I suppose you're writing all about this beady-eyed bug in a cap and gown!"

Raymond fairly shrieked with delight. "Caps and gowns! Great! Oh, man, this stuff writes itself!" When he pulled the sheet from the roller and handed it to Sean for inspection, it read:

"Fruit Fly" by Gavin Gunhold

Due to the tragically short life span of the average fruit fly,
College is not really an option.
Caps and gowns don't come in that size anyway.

Sean looked thunderstruck. "My God, it's terrible! It's so bad that — it sounds just like Gavin Gunhold wrote it!"

"I don't know," said Raymond critically. "I kind of like it."

"*You* liked 'Registration Day,' " Sean reminded him. "But this is — okay. Only, we're going to have to write an analysis. What can we say about 'Fruit Fly'?"

Raymond shrugged. "We can always put something about education, or the underprivileged. And if that doesn't work, we say that it comments on society. The important thing is, we just doubled Gavin Gunhold's total output, with one word out of a dictionary. Somewhere under that trolley car, I bet Gav is smiling." He picked up the dictionary and threw it open again. "Eyes closed, right — there."

"Consommé," read Sean.

"Consommé," mused Raymond. "Hmmm."

Sean blew up. "How could you even *try* to think

of a poem about consommé? It's soup, Raymond! Soup!"

"Well, yeah, but I mean, we're being artists here. We've got to use our creative imagination. Sure, on the surface soup isn't too interesting, but let's toss it around a bit."

"There's nothing to toss. It's consommé. You eat it with a spoon. You can't swim in it, paint a fence with it, or wax a floor with it. It's no good as insect spray or shampoo, and it won't cure athlete's foot, run your car — "

"Run your car!" Raymond howled. "That's it! What a Gunholdesque idea! Can you imagine if cars could run on consommé?"

"The oil companies wouldn't stand for it. Really, Raymond — "

"Oil companies!" cried Raymond, running back to the typewriter. "Come on! Keep thinking!"

"You're going too far!" Sean thundered. "Consommé is clear broth! The most poetic thing that ever happens to it is parsley!"

"Beautiful! *Beautiful!*" crowed Raymond, his index fingers working like pistons. He ripped out the sheet and handed it to Sean.

"Industrial Secret" by Gavin Gunhold

The oil companies don't want you to know
That the average car will run on
Consommé,
If you can figure out a way
To get the parsley out of the carburetor.

"Not bad," Sean said weakly. "Here, give me that dictionary."

Sean ended up with "multiple," which he and Raymond argued up through "multiple contusions" and "multiple birth" to settle finally on "multiple personality." Then the fight began in earnest, with Sean claiming that he was going crazy, and Raymond hacking at the typewriter and chortling with glee. When the dust cleared, the result was:

"Group Therapy" by Gavin Gunhold

When my psychiatrist went insane,
Only six of my multiple personalities
Were cured.
The rest of us want our money back.

Raymond flopped back in his chair. "Oh, we'd better give it a rest! With artists like us, you shouldn't overtax the creative muscle."

After a few minutes of relatively companionable silence, both boys realized that they were completely exhausted.

"Well, it's no wonder," said Sean. "Do you realize what we've been through in the last twenty-four hours? Yesterday at this time, the party hadn't even started yet. Just think of all that's happened to us since then."

"Yeah, life's like that sometimes," Raymond agreed. "It's another one of the ways they have of trying to get at Jardine. When I think about it, it's pretty amazing how well he came through this last bit."

112

"What do you mean 'get at Jardine'? Don't you remember who was with you every inch of the way, through that nightmare party? Through that pleasant little business at the library this morning? And through these hours of marvelous creativity that almost killed the two of us? How do you explain the fact that, over the last day, another person has had just as much bad luck as Jardine?"

"It's not the same," said Raymond simply. "You had a heavy twenty-four hours; Jardine had a heavy sixteen years."

Sean sighed. "Go home, Raymond."

"What were you two doing in there?" Gramp asked after Raymond had left. "It sounded like World War III."

"Oh, we were working on our poetry assignment."

"Huh! Well, I guess poetry is rougher stuff than I thought it was." Gramp lit up a Scrulnick's. He always smoked more when the hurricane season was over. "You and Jardine seem to fight a lot."

Sean shuddered. "Gramp, that guy drives me *crazy*."

Gramp shrugged. "Crazy's not so bad. It's a lot like prune juice — too much is a disaster, but a little can be just what the doctor ordered. You should learn to appreciate Jardine. That's one kid who's never going to turn into a robot. He reminds me of the old neighborhood."

"Why? Because he likes the Weather Channel and runs out of gas in front of your deli? He's a Looney Tune!"

Gramp smiled smugly, indicating he was not convinced. "I'm going to watch some weather. Jardine and I are betting on some early blizzards in the Midwest this year."

Sean groaned. Since kindergarten, Gramp had yet to approve of a single one of his friends. Why must he take to heart the one guy who seemed destined to ruin Sean's comfortable life?

On Monday morning, Q. David Hyatt, Engineers Sopwith and Johnson, and Senior Engineer Quisenberry led a delegation of six Korean energy specialists into a small presentation room adjoining the office.

"We've prepared a short videotape," Quisenberry explained, "to give you an overview of the project before you can see SACGEN itself." He popped a tape into the VCR as Sopwith dimmed the lights.

Mr. Hyatt had seen this tape at least fifteen or twenty times, but he never tired of it. He always felt a thrill of exhilaration when the music started, the theme from *2001: A Space Odyssey*. His ears perked up. Instead of the usual music, Bob Dylan was singing "Blowin' in the Wind." Well, this was something different. The Department of Energy must have updated the tape. There was a new narrator, too, a young, vibrant voice that instantly appealed to him, although virtually any one of the twenty-two hundred DeWitt students could have identified that voice as belonging to Howard Newman.

"What you are looking at is the windmill," announced the audio as the screen showed various angles of SACGEN. *"First, a little history. They built it over the summer. Now some technical data. It's bigger*

than a breadbox, but smaller than Pakistan. And if
you drop it on your foot, your career in ballet is pretty
much shot.''

In the dark, Quisenberry elbowed the principal.
"Hyatt, what the hell is this?" he hissed.

Hyatt looked bewildered. "This is your tape."

"No, it isn't! It's the school's tape!"

The video now showed the interior of the SAC-
GEN control room, with Sopwith and Johnson,
unfrazzled and smiling. *"This is the control center,*
where everybody goes to pretend that they can run the
windmill. Truth is, the windmill doesn't work.''

Everyone froze, and the visitors began whisper-
ing among themselves confusedly in Korean.

"I know what you're thinking,'' Howard's voice
continued pleasantly. *"You're asking yourselves why*
did my government send me halfway around the world
to look at a useless pile of scrap? Well, look on the bright
side. OUR government put up the thirty-three million
bucks to BUILD —''

Quisenberry lunged at the stop button and, had
the lights been on, his guests would have seen that
his face was bright purple as he said, "Ha, ha, ha.
We seem to be having a little difficulty with the
tape."

"Your attention, please," came Mr. Hyatt's voice
over the p.a. system. "Would the person responsible for tampering with the SACGEN orientation
cassette please report to the office immediately."

"No, no, no, Q-Dave!" said Howard in obvious
pleasure. He looked at the five poker players around
the table. "He's so dense! He tries the same thing

every time, and every time I don't show up." Howard was doubly happy, because he was making a killing at six-handed poker, ahead nineteen hundred toothpicks in scarcely half an hour.

One of the other five hands, and easily the morning's big loser, was Sean, who was personally out of pocket nearly six hundred toothpicks. He was making a valiant attempt to ignore the fact that Raymond was standing a few feet away from the table, signaling madly. Raymond just couldn't seem to figure out that poker was something Sean played to *avoid* him.

"What did you put on that tape, Howard?" asked Chris McDermott as he examined his cards.

"The truth, the whole truth, and nothing but the truth," said Howard piously. "I said the windmill's lousy." His eyes shifted around the table. "Raise seventy-five." A hum went up from the other players.

Raymond was still gesturing at Sean. He seemed to be pointing at the player to Howard's right, one Leland Fenster. Leland was the self-proclaimed "coolest guy" at DeWitt, and his clothes, his "shades," and his hairstyle backed that up. Not content with merely being in fashion, he kept himself several weeks ahead, consistently managing to look peculiar rather than avant-garde. Loud jackets and onyx earrings were his current trademark, along with an unimaginably expensive pair of sunglasses from Italy, which looked exactly like the kind that sold for three dollars on the street. Raymond was pointing at Leland, thumbing his nose, and pretending to gag himself with his index finger.

All the players dropped out of the hand except for Sean and Leland, who pushed their toothpicks into the sizable pot.

Leland said, "Fling the horizontals, baby." In keeping with his all-pervading coolness, he spoke only in "hip" words, most of which he made up as the occasion warranted. Sometimes he was downright impossible to understand. For example, in this instance he was saying "deal the cards." But it could get much more obscure, and often even his closest friends had difficulty. Some students were still trying to figure out what he'd meant that day last June when he'd stepped onto the school bus and announced, "Don't libe me that free-zone box, babies."

Sean pulled two cards, Leland three, and Howard stood pat. He had dealt himself a royal flush, and didn't feel he needed any assistance.

"Zung my nut," said Leland dejectedly when Howard revealed his hand and raked in the pot.

Sean could no longer ignore Raymond's gesturing. "What do you *want*?"

"Hey," said Randy Fowler, "he's the gangster. He was in Danny Eckerman's comedy sketch at the Halloween party. You know — with the helium balloon."

"It wasn't comedy," said Raymond. "It was real-life drama."

"I don't like this guy," said Howard to no one in particular.

"It was a great skit," said Chris. "The whole school's talking about it. Man, I laughed."

"Affirm, baby," agreed Leland enthusiastically.

"That vub zipped my thinkometer and orbed me out in guffaws."

Raymond looked politely interested. "Really? That neutron-bombs my gladometer with electric flaming shock-tingles."

Howard assumed a pained expression. "Get him out of here."

As Raymond and Sean headed away from the game, Howard called, "Sean, from now on you're responsible for keeping that guy out of my face."

Sean was so amazed over Raymond's hip comeback to Leland that his irritation vanished. "Raymond, what did you say to him? What did *he* say to *you*?"

"It doesn't matter," said Raymond tragically. "This morning he signed up for Theamelpos."

"Who, Leland? Don't worry about him. He gets lousy grades, and all the teachers think he's a freak."

"He *is* a freak," said Raymond, "but he can't miss. His mother's been president of the PTA for seven years."

"So what? That has nothing to do with him."

"You're a great guy, Delancey, but you're naive. Mrs. Fenster's nickname is The Piranha. They say Q-Dave is scared to death of her. There's no way he'd risk not sending Mr. Cool to Theamelpos. And this is getting pretty hairy, you know, because Mr. Cool, Vanderhoof, and Cementhead grab the first three spots, and that leaves eight of us fighting for the last three. And there are the Saps and some stiff competition in there." He held out his clipboard for Sean's inspection. "I put this together in a bit of a hurry. Can you add anything?"

FENSTER, L., 2331, Sophomore
Height: 5' 7" Weight: 135 lbs.
Hair: funky   Eyes: who knows what's
beneath those tacky sunglasses?
Grade point average: 2.2

Extracurricular activities: doesn't need any.
Comments: Mama's apron strings will get
him there. He'll set back Greek-American
relations a thousand years, baby!

Sean shook his head. "Is there anyone you don't hate?"

Mr. Kerr was late for English that morning, so Ashley used the time to throw the floor open to Raymond and Sean for any ideas they might have as to how she could meet Steve Semenski.

"Gee, Ashley," said Sean in perplexity, "that's a tough one."

"I'm a complete blank," said Raymond, shaking his head. "By the way, have you had a chance to talk to that Entwistle guy about his prize?"

She nodded. "We're going out next Friday, but I don't think he's too keen on it. He's kind of a weird guy — really shy. He loves his tire gauge, though."

Mr. Kerr breezed into the room. "Sorry I'm late, people. Today I want a progress report on all the poetry assignments. We'll start with the group of three — " he checked his list — "Delancey, Jardine, and Bach."

Sean panicked. "Raymond, what are we going

to do?" he whispered frantically. They had not anticipated the need to show Mr. Kerr the project until it was already finished. The three-quarter page analysis was not going to impress the teacher very much, since it represented the entire output of three people over a two-week period. As for the poems — well, there were four of them now, which was a triumph, under the circumstances. But Mr. Kerr didn't know the circumstances!

The teacher examined the material that was put before him. "Well, it's one of two things: You people either don't work very fast, or you don't work very much. What's the problem here?"

Raymond cleared his throat carefully. "Well, sir — uh — we didn't want to tell you this so soon, because it would spoil the surprise. . . ."

Sean stared at Raymond. What surprise? Even Ashley looked intrigued.

"Surprise me," said Mr. Kerr skeptically.

Raymond swallowed hard and forged ahead. "As you know, we've been working on Gavin Gunhold. Well, Mr. Kerr, you see, we know Mr. Gunhold, and — "

Sean felt a seizure coming on.

"Stop right there. Don't say another word. I know what's going on," the teacher said sternly. "You people picked Gunhold right from the beginning because you knew he could help you with your analysis. Why didn't you just come to me and explain the situation instead of making up a story about how you found this Canadian poet who caught your interest?"

"We — we thought you might not let us do him," said Raymond faintly.

"Nonsense," said Mr. Kerr. "Actually knowing the artist is an excellent opportunity for study. You could do analyses both before and after discussing it with Gunhold. Yes, that's what I'd like. Your project will, of course, be much longer than the others, but there are, after all, three of you."

Out of the corner of his eye, Sean caught Raymond glancing up at the ceiling.

"Now," said Mr. Kerr, "exactly how much poetry has Gunhold published?"

"Just the one back in Canada," Raymond confessed. "He gave up poetry to be a service station attendant full-time. But now that he lives in New York, there are new poems, and more on the way."

Sean put the poetry text, open to "Registration Day," in front of the teacher, and placed the typewritten sheets next to it. He held his breath and waited for Mr. Kerr to say, "The one in the book is a poem, but the other three *you* wrote."

Mr. Kerr scanned the work. "Yes, I see what you admire about the man. No vast literary merit, but very sensitive and appealing all the same."

"Thank you," beamed Raymond. Hastily, he added, "On behalf of Mr. Gunhold."

"Well," said Mr. Kerr. "Now that everything's up front, we see that you still have a very exciting project in the works. Next time we update, I want to see a whole lot more on paper."

Another group was called, and Jardine, Delancey, and Bach returned to their seats.

"I want to meet him," said Ashley in a whisper.

"Who, Steve?" said Sean. "Ashley, we'd help you if we could, but — "

"No!" Ashley dismissed this with a wave of her hand. "Gavin Gunhold! I want to meet Gavin Gunhold."

Most of the color drained out of Sean's face, and even Raymond looked stricken.

"Y-you don't want to meet him," Sean stammered. "He's — not your type." Raymond nodded vigorously in corroboration.

"Sure he is. I like all kinds of people. And besides, I've never met a real-live poet. Come on. Please?"

"Well, there's a problem," said Raymond. "Gunhold's eccentric. He doesn't see very many people, and if we just brought along someone he didn't know, he could freak out and stop helping us."

"Could you ask him?" Ashley pleaded. "Tell him I love his work."

"Okay," Raymond agreed finally. "But remember, we're not promising anything, so don't take it personally if he says no."

"Oh, thanks! And, you know, it's not only meeting a poet. You guys have been doing all the group work for this class, which was okay at first, because I had to get adjusted, and after that there was the party. But now I want to do my share."

After class, when Ashley headed off to art, Sean lit into Raymond. "Didn't anybody ever tell you about lies? Don't you remember George Washington and the cherry tree? You'd be the guy who tried to say that the cherry tree was still standing! I could *kill* you, Raymond, except that would leave me as the only living personal friend of Gavin Gunhold!"

"I can see why you're upset, Delancey, but when

I was standing up there in front of Kerr, I suddenly realized this was the only way. Otherwise we'd have to make up stuff about the poems, and fake books and magazines where they were published. We'd have tons of lies going, any one of which could blow up in our faces. So it just came to me — a way to swap all those little lies for a single big huge one. And Kerr's so sure he caught us trying to use Gunhold to make our work easier that he'll never consider that the guy's been dead for thirty-eight years. So, believe it or not, Delancey, we're pretty cool here."

That explanation seemed so logical to Sean that it alarmed him. Why were there no big gaping holes in Raymond's reasoning? There was only one explanation. The boy whose former biggest risk in life was a jump shot from long range was turning into a plotting, conniving, figuring-the-angles Jardine protégé. Yes, only Jardine logic could dictate that they were "pretty cool here." A normal person would be feeling like the blender operator of a nitroglycerine milkshake.

"Well, what about Ashley?" Sean asked finally. "She wants to be in on the project. Do we tell her?"

"Tell her what?"

"The truth, you idiot! That if she wants to meet Gavin Gunhold, she's going to have to take a trip to Toronto with a shovel! And that *we're* writing the poems!"

"God forbid!" said Raymond in horror. "I like Ashley as much as you do, but she talks a lot, and to everybody. If she knew a secret like ours, she'd be so proud of pulling off something that big that, sooner or later, she'd say it in front of the wrong person, and it would get back to Kerr."

"So what was all that about how we're going to try and fix it so she can meet our friend, the dead poet?"

"Don't worry about that," Raymond shrugged. "We'll put her off a few times, and pretty soon she'll forget the whole thing."

"Raymond, I feel like I'm drowning in this."

"Keep dog-paddling, Delancey."

"Good workout, group!" barked Coach Stryker at basketball practice that day. "That's enough for now." To Sean he added, "Nice shooting. Let's hope the slump is over."

In the locker room, Sean found himself beside Steve Semenski, and felt a bit guilty about how little time he'd been spending with his friend lately.

"You've been hiding out these days," Steve said.

"It's schoolwork, believe it or not," Sean replied glibly. "I've got this killer poetry assignment hauling me down." This was almost the truth. It was Raymond who was hauling Sean down, and that was directly related to poetry.

"I've seen you hanging around with that Raymond guy —" Steve began.

"Hold it," Sean interrupted. "I'm not hanging around with him; he's hanging around with me. He's like a virus. You can't shake him."

"Well, what I meant to ask — that girl, the amazing-looking one you guys are always with. What's the story with her?"

Sean swallowed hard. What could he say? "She doesn't talk about herself too much — wait — I seem to remember her saying something about a boyfriend. A wrestler. Tank Somebody. What's the big interest?"

"I thought I caught her looking at me a couple of times at Miami Beach."

"I didn't notice," said Sean through stiff lips. "I get the impression that she's pretty loyal to the Tank."

Steve nodded thoughtfully. "What's her name, just in case?"

"Ashley. Ashley Bach."

Sean knocked lightly on Nikki's door. "Nik, are you in there? I need to borrow your — " The door swung open on its own, and an amazing sight met his eyes. Nikki and her friends Marilyn and Carita were flopped in various poses around the room, examining, trading, and gushing over candid Polaroid snapshots of Raymond Jardine in different corridors and classrooms of Dewitt High.

"What the — ?"

"Sean, get out of here!" Nikki barked.

Dazed, Sean retreated into the hallway. Nikki followed a few seconds later, eyes afire. "How dare you barge into my room without knocking and embarrass my friends like that?"

"But Nik, I *did* knock. I was just — "

"Don't give me that! You just walked right in! You didn't care about anybody!"

"Well, how was I supposed to know — ?"

"I'll get you for this, Sean Delancey! Mark my words! I'll get you if it's the last thing I do!"

Sean slunk off to his own room, thoroughly shaken. This was definitely a complication he didn't need. Nicolette Delancey could carry a grudge into the twenty-third century and still be just as mad as if the offense had occurred yesterday. When Nikki said "I'll get you," you were a marked man. His mind wandered to the time three years before when he'd accidentally spilled pea soup on her autographed picture of David Bowie. She had sworn vengeance and bided her time for two months. Then, all on the same day, she had put grasshoppers in his lunch, dyed his favorite jeans pink, rolled his lucky penny down the sewer, and, for the *pièce de résistance*, written MISS COX IS AN IMMENSE FAT FREAK on his geography project in a marking pen so thick that it had gone through seven pages. Now, three years older, and comfortably settled at the center of a network of friends with access to virtually all of the twenty-two hundred students at DeWitt, who knew what vile evil she would devise to punish him?

He sighed. His only salvation appeared to be convincing Raymond to plead his case for him. Forget that idea! Take a weirdo like Raymond and let him know that suddenly he's the love of three lives, and there's no telling what might happen. And if there was anything worse than the wrath of Nicolette Delancey, it was having Raymond Jardine date your sister!

Seven

JARDINE, R., 8413, Junior
Height: 5' 10"   Weight: 150 lbs.
Grade point average: 2.85

Extracurricular activities: Student Social
Activities Planning Committee
Comments: *NO* luck

Sean squinted at the sheet in the uneven light.
SACGEN was having one of its flickering days. He
looked at Raymond impatiently. "So?"

"Well, what do you see? Or, more important,
what *don't* you see?"

"I *don't* see why you're pestering me. What do you want me to say, Raymond?"

"Sports! It's so obvious. You've got basketball, but my record doesn't say anything about me getting involved in sports. Even I wouldn't send Jardine to Theamelpos without some kind of athletic garbage. That's why you and I are joining the DeWitt varsity ice hockey team."

Sean frowned. "We don't have a hockey team."

"That's why this is such a great opportunity," Raymond replied with satisfaction. "Since we're forming the team, we go on the record as captain and assistant captain."

"But Raymond," Sean argued, "we couldn't play any games. There isn't a high school on Long Island with an ice hockey team."

Raymond grinned delightedly. "Don't you think I know that? It's a little trick I picked up from Cementhead — do nothing and get lots of credit. We can recruit players, hold meetings, assign positions, maybe even print up a notice or two. But there's no way we'd ever have to play a game, because we'd have no opponents; and there's no way we'd ever have to practice, because we have no games. Which means we get fantastic records without ever putting on a pair of skates. You may now go down on your knees and kiss Jardine's feet for such a display of brilliance."

"I'll pass," said Sean sarcastically. "The last time you displayed brilliance, it was to pick an unknown poet for our project. And I'll be paying for it the rest of the semester and possibly my whole life, depending on whether or not we get caught. I'm staying away from your hockey team."

"But your name is already up on the list outside guidance."

"Not anymore." With Raymond in tow, Sean marched down the hall to the guidance wing and the offending bulletin board. There it was in bold print: VARSITY ICE HOCKEY SIGN-UP. He stepped forward, pen in hand, to strike his name from the list, and suddenly found himself face to beautiful face with Ashley Bach.

"Oh, there you are. I was just coming to look for you. I'm so thrilled!"

"Thrilled?"

"That we're going to have a hockey team! I *love* hockey! It's my favorite sport. I used to go out with this guy from Minnesota; he was a fabulous hockey player."

"I'm the assistant captain," said Sean, hating himself. He shoved his pen into his back pocket.

"It's going to feel great to get on that old ice again," said Raymond nostalgically, winking at Sean and infuriating him further. "Feeling those blades cutting into the ice, stopping on a dime in a shower of snow — here's Jardine! He's got a breakaway! Look at him fly! He's coming in on goal! What a move! Another beautiful goal by Jardine! This kid can really make things happen out there!"

This had Ashley laughing so hard that she could barely stand up. Sean looked daggers at Raymond.

At the end of the day, Raymond and Sean came back to check their list at guidance to find there was a third man on their hockey team.

"It figures," said Raymond in disgust. "Cementhead."

Sean shrugged. "He's on all the other teams.

Why not this one?" As an afterthought, he added, "And quit calling him Cementhead."

"It's a good thing we're not going to be playing any games. We'd have to rent a U-Haul just to transport his helmet to the rink."

Yet, as the week progressed, Raymond and Sean found that there were many undiscovered hockey hopefuls at DeWitt, and their list was beginning to fill up. According to Raymond, sixteen or seventeen names were all they needed.

Ashley now looked at the team with double enthusiasm, as she was hoping to use it as a vehicle to meet Steve Semenski. Raymond and Sean promised to "do what we can," and privately vowed to die first. The two were also supposedly doing what they could to get her in to see Gavin Gunhold, but Mr. Gunhold was being stubborn.

"You know how artists are," said Sean, blushing. And Raymond promised to try again.

The Korean energy experts were apparently undeterred by Howard's creative sound track to the SACGEN video. Their government began negotiations with the Department of Energy for the purchase of two SACGEN units, and possibly more later.

Howard was unimpressed. "They'll be sorry," he commented, "when they're in the dark."

And, true to character, SACGEN was resting on its laurels after its triumph with the Koreans. The week was one breakdown after another, leading on Friday afternoon to a screaming fit by the computer teacher, Mr. Lai, followed by the handing in of his resignation, effective immediately. Of all the courses inconvenienced by power interruptions, computers was the hardest hit, because every time anyone tried to key in a program, a power blip would erase the memory or convert all entries into total gibberish. Here it was November and, according to Mr. Lai's progress chart, it was September eleventh. There was not one single piece of finished work to show for two months of effort. The last straw had come when SACGEN had conked out a scant three lines from the end of the video game he was designing so he could get rich and quit. He quit anyway.

In a parting gesture, Mr. Lai told Q. David Hyatt, in front of cheering crowds, where he could stick his windmill. Howard declared that Friday to be "Mr. Lai Appreciation Day."

Early Monday morning before class, the DeWitt varsity ice hockey team held a preliminary meeting in one of the math rooms. All eighteen signees were present, called there by team captain Raymond Jardine. The only nonplayer in attendance was Ashley Bach, acting in her official capacity as team secretary, equipment manager, and the only person Raymond and Sean knew who owned a book of hockey rules. .

Raymond had Ashley record everybody's name, position, and hockey experience, and then tried to adjourn the meeting. But unfortunately there were questions. When a single hand shot up, Raymond turned to Sean and mouthed the words, "Who else? Cementhead."

"When's our first game, Ray?" Steve asked.

"I'm not sure," Raymond replied glibly. "The schedule hasn't been released."

"Well, then, when's our first practice?" Steve persisted.

"Our uniforms aren't ready yet."

Steve seemed to accept this.

The team actually appeared to be a fairly dedicated lot. Randy Fowler and Chris McDermott had both played in house league when they were much younger, and seemed excited at the prospect of skating for DeWitt. Chris, as well as Steve Semenski, also played varsity football (although Steve never got off the bench), as did Ten-Ton Tomlinson, who was a great skater, and was sure that his talents as a tackle would be of good use on the ice. No one understood why Leland Fenster had signed up, even though he explained himself, saying, "Hockey is some high-powered vub, babies."

Not once did Raymond so much as hint at the fact that they were a hockey team in name only. Oh, yes, they would train, and play, and have their moments of glory — sometime in the future. He pointed out that varsity ice hockey had a very late season, and everyone assumed that he knew what he was talking about. Sean was already plotting how to deny all responsibility when this team was uncovered as a fraud. Most of the people he hung out with were in this room, so he stood to lose a lot if he was blamed along with Raymond when it all came out.

After everyone was gone, and Raymond was drawing up an official summary of the meeting to submit to the office so the staff would know that he, Jardine, was involved in athletics, Sean got the chance to ask Ashley how her prize date with Sheldon Entwistle had gone Friday night.

"Don't ask," said Ashley. "When I'm in the city, I love taking carriage rides through Central Park. Did you know there are some people who are allergic to horses?"

Raymond looked up. "What happened?"

"His throat closed up! The poor guy could hardly breathe! We had to gallop to the hospital! And while we were in emergency, someone spray-painted 'Eric loves Jean' on the horse! The driver was *sooo* mad!"

"Is Entwistle okay?" asked Sean.

"He's fine. But we went straight home after the hospital, so it wasn't much of a night."

"Well, he got a good tire gauge out of it, anyway," said Raymond. "You did a great job, Ashley. We appreciate it."

"It's too bad I didn't get a chance to meet Steve at this meeting," Ashley reflected wistfully. "If I were the coach, I'd put Steve at center. He looks like a center — the broad shoulders, the sleek figure, the *face* of a great goal-scorer — do you think Steve'll get to play center?"

"It's hard to say," said Raymond, secure in the knowledge that there would never be a hockey game. But from the expression on the team captain's face, Sean could tell that, in Raymond's opinion, the only position Steve was fitted for was cleaning the locker room floor with his tongue.

"I've also been spending a lot of time studying Gavin Gunhold's poems," said Ashley. "I'm really anxious to start helping you guys with the work —

133

as soon as I can go and meet Mr. Gunhold. I was thinking of maybe having him autograph my Xerox copy of 'Fruit Fly.' It's my favorite."

"You know, Ash," said Raymond, "he hasn't written anything in a while, and he's really cranky about it. So we figured it wasn't the time to hit him up for favors. We'll ask again when he gets over his writer's block."

To combat Gavin Gunhold's writer's block, Raymond and Sean decided to try their hands at some more poetry. But today Sean's house was off limits. Mr. Delancey was coming home from work early, and bringing with him the people from Stead-E-Rain to install the revolutionary new weather-sensitive fully automatic sprinkler system for the lawn. So Raymond and Sean traveled on the motor scooter out to the DeWitt-Seaford town line to tap the creative energy of Raymond's home.

Raymond's neighborhood was much older than Sean's, lined with small neat houses, and so abundant with weeping willow trees that the bright afternoon sun touched the pavement only here and there. The front lawns, sidewalks, and streets were teeming with kids at play, ranging from toddlers up to eight- or nine-year-olds, all of whom stopped what they were doing to greet Raymond.

"Hey, everybody, it's Jardine!" announced one seven-year-old. He picked up a large dirt bomb and fired it with deadly accuracy against the mudguard of the scooter.

"That's the kid who loaned me the machine gun," Raymond called over his shoulder to Sean as children mobbed the scooter and gave them a cheering escort down the street.

"Yo, Jardine! What's up?" asked a little boy on a tricycle.

"Keeping ahead of the snipers, kiddo," Raymond replied.

"Jardine, could you play house with us?" called a little girl holding a baby doll.

"Not today. Jardine's a serious student. Taking a trip this summer, you know."

There was a loud chorus of boos from the kids.

"No one's going to send you to Theamelpos, Jardine," said one of the bigger boys.

"Yeah! Stay in Secaucus, and you can come and visit us!"

"No dice!"

The crowd parted, and Raymond pulled into the driveway of his house. Automatically, Sean headed for the front door, but Raymond called him back.

"Not there, Delancey. That's Jardine's parents' place. Jardine lives over here." He indicated the garage, a small brick structure detached from the rest of the house. The garage door had been replaced by a permanent wall of aluminum siding, on which was painted JARDINE in large black letters.

Sean was incredulous. "You live in the garage?"

Raymond shrugged. "We only have one car, and there's plenty of room on the driveway. Let me tell you, it took a lot of nagging to get this place. You know what they say — 'leavin' home ain't easy' — even when you're only going eight feet from the house." He took Sean to the rear, where a built-in wooden ladder led up to a padlocked window at the very top of the sloped roof. He unlocked the window, propped it open, and climbed inside, helping Sean in after him.

"Welcome to Jardine's castle. This is the bedroom."

Crouching down because of the low ceiling, Sean examined his surroundings. The "room" was a low, atticlike loft with sloping ceiling. It held only Raymond's bed and a small dresser, on which was placed a black-and-white twelve-inch TV.

"Don't you bang your head when you get up in the morning?" asked Sean, noting that the ceiling literally met the floor just beyond Raymond's pillow.

"Every day. It reminds me that I'm Jardine, just in case I'm dreaming I'm someone else."

Another ladder led down to the main floor, which was a standard size for a one-car garage. This Raymond had turned into a sitting room, with carpets on the floor and comfortable, although beat-up, furniture. The decor was dominated by the large poster of the beach at Theamelpos, which had once been in the travel agent's office at the DeWitt Mall. The rest of the room was plastered with newspaper and magazine clippings about people who had visited Theamelpos and become rich, famous, and successful immediately afterward. References to the island were carefully highlighted in fluorescent blue magic marker. Sean stared. Raymond had certainly done his homework. There were lottery winners, Oscar nominees, millionaire businessmen, oil tycoons, best-selling authors, chefs, and art dealers, all of whom had been struggling in obscurity before that fateful trip to Theamelpos. Stock portfolios had skyrocketed, businesses had thrived, record albums had gone quadruple platinum, and all manner of incredible instances of luck had occurred while the people involved soaked up the Theamelpos sun. One Montana farm boy on his first trip away from home had married a Scandinavian actress, won the National Ouzo Sweepstakes, and returned home to discover they had struck gold on his property.

"Have a seat," Raymond invited, indicating a large armchair. "Watch out for the broken spring."

They were just about to get to work when the telephone rang — once, twice, three times. But Raymond ignored it. "Don't worry about it. I've got an answering machine. Fish guts aren't fun, but the pay is pretty good."

There was a click, and the recorded message came through the machine's speaker. *Hello. This is Jardine. There's going to be a beep in a couple of seconds, so if you're really into talking to Jardine, you can leave a message. Thank you.*

After the beep, a woman's voice said, "Hello, this is Jardine's mother. Don't pretend you're not home, Raymond. I saw you come in. I've got fresh blueberry pie. Why don't you and your friend come over and have some? You've also got a letter from the Greek Ministry of Tourism. Are you sending away for Theamelpos brochures again? You know Uncle Alex says — "And the tape cut her off.

Raymond heaved a great sigh. "Come on, Delancey. Let's go meet my mom. If we don't go, she'll just throw pebbles at the window."

Mrs. Jardine was waiting for them in her kitchen

137

as Raymond entered and snapped her a salute. "Reporting as ordered, Kommandant. This is my friend Delancey from school."

"Hello, Delancey," said Mrs. Jardine. "I don't expect Raymond to know it, but do you by any chance have a first name?"

"It's Sean. Nice to meet you."

"Great pie, Kommandant," Raymond commented after they'd each had a slice.

Mrs. Jardine was looking through the Theamelpos tourist brochures that had come in the mail. "You know, Uncle Alex thinks you're going to be working with him in New Jersey this summer. And if you don't work, how are you going to be able to keep up your place?"

Raymond set down his glass of milk. "Jardine will be too lucky to have to work after he goes to Theamelpos."

Mrs. Jardine regarded Sean. "How does a nice, sensible boy like you end up spending time with Jardine?"

Sean had aked himself that question many times. "We're working together on a poetry assignment," he said finally.

"Speaking of which," said Raymond, rising, "I've got to borrow the big dictionary from Dad's study. Okay, Kommandant?" He headed out of the kitchen into the hall.

"Just keep at it, Raymond," she called after him. "Slowly but surely, everything that your father and I used to own is finding its way over to 'the apartment.' " She smiled at Sean. "He's nice, though. Any time we want, we can borrow our stuff back." She called to her son once more. "We should start charging you rent for that place, Raymond. What do you think it's worth? Two hundred? Three hundred?"

"Just take a pound of flesh every month, Kommandant," Raymond replied from upstairs, "and that way, by June, I'll still have a hundred and forty-two pounds left to take to Theamelpos."

Mrs. Jardine turned momentarily serious. "I'm glad to see that Raymond has someone nice to spend time with," she told Sean, "because underneath all that 'no luck' business, he really is a good person."

Sean nodded vaguely. Maybe so. But *how far* underneath?

"The Bargain" by Gavin Gunhold

After the hair tonic salesman's toupee fell off
He decided to lower the price.
So I bought six cases.
A bargain is a bargain.

"It's okay," said Sean thoughtfully, "but I don't think it's as good as the others."

"Don't worry about it," said Raymond. "Even a brilliant Canadian poet has an off day now and then. We can write all about how this one comes from his mediocre period."

They played around with a few other ideas, and tried some experimental words out of the dictionary, but without results.

Sean, who had at first thought Raymond's living arrangements to be a lunatic idea, felt strangely at home in the garage apartment now. After all, what else could be expected from Raymond Jardine, garbage bag? Idly, he imagined the fireworks if he asked if he could move into the Delancey garage. Hah! They wouldn't even let Gramp, a grown man, have his own apartment in Brooklyn. Besides which, the garage was piled high with discarded revolutionary inventions — more little windmills that worked about as well as the big one at school.

Until a replacement could be found for Mr. Lai, the Nassau County pool of supply teachers sent a different substitute every day. On Wednesday, it was Mrs. Hurtig, a wonderfully jolly but completely unqualified lady who normally filled in for absent kindergarten teachers.

"I don't know a computer from a toaster oven," she announced pleasantly at the start of the class. "I can't help you with your programs, but if you like, I can organize a singalong about "Rosie the Little Red Car."

The whole class loved her instantly, and they spent a companionable half hour just chatting.

They were interrupted by Mr. Hyatt's voice on the p.a. system. "Attention, staff and students. There is no cause for alarm. Please evacuate the building by the shortest route. Once again, there is no cause for alarm."

In the background, scuffling could be heard, and Engineer Johnson suddenly shouted, *"Hit the deck!"*

There was a series of sharp cracklings, and the p.a. system went dead along with the lights.

"Oh, dear," said Mrs. Hurtig. "I suppose I should do something. I am the teacher, after all." She looked thoughtful for a moment, and then bellowed, *"Every man for himself!"* and led the laughing, good-natured stampede to safety.

Out on the front lawn, the entire population of DeWitt High School was milling around in a sociable carnival of griping. Their irritation at being hit with yet another SACGEN inconvenience was mellowed by the opportunity to take a break from classes, and the students spent a pleasant few minutes mingling with friends. The prevailing attitude went from pleased to joyous when Engineers Sopwith and Johnson came running out of the building, their faces and clothing darkened with soot from a series of small explosions. The outbreak, however, wasn't too serious, and the DeWitt Fire Department had everything under control in a matter of minutes.

"You can't win 'em all," said Howard philosophically. As soon as Mr. Hyatt had come on the p.a., Howard had grabbed his table and chairs and set up his poker game on the lawn. Leland, Randy, and Chris were playing when Sean found them. Sean would have liked to join them, but he had left his toothpicks in his locker, and Howard refused to negotiate a line of credit.

"Wood only, baby," said Leland, summarizing house policy. To Leland, toothpicks were *wood*, except when the bet went really high, when they became *lumber*. "That's a lot of lumber, baby," he would often protest one of Howard's super raises. And sometimes, when the game organizer raked in a particularly large pot, he would exclaim, "Lumberyard! Zunging lumberyard!"

Sean stayed on as a spectator, though, and soon Raymond came by, but fortunately, Howard was too involved in the game to growl at him.

Raymond was already in a bad mood. "Did you see Eckerman over there? He's making a speech all about how everything is under control, thanks to the Danny Eckerman evacuation plan! How come you can never find a helium balloon when you really need one?"

Sean did not reply. He was staring across the lawn at a sight so unbelievably terrible that all he could manage to say was, "Raymond — look!"

Raymond followed Sean's gaze. There, not too far from the spot where a frantic Q. David Hyatt was tearing his hair over SACGEN's well-being, stood Ashley Bach and Steve Semenski, holding an intimate conversation, obviously totally absorbed in one another.

Raymond turned beseeching eyes to the sky. "That's right. We were overdue for another devastating strike against Jardine. This is just what the doctor ordered. Sure. Give her to Cementhead. Jardine doesn't care. Young love is a wonderful thing." He turned to Sean. "Delancey, *how* did this happen?"

"How did what happen?" asked Randy. He spotted the object of their scrutiny. "Oh, yeah. Steve and that new girl, the one you guys always hang out with. The whole school's buzzing about it."

"But he didn't even know her," offered Sean weakly.

Randy looked confused. "Why is it such a mystery to you, Sean? It was *your* sister who introduced them. Just today."

Sean choked. There it was, the revenge of Nicolette Delancey. She had pledged to "get him," and she had devised the one plan guaranteed to wipe him out. She had carefully considered all the options, and instead of being merciful and just running him over with the family car, she had set up Ashley and Steve Cementhead!

"Steve's a lucky guy," Randy continued, shaking his head. "She's really something. They're going out Friday night."

"This is all over the school, and Jardine is the last to know!" Raymond lamented. "They even publicize what night they're going out!"

Randy laughed. "It's not *that* much of a top story. I just know that Steve's going with his family to Saratoga on Saturday, so when I heard they had a date, I figured it had to be Friday."

Raymond turned on Sean. "Jardine is holding you personally responsible for this, Delancey! How could you let your sister do such a thing?"

"Well, she didn't exactly consult me on it, did she?" Sean cried irritably.

At that point, the students began to file back into the school. Sean could see Ashley and Steve holding hands as they headed for the door.

"There's no way Jardine is going back to class after a blow like this," Raymond muttered darkly as he followed Sean inside. "This is the least cool thing that could possibly have happened. Think about it. A *totally* terrific thing is about to happen to Cementhead. Cementhead! The man who *surfs* on a cafeteria tray! The man who wears muscle armor for Halloween! The man who, when they were giving out luck, cut the line and went twice so there was none left for Jardine!"

"Come on, Raymond. Don't be a baby. How can

you get mad at Steve for doing exactly what any other guy would do in his place?" Sean's face twisted. "Even if he *was* born with a horseshoe up his diaper — a great big twenty-four karat *gold* horseshoe!" He reared his foot back to kick the nearest locker, but stopped short. Where did he get off being this upset over a girl? He was Sean Delancey, a popular guy, star of the basketball team, a regular at Howard's poker game. And Steve was a close friend, too. Raymond had planted these anti-Steve sentiments in Sean's mind, but here was where it ended. He should be happy that a friend of his was getting a fantastic girl like Ashley. There was nothing to be upset about. So why did he feel like the world had just ended?

He sighed. Forget class. There was no sense getting an education now. He would tell Raymond to get lost, and find a nice quiet place to do his mourning. Then he would go home and kill Nikki. He looked up to see Ashley bearing down on them, her face aglow.

"Here you are! I've been looking all over for you! I've got the most wonderful news in the world! You'll be so happy — "

"We've got wonderful news, too!" Sean suddenly heard himself cry out. He paused, having a vision of the triumphant Steve brandishing Karen Whitehead's stolen underwear. Steve, the winner — and beside him, Sean, the guy who was there, but that's all. Sorry, Steve. Not this time. "This is such great news, we just have to go first!" He caught a confused look from Raymond, and forged ahead. "Ashley, we've finally convinced Mr. Gunhold to let you come into the city and see him — on Friday night."

Ashley smiled even wider. "That's marvelous! That's fabulous! That's — Friday night?" She looked stricken. "I can't go Friday night! I've got plans! Couldn't we make it Saturday?"

"Oh, Ashley, no," said Sean in great concern. "Raymond and I have been pestering Mr. Gunhold about this for so long. If we don't turn up with you on Friday night, it's all over for our project."

Ashley was the picture of despair. "But — but — oh — okay, I'll come with you on Friday. It's really a bad night for me, but if it's the *only* time Mr. Gunhold'll see me — "

A slow smile was taking root on Raymond's face, but he covered it up. "Oh, it is. The only time. Friday or never." He chuckled, shaking his head. "Aren't poets the darndest people?"

"Well, then, I guess I'm going with you guys," she sighed. "Thanks for arranging it for me. I'm sorry I'm not happier, but — well, anyway."

"Oh, yeah," said Raymond, remembering. "What was *your* good news?"

Ashley sighed yet again. "Oh, nothing. Nothing at all."

The scene that followed was positively eerie. In total silence, Raymond and Sean got their jackets, left the school, and walked to the nearby DeWitt Park.

Raymond reached into his pocket, produced a stale peanut, and listlessly beaned a squirrel. The animal retreated a couple of yards, then stopped, and made a remarkably Jardine-like gesture, pointing its little paws skyward.

Finally, Raymond spoke. "I just want you to know, Delancey, that I've never been so proud of you as I am right now."

Sean shook his head. "How could I have been so *stupid*?"

"That's easy. Sheer jealousy. You couldn't stand by and let Cementhead have Ashley. No fancy explanations. No excuses. We're worms, but let it never be said that we won't admit it."

"But Gavin Gunhold is dead," Sean said quietly.

"That's the beauty of it. You saw a plan of attack, and even though there were a lot of sticky details to work out, you went right ahead. It brought tears to my eyes."

Sean's face was pale. "The fact that the guy is dead qualifies as a lot more than sticky details, Raymond."

"That made it even more beautiful. If you ever run for President, I'll tell you right now, you've got Jardine's vote."

"I can't believe I did it," Sean lamented. "Raymond, if they like each other, throwing a monkey wrench into Friday night isn't going to do anything. They'll just go out the next night, or the night after that."

"But Mr. and Mrs. Cementhead are taking their little chip off the old block to Saratoga, remember? Chances are they won't be able to have their date until next weekend. Who knows what could happen between now and then? Cementhead could decide he doesn't like her. He's stupid enough. Or she might start to fall madly in love with some other guy. Maybe even you, Delancey, or — dare we say it? — Jardine."

"I know what she's *not* going to do," said Sean sadly. "She's *not* going to meet Gavin Gunhold."

Raymond shrugged. "Maybe she is. We can dress up some guy, take her someplace dark, and blow it by her fast."

Sean shook his head. "No way, Raymond. Ashley may not be good at school, but she's got more common sense than the two of us put together. If we dress up somebody like Howard in glasses and a fake beard, she'll see through it in a minute."

Raymond nodded. "Especially when he asks if she's got any toothpicks."

"Seriously! And then not only will we lose her to Steve, but she'll also never talk to us again. And I think Ashley's a pretty good friend of ours by this point. She bailed us out on the party, and forgave me when I set her up with that Entwistle guy, and now she's giving up her date just because she thinks she's being helpful on the poetry assignment. Raymond, I enjoy her company. I like watching her count calories. I like sneaking into Miami Beach early every day to avoid her health food. I like Ashley!"

Raymond looked surprised. "Good point, Delancey. I like her, too." His face grew animated. "So we have to do right by her. We have to come up with a Gavin Gunhold so perfect that she'll never suspect we're snowing her. Now, let's see — what would Gav be like today if that trolley car hadn't offed him?"

"The world's oldest gas jockey," said Sean irritably.

"That's right! He was born in 1899. That would make him — let's see — eighty-eight." An enormous grin spread all across his face. "Eighty-eight! Yeah!"

"What are you beaming about?" Sean asked suspiciously. "What are you thinking?"

"Who do we know who's eighty-eight, bored, needs something to do, and would really appreciate a little change of pace?"

Sean leaped to his feet. "Oh, no, you don't! Not Gramp! No way!"

"But Delancey, he's perfect!"

"*No*, Raymond! No chance!"

"But — "

"Forget it! End of story!"

Eight

The first frost of the year had come the very night Mr. Delancey had installed his Stead-E-Rain sprinkler system, but the technological marvel didn't seem to notice. According to Stead-E-Rain, the temperature was hovering in and around one hundred fifteen degrees Fahrenheit, and the town of DeWitt was experiencing a Sahara desert drought.

For this reason, all sprinkler valves had been going full blast for almost a week now. The lawn had been converted to semiswamp, and the bushes were wilting. One thing Mr. Delancey had neglected to ask the people from Stead-E-Rain was how the system could be deactivated. There was no on/off switch, and when Sean tried to yank the control system out of the wall, he received a jarring electric shock. Strangely, there had been no answer at the Stead-E-Rain offices for several days now.

"Don't blame me," was Mr. Delancey's statement.

A seepage problem was beginning in several parts of the house. In the TV room, the sound of water dripping into buckets formed the background for exclusive Weather Channel footage of National Guard troops vainly trying to dig Denver out of a mountain of snow. Gramp watched smugly, loving every minute of it, drinking a glass of prune juice and smoking a Scrulnick's. With effort, he pulled his eyes from the set and regarded Raymond and Sean.

"It sounds to me like you kids have been pulling some stuff here."

Raymond had just recounted a reasonably accurate summary of the Gavin Gunhold affair, leading up to the need for a bogus poet on Friday night. At Sean's request, Raymond had left out any mention of Steve Semenski, and described Ashley merely as a doubter who needed convincing.

Sean flushed. "We promised up and down that Gavin Gunhold had tons of poetry, Gramp, and it turned out that he had only the one. So we *had* to write the poems."

"Now this Ashley girl is getting on our case to meet you — uh — him," Raymond added. "So if we can't produce our poet, it'll look like something's not kosher, and there's a chance we'll get found out. Then Kerr'll flunk us for sure."

Gramp leaned back and took a long puff of his

Scrulnick's. "Well, I want you to know that I think this is just great."

"You do?" Sean asked in amazement.

"Of course!" The old man put an arm around each boy. "This is what getting an education is really about. Being alive! Feeling the blood pumping through those arteries! Having your back up against the wall every now and then!"

"So you'll do it?" Sean prompted.

"Well, I'll have to check my social calendar," said Gramp sarcastically. "After all, I *am* in Long Island, the excitement capital of the world."

Raymond grinned. "This is fantastic! Thanks a lot, Gramp!" From his pocket he produced a crumpled dollar bill and held it out to the old man. "You were right. Denver was first. I could have sworn it was going to be Cincinnati."

Gramp motioned for him to put his money away. "Double or nothing northern Texas is next."

"Northern Texas? No way!"

"Don't be so sure, Jardine. Picture the national weather map. . . ."

As Sean was on his way to English class the next morning, Steve Semenski approached him and begged for a moment of his time. Steve's normally happy, devil-may-care expression seemed to be missing that day. In fact, if his complexion had been any paler, it would have matched his light green CLUB MED muscle shirt.

"The part that freaks me out is the *lame* excuse she gave!" Steve exclaimed, after telling Sean with wonder in his eyes that Ashley had broken their date. "She said she was going to New York for English class to meet a poet! Can you believe it? Isn't that the *lamest* excuse you've ever heard in your life?"

Sean swallowed hard. It was wrong to keep Ashley from Steve when they were both so drawn to one another. Where was his respect for friendship? What about the secret society they had once pledged to be faithful to? Steve was a good friend, too, never pointing out that Sean was the least adventurous of the group's five members. It still bothered Sean that he was the only one out of the five who had never had the guts to steal Karen Whitehead's underwear. Even now, as a varsity athlete, he felt vaguely uncomfortable talking with Steve, for some reason expecting him to bring it up.

"Well, Steve, maybe she feels funny on account of her boyfriend, Tank," he mumbled, blushing.

Steve thought it over. "I don't know. Maybe it was because of Tank — "

Raymond approached them. "Who's Tank?"

"You know Tank," Sean said meaningfully. "Ashley's *boyfriend*."

"But Ashley doesn't — oh, *Tank*!" To Steve he said, "He's a boxer, you know."

Steve looked confused. "Sean said he was a wrestler."

"Oh, *that* Tank!" exclaimed Raymond. "Right. Big guy. Mean."

"I was going to show the chick a real class time, too," Steve lamented. "You know. A movie, some chow, and then a cruise in the Stevemobile."

"You mean that '72 Catalina you drive?" Raymond slapped his forehead. "Ashley ought to have her head examined for blowing off *this* date!"

"I put wide tires on that car. Wide tires! It has a four-forty engine and a four-barrel carburetor!"

"And imitation fur dice hanging from the rearview mirror!" Raymond added in disbelief.

Later, after Steve had gone off, still shaking his head, Raymond awarded Sean a hearty slap on the shoulder. "Tank! I love it!"

"Shut up, Raymond," snapped Sean. "I'm not proud of this."

So the wide tires of the Stevemobile cruised with only the driver on Friday night as Ashley rode into New York on the Long Island Railroad with Raymond and Sean. Their destination: The Euripides Café, a dilapidated basement bistro in Greenwich Village, soon to be condemned by the Board of Health, but a favorite hangout of poets, especially expatriate Canadians. There Gramp would be waiting for them, ready to play Gavin Gunhold. Gramp had left on an earlier train, so delighted by the prospect of secret scheming that he had been chain-smoking Scrulnick's all afternoon.

The café was dark, damp, and smoky as Raymond and Sean led Ashley, who was dressed as though she were about to meet the governor, down the stairs and through the battered door. The all-classical jukebox was playing quiet chamber music so as not to drown out the strange tip-tapping noise that was the trademark of the Euripides. The building commissioner claimed the unexplained sound, which came from all four walls and the ceiling, was just bad plumbing, but the management insisted that the café was home to the largest rat in New York City.

Poet Gavin Gunhold was already in a fight with the management and a few patrons when Raymond, Sean, and Ashley walked in.

"The guests are complaining about his cigars," the manager informed Sean.

"Don't you have a smoking section?" Raymond asked.

"He's *in* it! It's the *smokers* who are complaining! The nonsmokers are lucky. They're on the other side of the room."

"You ignoramus!" Gramp accused the manager. "These are the finest cigars in the world!"

"They smell like the morning after the night the outdoor toilet burned down," exclaimed a woman sitting at the table next to Gramp.

"What do *you* know?" Gramp snapped back, whereupon the woman's husband became upset, and the manager had to step in. In minutes, the whole café was one big shouting match, with Gramp at the center, ready to defend his Scrulnick's to the end.

"Wait a minute!" cried Ashley. Silence fell, and staff and patrons turned their attention from their bickering to her. "Don't you know who you're talking to? This is Gavin Gunhold, the famous Canadian poet!"

Sean covered his eyes.

"Yeah, well, I've never heard of you!" piped the man whose wife Gramp had just insulted.

"That's because the most challenging thing you've

ever read is the free gift offer on the back of a box of Snappy Wappies!" Gramp retorted, and the bickering started up again.

"Well, I never!" exclaimed Ashley indignantly. She grabbed Gramp's arm and led him toward the exit. "Come on, Mr. Gunhold. You don't have to take this. You're an artist."

"Yeah," agreed Gramp, turning to thumb his nose at the couple at the next table.

Outside, Sean finally got the chance to take a look at Gramp, and realized what a perfect poet his grandfather had become. The arguments at The Euripides had made his eyes wild, and he wore an ancient, battered suit that looked like it had been thrown over Niagara Falls and sun-dried in the Mojave Desert.

It was quite a warm night so, after Raymond performed the introductions, they adjourned to a nearby park bench, where Ashley held her first-ever meeting with a poet. She asked dozens of questions, most of which Gramp didn't really answer, so Sean wasn't quite sure what kind of impression Gavin Gunhold was making. Raymond, apparently, didn't think things were going too well, as he was constantly looking up at the sky. He eventually left the meeting altogether to strike up a conversation with a bum who claimed he'd been to Theamelpos.

"I should've known no one who lives in a park could have gone to Theamelpos," Raymond complained to Sean on his return to their bench. "They all win lotteries and become bank presidents and stuff. He hit me up for a quarter, and it turns out he thinks Theamelpos is in Connecticut."

"Take off on me again and you're dead!" Sean hissed.

The boys didn't get an indication of the night's success or failure until it was time to head back to Long Island.

"Mr. Gunhold, meeting you was one of the greatest experiences of my life," said Ashley honestly. "Thank you for seeing me."

"Call me Gavin," Gramp said generously.

Ashley raved about Gavin Gunhold all the way home. Sean ducked out at a McDonald's near the station until Gramp came in on the next train, flushed with victory.

"Now, *that* was a good evening," he declared, stretching out his arms.

"You were thrown out of a restaurant," Sean pointed out.

"We showed those robots. Your friend Ashley's really something."

Sean smiled sadly. "I know."

"Household Security" by Gavin Gunhold

As a positive step against crime
I bought a watchdog,
And am training him personally.
This week we study full contact karate.

"It's fantastic!" said Ashley honestly. "Gavin's stuff just blows my mind."

Sean flushed. "He's a — uh — developing artist."

Ashley nodded enthusiastically. The two were

eating lunch at Miami Beach, listening to the tantrums from the poker game and the cheers from the tray-surfing. Ashley, a serious student of modern poetry, wasn't paying attention to these distractions, except when Steve surfed. Then she would stand on her chair, waving and shouting encouragement. It was turning Sean's stomach so badly he could hardly eat.

Raymond had had to rush off to help Miss Ritchie with some filing. This was not the first time, either. Miss Ritchie seemed to have plenty of odd jobs for Raymond, both at lunch and after classes.

"It's blackmail," was Raymond's opinion. "She's got me by the throat because King Phidor, the bozo, couldn't run a country worth beans. So all Jardine can say is, 'Sure thing, Miss Ritchie. I'll do your filing. No problem.' She's a very sick individual."

Nikki came by, and instantly Sean was on his guard. There was a bit of a cold war going on between the Delancey children lately, since Sean now refused to talk to Nikki, and Nikki seemed equally up to the task of not talking to Sean. This left a lot more space in the dinner conversation for miracles of technology (Mr. Delancey), Brooklyn (Gramp), and "Why can't the students at DeWitt appreciate SACGEN?" (Mrs. Delancey).

"So how did your big date with Steve go?" Nikki asked Ashley, smiling maliciously at Sean.

"It didn't," Ashley replied. "I had to go into the city with Raymond and Sean, so we canceled."

"That's terrible!" Nikki exclaimed. The broken date didn't bother her so much as the fact that her brother had stolen her grin, leaving her with a look of dismay.

"Don't worry," said Ashley. "We're going out this Friday for sure!"

Once again, Nikki had possession of the grin, while Sean reflected that his lunch was only half eaten, and he had completely lost his appetite.

Sean was riding home that night on the local transit from the DeWitt Mall, carrying a bag of groceries for his mother. He was thinking about the injustice of Ashley's falling in love with Steve, who never got off the bench, when Sean, the star, was available. Squinting through the dirty scratched glass of the bus window, he noticed the lights were still on at DeWitt High. Someone was carrying a large carton from a stack in the parking lot into the school building. Then he saw the scooter leaning against the fence. He pulled the cord just as the bus was passing its stop, and caught a few mild curses from the driver as he grabbed his parcel and headed for the school.

"What's this all about, Raymond?"

"It's a scientific study," Raymond replied, his voice strained by the effort of his lifting. "To see how many hundred-pound crates the average high school student can carry around before he drops dead. Just inside that door, there's a scientist with a stopwatch."

"No. Seriously."

"Miss Ritchie volunteered me to carry in this beautiful two-thousand-pound paper shipment because of my Pefkakia project," Raymond puffed. He made a face. "And you can't know what a wonderful feeling it is that children are going to have supplies for their education because of Jardine's efforts tonight."

"Can she do that?" Sean asked.

"Because Jardine wants to go to Theamelpos, he opted not to say, 'Stuff your shipment, Miss Ritchie.' " He stood up again. "Grab a box, Delancey. Let's get this over with."

"Why me? I never did a project on Pefkakia."

"Well, you can't just stand there and watch while I kill myself here."

"Why not?" Sean grinned. "You look good doing manual labor. It suits you."

Raymond looked up at the sky. "That's right. Send Jardine a sadist. Terrific. Now grab a box."

"These are hundred-pound cartons," Sean protested, really enjoying the look of aggravation on his English partner's face.

Raymond was livid. "Listen, Delancey, I've been at this for over an hour, and I let my hernia insurance lapse, so I'm in no mood for your cute little jokes. If you don't help me, I'm going to order a twenty-seven-inch pizza to be delivered to your house at two o'clock in the morning. So just *grab a box, huh*?"

Fortunately, Raymond had already done most of the work, but it still took the boys half an hour. Sean's muscles were aching, but Raymond was in such pain that Sean had to drive home.

"It's just like riding a bike, Delancey, except that you don't have to pedal. I'd do it, but I feel like I've been run over by a train. Even my cramps have cramps!"

So Sean took over the helm, piloting the scooter

carefully through back streets as Raymond slumped at the rear with Sean's grocery bag, holding an impassioned conversation with the sky.

"You know, Raymond, Ashley and Steve have another date this Friday."

"To a person in my condition you give this kind of news?" Raymond asked. "What's our plan?"

"There is no plan," Sean called back. "It's stupid to try to keep them apart. First of all, it's childish; second, it's a rotten thing to do to both Ashley and Steve; and third, it'll never work. How many times can we dynamite their dates?"

Raymond looked disgusted. "This is your department, Delancey. Jardine relies on you to keep Ashley away from the Cementmobile. You can't give up now. You've become one of the master strategists of the twentieth century — giving the prize to Entwistle, taking her to meet our dead poet, dreaming up Tank. Think!"

"There's no point. Even if we could throw a monkey wrench into date after date, which is impossible, they'd start to get suspicious."

Raymond looked up to the sky. "A quitter. Thanks."

"Hey! I'm not a quitter! I just know when it's over!"

Raymond shrugged expansively. "You want Ashley to get together with Cementhead? Who's Jardine to argue? I even volunteer to play the violin for them. You know, you're allowed to go faster than five miles an hour."

Sean bristled. "Hey, I'm being cautious, okay?"

"I need the breeze. It eases my pains."

As he rounded the corner onto his own block,

Sean could see the even spray of the Stead-E-Rain sprinklers refracting the light of a nearby streetlamp.

"Far out," said Raymond. "A rainbow at night."

The scooter was hard to control because the road was covered by at least two inches of water, as the sewers were unable to keep up with the output of the Stead-E-Rain. Their shoes and the bottoms of their pants were soaked from the splashing of the scooter.

Sean was getting nervous. "Raymond, I'm having trouble steering in all this water!"

"No problem, Delancey. You're doing fine." Suddenly, he pointed. "There's a whole crowd in front of your house. Did you ever see so many umbrellas?"

Involuntarily, Sean slammed on the brakes, and the scooter went into a long skid, cutting a wide arc across the street, spraying water everywhere.

A big Lincoln Continental turned the corner. Sean swerved to the right, jumped the curb, and ditched himself, Raymond, and the scooter in a tall hedge of unpruned bushes. The groceries went flying, scattering in all directions.

Gingerly, Raymond sat up, pulling a stray branch away from his face. "Not bad, Delancey. Next lesson we'll study not crashing."

Sean pulled himself away from the scooter and stepped down. The ground was so wet from the sprinklers that his sneaker sank in the mud. He flipped his soaking hair back from his eyes and regarded the wreckage of the groceries. The eggs were all broken, and the dehydrated milk was hydrating in the street. As he watched, the oatmeal broke out of its box and began oozing in all directions as though it were a swamp creature with a mind of its own.

Gramp's face appeared above the top of the hedge. "Sean! Jardine! Are you all right?"

"We had a little accident," Sean admitted.

Raymond tried to sit up. "I'm stuck," he observed.

"What's going on at the house?" Sean asked.

Gramp snorted. "Schnitzenberger's got together a lynch mob of neighbors to complain about the rainy season. Seems he doesn't buy your father's 'miracle of technology' speech." He grinned. "You should see Schnitzenberger's face. If it gets him that mad, it *must* be a miracle of technology!"

Raymond was still engaged in the process of disentangling himself from the hedge. Finally, hopelessly caged in by scratchy branches, he gave up and lay back in the brush and mud, folding his arms in front of him. He might have slept there, too, if Sean and his grandfather hadn't dragged him out, hosed him down, and set him up in the Delancey spare room.

Just after seven, Sean was awakened by the insistent ringing of the telephone. No. There was no way he was getting out of his warm bed to tell some broke college student he wasn't interested in subscribing to *American Quantity Surveyor* magazine. He was going to sleep until ten minutes before school. Longer, maybe.

The ringing stopped, and then his mother was knocking on his bedroom door. "Sean, telephone. Someone named Ashley."

Sean set a record getting to the phone. Eat your heart out, Cementhead. She's finally realized who the real man is. He picked up the receiver. "Ashley — hi."

"Sean, I have the most incredible news! You're not going to be able to believe it!"

"Yeah?" Sean prompted expectantly.

"I was in the city last night, and I ran into an old friend. He's got a job with *Spice of Life* — you know, the TV show? He's an idea-thinker-upper — I forget the official name. He comes up with ideas for interviews. So guess what?"

"What?" Sean asked suspiciously.

"I told him all about Gavin, and they're going to interview him on *Spice of Life* next week! Isn't that fabulous?"

Sean almost dropped the phone. "I — I — I'll put Raymond on!"

Raymond had other ideas. "The way I feel this morning, I wouldn't get up to talk to anybody short of the Greek Minister of Tourism."

"Raymond, Ashley's set up a TV interview for Gavin Gunhold!"

"Hi, Ash," Raymond said into the phone. "Yeah, I just heard. That's great!"

"Great?!" Sean hissed. "It's terrible! Tell her no way!"

Raymond ignored him. "Beautiful, Ash. Nice work. He'll be there."

"No, he won't!" Sean was in a frenzy. "Cancel! Cancel!"

"Oh, I agree. He'll be amazing on TV."

"How can you be so stupid? Give me that phone!"

"I've got to go, Ash. 'Bye." Just as Sean reached

for the receiver, Raymond hung up. "Cool out, Delancey."

"*Cool out?* Our dead poet has a live interview, and you want me to cool out?"

Raymond shook his head. "He's not dead anymore, thanks to you. *Gramp* is Gavin Gunhold. Think, Delancey! What starts with *T* and rhymes with *eamelpos*?"

Sean frowned. "I don't see how forcing *my* grandfather to impersonate a poet on national television will get you to Theamelpos."

Raymond looked exasperated. "*We* discovered him, which wouldn't be worth beans if he was a total nobody. But as soon as he goes on that show, he's a somebody. It'll make points with Kerr. I'll get the kid who loaned me the machine gun to tape the interview on his VCR, and then we'll have a poetry assignment with accompanying videocassette material. They've *got* to send us to Theamelpos if we've got accompanying videocassette material."

"I don't like it," said Sean. "Before we were just lying to Ashley and Kerr. Now we're going to be lying to millions of people on network TV."

"That's a downer way of looking at it. There's only one true test for this. We talk to Gramp and see what he thinks." He opened the door to reveal a pajama-clad Patrick Delancey, crouched right there with a hand to his ear.

"Gramp, were you spying on us?" Sean demanded.

"What are you complaining about? It saved you the trouble of coming to find me and con me into it. Show a little respect for a TV personality."

"So you'll do it?" asked Raymond.

"Of course I'll do it," said Gramp. "Weather systems develop so slowly that it leaves us a lot of spare time, Jardine. Besides prune juice and fine cigars, my poetry is all I've got these days." He assumed a smile that was remarkably boyish for a man of his years. "And I've always wanted to be on television."

Late Friday afternoon, Sean was just sitting down to work on his map of Central America for geography class when Raymond showed up at the door. "I was just starting on my map," said Sean hopefully. "It looks like a lot of work."

"I came right over," said Raymond, "to let you know how much Jardine appreciates all your efforts to prevent Ashley from going out with Cementhead tonight."

"Don't be an idiot, Raymond. You know we didn't do anything."

Raymond pretended to be surprised. "Oh! That must be why I saw the Cementmobile getting a hot-wax treatment at the car wash in the mall. And, you know, that would explain Cementhead buying a brand new muscle shirt. Jardine certainly wishes them a lovely evening. But with Cementhead, the man born with a horseshoe up his diaper, how can it miss?" His brow clouded. "Grab your coat, Delancey. You're coming with me."

"I refuse to follow Ashley and Steve around on their date."

Raymond shook his head. "It's not that at all. We've got a long night before us, and we'd better get a head start sulking. Jardine requires your presence, because you are the only other person in the universe who realizes just how terrible this really is."

Sean thought it over. There was no refuting the logic, but he sure didn't feel like spending a whole evening listening to Raymond crab and complain. He was upset enough as it was over Ashley and Steve. "You know, my mom's making a big dinner tonight, and — "

Mrs. Delancey peered out of the kitchen. "No, I'm not, dear. We're having leftover liver, remember?"

Sean turned back to Raymond. "Why do you want to go out somewhere with me? Since this is supposed to be my fault, you should be avoiding me."

"I'm not blaming you," said Raymond. "You were made not to do anything by *them*." He glanced up at the ceiling. "So *they* could get a few more licks in at Jardine."

With a huge sigh, Sean went for his coat. There really was no avoiding Raymond Jardine, not even in moments of stress.

Raymond decided that they should grab some dinner at the Underwood Colonial Diner in Massapequa.

"Why there?" Sean asked.

"Because they have the worst food on Long Island," Raymond replied grimly.

After dinner, they went to a broken-down theater in Bellmore to see an old black-and-white detective film from the 1950s.

"It's the lousiest movie I've ever seen," Raymond explained as they bought their tickets.

When the movie was over, they picked up two

jumbo orders of stale popcorn and went to hang out in Schuyler Park.

"The ugliest place in Nassau County," Raymond reasoned.

They left the park at ten and returned to the Delancey TV room to cap off the night watching a *Gunsmoke* rerun dubbed in Serbo-Croatian on cable, and sipping enormous glasses of tomato juice.

"Why tomato juice?" Sean asked as he headed for the kitchen.

"Jardine *hates* tomato juice," Raymond replied.

They watched in silence for a while, then Raymond scratched his head thoughtfully. "It's not too late, you know. I can still call the police and tell them I've planted a five-megaton hydrogen bomb somewhere in southern Long Island."

Sean stared dully right through the TV set. Ashley Bach was just a girl. Like any other girl. What was the big deal?

"They'd call in the National Guard and evacuate everyone," Raymond mused. "Ashley and Cementhead would have to rejoin their families at some evacuation station." He paused. "Of course, they'd also evacuate Jardine."

Sean frowned. It wasn't as though he'd never had a girl friend before, or would never have one again.

"They'd probably send Jardine to an evacuation station in Secaucus." Raymond's brow clouded. "My uncle would say, 'Jardine, as long as you're here, why don't you pick up some extra money?' Oh, no!" He took a large gulp of tomato juice and winced from the taste.

A varsity basketball star doesn't have to worry

about girls. *They* line up for *him*. . . . So where were they? Even Mindy didn't want him anymore; she preferred a sleazebag like Danny to one of the most popular guys in the school!

"But what if they sent Jardine to an evacuation station in Connecticut? Or Pennsylvania? What if they sent Ashley and Cementhead to the *same* evacuation station? What if. . . ."

So what was the use of the best jump shot in town? Here he was, sitting home on Friday night, watching Marshal Dillon babbling in some foreign language — drawing moral support from the likes of Raymond Jardine. This Ashley-Steve thing must have affected him more than he'd thought. He was losing all sense of perspective.

Raymond sat forward in his chair. "Well, Delancey, Jardine had a putrid time. I hope you had the same. I'd better get going so we can both burst into tears in the privacy of our own rooms."

A smile tugged at the corner of Sean's mouth. "Raymond, dinner was lousy, the movie stank, and the park was ugly and boring. What less could I ask for? I hope the tomato juice was to your disliking?"

Raymond was clearly impressed. "Hey, Delancey, you're starting to think like Jardine. Bad move."

Nine

Neither Sean nor Raymond was upset when Mr. Kerr wanted another update on the poetry assignments on Monday morning. Ashley seemed to be revving up for a blow by blow account of her big date, and a change of subject was most welcome.

This time, Jardine, Delancey, and Bach pulled through their interview fairly well. They only had work relating to six poems (there *were* only six poems — "Registration Day" and five by Raymond and Sean), but Mr. Kerr seemed to accept that things were rolling along. Raymond explained how his paper on "Industrial Secret" described his view of the poem both before and after discussion with Mr. Gunhold. Ashley gave rapturous details about the poet himself, and talked about "Fruit Fly." Sean smiled a lot, and tried not to blush.

"By the way," said Raymond in an offhand manner. "In case you're interested, Mr. Gunhold's being featured on *Spice of Life* this week, so you might want to check it out."

Sean winced as though receiving a blow to the head. He had known Raymond would do this, yet hearing it out loud was a painful experience.

Mr. Kerr perked up. "I'll certainly watch. Your Canadian poet is beginning to intrigue me."

After class, as the three partners headed out into the hall, Steve Semenski jogged up, calling greetings. He kissed Ashley briskly, and beamed at Raymond and Sean. "Hi, guys. What's up?"

"Nothing much," Sean rasped.

"Any news on our first hockey game, Ray?"

"The schedule should be released any day now," Raymond replied.

Steve pulled Sean aside. "She doesn't have a boyfriend named Tank," he whispered.

"She doesn't?" Sean said woodenly. "I must have been thinking of somebody else."

After Steve waltzed off, Ashley on his arm, Raymond turned on Sean. "Now look what you've done. I hope you're satisfied."

Sean was in no mood for this. "Raymond, just — stay out of my life, okay?" With the girl of his dreams out of reach, and Gramp two days away from his television interview, aggravation from Jardine was the last thing Sean was willing to accept.

Spice of Life was an hour-long variety talk show on every Wednesday night at nine. Ashley, Raymond, and Sean rode in on the train and met Gramp in front of the Euripides Café to take him to the studio. Raymond called his neighbors from a pay phone to make sure they were videotaping the show. Sean called his own home to make sure no one was there. Both his parents and Nikki were with friends that evening, preferably with the TV sets switched off. Sean wasn't sure how his family would react to Gramp masquerading as a poet on national television, but one thing he *was* sure of: He didn't want to find out.

At the studio, Ashley and Gramp were whisked off to the Green Room, and Raymond and Sean were deposited in two spare seats in the studio audience.

Before parting, Sean advised Gramp, "Don't be nervous," which he now realized was stupid, since it was he himself with the sweaty palms, while Patrick Delancey looked completely serene.

The show began, and Raymond was a participating member of the audience, laughing at all the host's bad jokes, and cheering madly whenever the applause sign came on. But not Sean. He sat rigid in his seat, playing nervously with his shirt collar.

"Lighten up, Delancey. Jardine's never been to a TV show before. I dig this."

"I can tell," said Sean sarcastically.

Spice of Life, which had a reputation for unusual guests, proceeded from one segment to another as Raymond drank it all in and Sean grew stiffer in his chair. Finally, it was Gramp's turn.

Michael Donovan, the host, was standing at the front of the stage as the audience cheered the previous act. "That was Dr. Marc Desjardins and his psychic orangutans! Weren't they terrific? Our next guest has been making great strides in the area of short poetry. Originally from Canada, Mr. Gavin Gunhold has been thrilling American readers with his unique blend of humor and social observation. Please welcome Gavin Gunhold."

Sean's heart was in his knees as the curtain swept aside to reveal Gramp, shuffling papers on a small wooden lectern. Dwarfed by the enormous set, the old man looked tiny, and about a hundred and fifty. Suddenly, Sean felt incredibly guilty for having done this to his poor grandfather. How could he have allowed it to happen?

Then a crabby, opinionated voice boomed through the studio, a voice that was usually making statements about prune juice, Scrulnick's, and Brooklyn.

"On registration day at taxidermy school
I distinctly saw the eyes of the stuffed moose
Move."

In the glassed-in control room, the producer slapped his forehead. "Why me? Honest to God! Why me? Did you hear that *stupid* poem?"

"I don't know, Malcolm," said one of the engineers. "I kind of liked it. You see, the moose is looking accusingly at the student taxidermists to bring out their guilt — "

"That's not it at all," the assistant producer interjected. "The moose represents the environment, and — "

"What a show!" moaned the producer. "First

the psychic orangutans, and now this! I should have taken the job on *Bowling for Dollars*!"

"He's not doing too bad, boss," the switcher called back. "The audience likes it. It's going over way better than the orangutans."

On stage, Gramp was reading "Industrial Secret," "Household Security," and "Fruit Fly" in rapid-fire succession.

"This is great, Delancey!" Raymond crowed. "Listen to the laughs we're getting!"

"Shhh!" Sean could not take his eyes off Gramp, who was really warming to his role as poet, reading with cantankerous passion at top volume.

In the Green Room, Ashley was staring at the monitor, clasping her hands in adoring pride.

"He stinks!" said the orangutan trainer. "How'd he get on this show?"

"I like it," said the guest who was scheduled to go on next. "I hope I do this well with my watermelon act."

Gramp read through Gavin Gunhold's skimpy repertoire, finishing off with "Group Therapy," which got the biggest cheer of the lot. He acknowledged the applause with a casual wave, looked over at the control room, and announced impatiently, "Well, I've got nothing else to read. What do you want me to do — tap-dance?"

"Oh, my God!" The producer held his head. "Get him over to Donovan, ask him a couple of questions, and get him out of my face!"

A *Spice of Life* hostess hurried over and escorted the poet to the interviewee's seat.

"Excellent! Excellent, Mr. Gunhold! Welcome to

the show. Is it true that you were discovered recently by three Long Island high school students doing an English assignment?"

"Great kids," said Gramp definitely. "With so many robots around these days, it's amazing to find such levelheaded youngsters."

"Obviously," said Donovan, "your poems are highly symbolic. Could you tell us something about the hidden images in your work?"

"No."

Donovan frowned. "No?"

"There aren't any hidden messages. Whatever my poems say, that's it." He folded his arms and nodded for emphasis. There were titters from the crowd.

"But surely you must feel some *need* when you write your poems — " the host persisted.

"There you go again. The poems — the poems. Who cares about the poems? Let *me* ask *you* a question for a change: You're a handsome enough fellow, bright, successful, a good talker. What's the point of that great big bushy soup-strainer you've got under your nose?"

A hoot of laughter escaped Raymond as Sean jerked forward in his chair. In the glass booth, the producer leaped to his feet and glared out at Gramp as though willing him to disappear.

Donovan was flustered. "A lot of men like to wear a mustache — "

"A mustache is one thing. But when my rosebushes get too long, I prune them, if you know what I mean."

A buzz of embarrassed laughter swept the audience.

174

Before Donovan could speak up in defense of his mustache, Gramp was on his feet, marching out into the seats.

"Oh, my God, what's he doing?" the floor manager exclaimed. "Get a camera on him!"

The producer was having hysterics. "My career is over! I'm lucky if they let me answer phones for a Channel Thirteen pledge drive! Would somebody please shoot that guy!"

Raymond and Sean were on their feet. "Raymond, can you see where he's going?"

"Second row!" gasped Raymond. "There's a kid playing with a yo-yo!"

"Son, let me show you how you're really supposed to use that thing."

The mystified child surrendered his yo-yo, and Gramp tossed it down and up experimentally a few times. "Now, I may be a little rusty at this — " He then began a demonstration worthy of the world yo-yo championship, executing complicated tricks while shouting their names out to the amazed crowd. "Walk the Dog! . . . Around the World! . . . Rock the Cradle! . . . Now, this is a trick I made up when I was a boy." It was a *tour de force*, with the spinning yo-yo flying in all directions, and Gramp leaping over and about, his face a study in concentration. "And if it wasn't for my rheumatism," he panted, handing the yo-yo back, "I'd have *really* shown you something!"

The crowd rose to its feet in a thunder of cheering, and Sean rose, too, filled with pride and wonder for this little old man who was his grandfather. Even the technical crew was clapping. In all the excitement, Gramp forgot to go back to the stage.

Instead, he tried to make his way through the crowd to Raymond and Sean, but he was mobbed by well-wishers on the way.

Total chaos reigned. Michael Donovan stood staring at the control room for some kind of instruction until the producer, now close to tears, junked the script and cut away into a three-minute film clip on covered bridges in Vermont. This bumped the watermelon act from the show, which caused the watermelon man to storm onto the set and hurl a twenty-two pound melon through the control room window. He was restrained by network security.

"Get me something to roll credits on!" howled the producer, and back came the covered bridges, this time upside down.

Ashley came sprinting out of the Green Room. "Gavin Gunhold, you're *wonderful!*"

And the studio audience agreed.

"A marvelous eccentric," proclaimed Mr. Kerr the next day in English.

"Not bad," said Raymond, winking at Sean. "But he's even better on a one-to-one basis."

"He's wonderful," said Ashley without reservation. "He's funny, smart, and cute."

Cute? thought Sean. Gramp?

"Well," said the teacher, "each day I'm more and more pleased with my decision to allow you to study Gunhold. You're on the edge of something very fascinating."

"Not half as fascinating as if he knew where Gav *really* is right now," Raymond whispered to Sean.

"Shhh! Raymond!"

In fact, a number of the students had seen the Gunhold interview the night before. But the big interest came from the last person Sean would have expected to become a poetry fan.

"Danny was really impressed by the interview last night," Mindy O'Toole informed Sean and Raymond, while the student body president stood at her side, smiling with all his teeth. "He was wondering if you could work it so he could meet Mr. Gunhold."

"If it's Danny who wants to meet Mr. Gunhold," said Raymond, "why doesn't he ask us himself?"

"All right," Danny chuckled. "Could you fix it so I could meet the poet?"

"No," said Raymond honestly, and walked away.

Danny addressed Sean. "What's eating him?"

Sean studied the ground. "It's just that Mr. Gunhold doesn't like to meet with that many people. He's a little, you know, strange."

Mindy was still watching Raymond's receding back as he headed down the hall for second period. "It's not Mr. Gunhold who's strange," she said, her eyes wide. "Your friend Raymond is *scary*! First he came up with that crazy EARS thing, then he got threatening when I asked him about it. Then he attacked Danny with a balloon. I've even heard he's been banned from Howard's poker game."

Sean nodded. "It's true."

"And you're the only one who can control him," she marveled.

"Well, do what you can for me, Sean, okay?"

said Danny. With Mindy in tow, he headed into the crowded hall, en route to second period.

The next Monday, Ashley was in such a good mood that she cut her third period class and met Raymond and Sean at Miami Beach with lunch already picked out.

"Uh — thanks," said Sean painfully as he gazed bleakly into the green of the Amazon rain forest.

"Gavin was fantastic on *Spice of Life*!" Ashley raved. "They've been ringing the phone down to get him!"

A mouth-bound forkful of spinach froze in front of Sean's face. "Ringing the phone down?"

"Other shows," said Ashley enthusiastically. "Isn't it fabulous? Already three other shows have phoned *Spice of Life* about having him on. I've got the messages right here in my purse. I'm going to call them back just as soon as you get me some dates when Gavin is free."

Raymond was jubilant. "Any time! You go right ahead and book whatever you can!"

Sean felt his stomach curling into a knot, and as Ashley and Raymond raved on about how great Gavin Gunhold was, and how big a star they were going to make him, Sean was having a flashback to the close of the *Spice of Life* interview. Oh, the relief he had felt! He could remember thinking, Thank God it's over!

He didn't voice these thoughts until he and Raymond were navigating the halls on the way to fifth period. "Sometimes I hate your guts, you know that? Where do you get off setting up TV guest spots for *my* grandfather like that? Especially when you saw how wiped out he was after *Spice of Life*!"

Raymond looked surprised. "Gramp wasn't wiped out, Delancey; *you* were. Gramp said he had the time of his life, and that it reminded him of the good old days when he was the yo-yo champion of Brooklyn. He said he'd love to do it again, and now he's going to get the chance."

Sean was flustered. "Well, he *did* say all that, but — " He stopped short. He'd been about to say, "It isn't good for him," but Gramp had been a changed man since his TV debut, bouncing energetically around the house, humming "You Ought To Be in Pictures." He had even let up a little in his sarcasm attack on his son, grudgingly admitting that it was probably not Dan's fault that the Stead-E-Rain Company had folded its tent and silently stolen away, leaving the Delancey family underwater.

"It's good for him, and it's good for us," Raymond went on. "If Gavin Gunhold becomes big enough, we're talking guaranteed Theamelpos. So don't hassle it."

Sean wished he had an argument but, failing that, he decided to take a stab at being nasty. "Don't tell me things are going well for Jardine, the man with no luck, none at all, zero, zip, zilch?"

Raymond grinned. "Well, there *is* one slightly shady tiny detail we have to take care of. Nothing heavy. . . ."

"Raymond, this is crazy," Sean whispered. They were sitting in a cramped cubicle at the New York Public Library, waiting for the poetry specialist to retrieve the Gavin Gunhold file.

"I agree with you. But believe me, Delancey, this is the only way. We have to make sure that no one can roll into the library and look up the obituary of the guy who was playing with a yo-yo on TV, looking not very dead at all."

The same thin file was placed on the cubicle desk. They opened it and stared. "Registration Day" was there. The blank notepaper was there. But the obituary was gone. Sean checked each and every page to see if the newsprint sheet was stuck to the back. He checked the floor to see if it had fallen out. He went back to the folder to see if, by some miracle, the clipping had returned. Nothing.

Raymond clutched at his heart. "Calm down. Jardine," he told himself. "Keep cool."

"But where's the obituary?" Sean barely whispered.

"Good question." Raymond scanned the room briefly and shrugged. "Let's just hope it got lost, because there's no way we can stop now. We're committed. And if someone surfaces in the middle of everything with Gunhold's obituary, we'll flunk English and kiss Theamelpos good-bye."

"And Gramp will go to jail for fraud," said Sean nervously.

"We'll take all blame," Raymond assured him. This was no great comfort.

"You're going out again tonight, Pop?" Mrs. Delancey asked at dinner on Tuesday. "Don't you think you're overdoing it a little?"

"Gee, once a week for three weeks," said Gramp. "I'm really burning up the track here."

"But why is it always to New York? There are

plenty of older people on the Island for you to associate with closer to home."

"They're boring," said Gramp. "Pure and simple."

"What's so exciting about the people you're with in the city?" Mr. Delaney asked. "And why are you so secretive about them?"

"A man is entitled to his privacy," Gramp declared defensively. "Do I pester you about your techno-junk?"

"You pester him, Pop," said Mrs. Delancey. "Remember?"

"Sure. Okay. Because none of those fancy gadgets ever works."

"That's not true," said Mr. Delancey. "The laser's been working perfectly since the day we set it up!"

"Doing what?" Gramp challenged. "It puts a red dot on the bookcase. Whoop-dee-do."

"Pop, that beam is so concentrated that if I shone it all the way to the moon, the dot would only be a few feet wide!"

"Which proves," said Gramp, "that the bookcase is closer than the moon. A scientific discovery!"

"I think Gramp has a girl friend," said Nikki mischievously. "That's why he goes out so much."

Gramp laughed. "Right. I'm meeting a sixteen-year-old high school girl who thinks everything that comes out of my mouth is poetry." He winked at Sean.

Sean glared at his grandfather. Raymond always pulled that kind of thing, and it drove Sean crazy.

"Well," said Mr. Delancey, stretching, "I'm looking forward to a night of pure relaxation. I'm going to sit myself down in front of that television set, and I'm not getting up until bedtime. That new variety show everybody's talking about is on — *What's Up?* I want to see what all the fuss is."

Sean choked, and even Gramp looked a little pale. In less than three hours, *What's Up?* was featuring Gavin Gunhold, complete with a new world-premiere poem.

"You can't watch TV," Sean protested. "You still have to pump out the basement."

"That's right," Gramp jumped in. "Just because you finally managed to turn off the rain doesn't mean the flood waters aren't still rising!"

"I finished before dinner," said Mr. Delancey. "That electronically calibrated pump is a miracle of technology!"

"Well, the electric toenail clippers need sharpening," Gramp persisted. "This morning they wouldn't even snip the end off a cigar."

Nikki made a face. "That's disgusting!"

"That can wait until tomorrow," said his son. "Tonight's my night off. I need this after last week. Who'd have thought that a classy company like Stead-E-Rain would go out of business so quickly?"

As soon as he finished dinner, Sean ran to the phone to inform Raymond of the latest crisis.

"No problem, Delancey. Here's the plan. Gramp meets Ashley in front of the Euripides — *What's Up?* is sending a limo. We stay here."

"Why?" Sean asked.

"To knock out your TV set," Raymond replied. "Some megacontraption is always blowing up at your place. A TV'll be a piece of cake. Has Gramp got the new poem?"

"I was just about to give it to him," Sean said.

"Great. Tell him to knock 'em dead."

Why did Raymond always know exactly what to say to Gramp?

What's Up? was on at nine, and the Delancey family, minus Gramp, sat in front of the TV, waiting. Gramp had left around seven, but Raymond had stayed on until eight-thirty, watching reruns and listening to Mr. Delancey talk about his revolutionary new pump. Now Raymond was skulking around the Delancey bushes, waiting to disconnect the cable until the show was over.

It was during the opening music that the picture suddenly fizzled into snow and white noise. Mr. Delancey grabbed the remote control and began pushing buttons. Nothing helped. "Wouldn't you know it!" he exclaimed in frustration. "The first time in months that I really want to watch a show, and the TV goes on the fritz! Maybe it's a loose wire or something." He rushed into the kitchen and began opening drawers. "Tina, where are my electromagnetic pliers?"

Actually, it was those pliers that Raymond had used to disconnect the cable. He and the pliers were hiding right underneath the TV room window, listening to the conversation. Suddenly, the neighbors' poodle, a cranky old dog, attacked, and Raymond let out a startled, "Hey!"

"What was that?" asked Mrs. Delancey, looking around.

"I didn't hear anything." Sean went to check the window, just to make sure no one else did. He looked down to see Raymond, half trussed up in the branches of a juniper bush, trying to swat the poodle's nose. Involuntarily, Sean smiled.

"Maybe the picture'll come back, Daddy," called Nikki, as her father continued to ransack the kitchen for the electromagnetic pliers. "Forget it," he said finally, giving up. "I'm going to sharpen the clippers."

"Well, I'm certainly not going to stay here and watch nothing," said Mrs. Delancey. She turned off the set and walked out. Nikki followed.

Sean looked out the window and signaled to Raymond that the coast was clear. He caught his English partner in the act of growling back at the dog with an expression so fierce that the poodle scurried away with a yelp. Raymond gingerly extracted himself from the bushes and set to restoring the cable. Sean wiped his brow and noticed in some surprise that, for such a cool night, he'd been sweating quite a bit.

"Okay, the poet's on next," the *What's Up?* producer told his technical crew. "You've all heard what the old buzzard did on *Spice of Life.* So we know he's good, but he's a little unpredictable. Just keep a camera on him at all times, no matter what happens."

In the Green Room, Ashley and several others were watching the monitor.

"Hey, who's this Gavin Gunhold coming up next?"

"Only the greatest poet ever to come out of Canada!"

Onstage, Gavin Gunhold stepped up to the podium, and shuffled a few papers. "This is a new

184

poem," he told the audience in an offhand way. "It's called 'Green Thumb.'

> *"To make sure my aspidistra gets enough carbon*
>   *dioxide*
> *I'm reading it*
> The Great Gatsby.
> *During the boring parts*
> *The leaves turn brown."*

In the control room, a network observer stared through the glass in disbelief. "You mean to tell me that, out of all the interesting people in America, you picked this old geezer?"

"Nah," said the switcher. "This guy's from Canada."

"Take my word for it, he's great," the producer said confidently. "I saw his *Spice of Life* tape. You won't believe what the old fellow can do with a yo-yo."

The network observer held his head, gazing bleakly at Gramp, who continued his poetry reading to the appreciation of the audience.

Meanwhile, Sean was seated in front of the dark TV screen, dying to tune in and see the interview, but afraid that one of his parents or Nikki might hear the audio and demand to see the show. After a few minutes, he crawled furtively up to the set and switched it on.

Vast waves of laughter came through the speaker, and when the picture came on, there sat the host, completely drenched with water, staring at Gramp in deep shock. Gramp sat in the interviewee's seat, the dripping water pitcher still in his hands.

"What was that for?" the host bawled.

Gramp drew himself up indignantly. "Well, that's the gratitude you get from some people!" he told the audience. He turned back to the interviewer. "A live ash from my cigar blew onto your jacket. In another few seconds, you could have gone up in smoke. I just saved your life, son!"

"Sean, is that the television back on?" came Mrs. Delancey's voice from the living room.

"No, Mom, it's the radio," Sean replied, switching off the set and leaving the room.

Raymond pulled up in front of the Jardine garage, shot up the ladder, and scrambled in the window. He darted down to his TV and turned it on.

Something amazing was taking place. The cameras were panning the studio audience, a group bowled over with fascination. Most of them were on their feet, staring intently at something that was happening onstage.

Gavin Gunhold was performing yo-yo again, only this time he had been given two yo-yos, one for each hand, and the result was an incredible display. Gramp was just a blur, moving almost as quickly as the yo-yos, calling out the names of the tricks as he performed them. The grand finale was the two-handed version of Gramp's own special trick, and it brought the house down. Even the interviewer, soaked and uncomfortable, was on his feet, cheering this amazing eighty-eight-year-old poet.

The producer was jumping up and down in the control room. "I love it! This is our best show since the boxing kangaroos!"

The network observer shook his head. "I remember the days when a talk show was a *talk* show. Now everything's boxing kangaroos and old poets with yo-yos. . . ."

Raymond smiled. It was an honor to be the almost-grandson of such a man.

Ten

"He's a monster talent," Ashley said positively in English class the next day. "With the right management, he could be a major star."

"What do you mean by 'the right management'?" Sean asked nervously.

"Me," Ashley replied. "I think I have a gift for being a poet's agent. I don't know if there's a future for me in modeling stuff. I'm not getting any younger, you know. I'll be seventeen in January."

"Exactly what kind of plans do you have?" asked Raymond.

"Gavin's done two TV things, and he's got two more coming. I want to try for newspapers and magazines. I'm *this* far away from a *New York Times* profile." She held her thumb and forefinger an eighth of an inch apart. "After last night, I bet we're in!"

Sean turned pale. If Ashley succeeded in making Gavin Gunhold a household word, there was no way he'd be able to keep Gramp's secret life from his parents. He could not help comparing his own white face to the beaming smiles sported by Raymond and Ashley.

Mr. Kerr breezed in. "Good morning, class." He focused his attention on the three partners seated in the corner. "Ah, the Gunhold group. I see your man was in the public eye again last night."

"He's been described as a monster talent," said Raymond, winking at Sean. Sean squirmed while Ashley beamed.

"How does Mr. Gunhold arrange all these media events?" the teacher inquired. "He has no publisher to do it for him."

"Oh, I handle Gavin," said Ashley casually.

Mr. Kerr smiled sardonically. "He's very lucky to have found you, then. He's making quite a name for himself."

Mr. Kerr was right, and with Ashley on the case, there were great days ahead. At least, that was the way Raymond put it.

The three cut a half day of school to escort Gavin Gunhold personally to his *New York Times* interview. Before leaving the city, they stopped by the studios of *Spice of Life* and *What's Up?* to pick up the handful of letters that had been trickling in for the poet. Sean felt a chill every time he looked at the addressee's name.

Gramp was so thrilled with his seven fan letters

that he rushed right home to answer them personally. "In a world full of robots," he pronounced, "here's proof that there are at least seven intelligent, alive people out there somewhere!"

SACGEN was worse than ever, plunging the school into total darkness even more frequently than before. But Howard Newman's candlelight poker game continued to forge on until the art department ran out of wax. Howard was recruiting more and more new opponents, since virtually all of his regulars were deserting him. Randy and Chris were so excited about the upcoming varsity ice hockey season that they spent every spare second at Schuyler Arena, practicing their skating and shooting. This made Sean feel horribly guilty, and miffed Howard so much that he set fire to Randy's toothpicks with one of the candles. Sean, too, rarely played now, because he was devoting so much of his time to being a member of the Gunhold entourage. Between that, basketball practice, and scrambling to keep up his classes, his spare time had dwindled to zero. Only Leland remained, since he had nothing better to do during school hours.

"Playing horizontals orbs my nut positive," he explained, although Raymond claimed that the main reason for Leland's playing so often was that he was sure the reflection of the candles in his sunglasses made him look even cooler.

Raymond was still doing the occasional odd job for Miss Ritchie, and complaining all the way. "When I burn off this Pefkakia thing," he promised, "I'm not coming near her side of the building!"

He was even more irritated by *The Eckerman Report*, a bimonthly newsletter published by Danny Eckerman to keep the students up-to-date on what the president was doing to represent their best interests.

"Hah!" said Raymond hotly. "There's no way Eckerman wrote a word of this. That would require lifting up his presidential butt and *doing* something. He conned people into writing it, roped people into editing it, and shanghaied people into printing it!"

Sean finally got a chance to read *The Eckerman Report* in last period, since the school had still not found a full-time replacement for Mr. Lai. The ex-computer teacher had apparently warned all his colleagues of the frustrations of teaching with SAC-GEN breaking down, shorting out, and creating power surges all the time. So computer class became study hall, with another substitute teacher biding his/her time until three-twenty dismissal.

There was a large article on the Halloween party, complete with pictures, and even a mention of the "hilarious comedy sketch" where Raymond fed the balloonful of helium to the president to curtail his speech. His name was listed as Raymond Jardinsky, and he was billed as Danny's "comedy partner."

There was also a piece on the hockey team, "personally sponsored by Danny Eckerman," which told how Danny, "working arm in arm with team captain Raymond Jardinsky, makes ours the only high school on Long Island with a varsity ice hockey team." But the real crusher was the article on poet Gavin Gunhold, discovered by students Sean Delancey and Raymond Jardinsky, in close association with classmate and student body president

Danny Eckerman. It said that Danny was scheduled to meet with the poet to discuss possible projects between him and the school.

Right at three-twenty, Sean ran to look for Raymond to find out if he'd read the articles and, if yes, to keep him from doing violence. He located Raymond prowling the dark DeWitt halls, collecting as many copies of the paper as he could pick up.

"Jardinsky is red-hot steaming mad about this!" Raymond declared. "You see these papers? Eckerman is going to eat them! What's more, he's going to enjoy them!"

He couldn't find Danny, though, since the president had last period free and always caught a ride home with a friend. He did find Mindy, and passed on his message through her. Poor Mindy looked so frightened by the time Raymond was through with her, that Sean had to calm her down.

"But Danny's in danger!" she quaked. "That guy's a homicidal maniac!"

"No, he's not," Sean soothed. "He's just a little upset about the paper. He'll cool off." If there was one Jardine quality Sean admired, it was his ability to strike instant terror in the heart of Mindy O'Toole.

Q. David Hyatt paced back and forth in his office, his thumbs in the pockets of his custom-tailored double-breasted jacket. "I just want you young gentlemen to know that I'm proud of you, the school's proud of you, and the Department of Energy's proud of you."

Seated beside Raymond in a padded swivel chair,

Sean marveled at how the principal always managed to weasel a reference to SACGEN into everything that came out of his mouth. Lying on Mr. Hyatt's desk was that week's Sunday *Times*, open to the profile article on Gavin Gunhold.

"As I was saying to Miss Bach earlier this morning, this is exactly the kind of image we like our students to project," Mr. Hyatt went on. "Incidentally, why was it that you two were unable to come when I paged all three of you right at nine?"

"My scooter ran out of gas," Raymond admitted.

The principal nodded understandingly. "These things happen. I drive a Cadillac, you know. It's a beautiful car, but it uses gas very quickly. Well, Miss Bach told me all about you two boys, and I'm very impressed. Athletes, social planners, and creative scholars." He pointed to the newspaper. "This article is a credit to me and to SACGEN."

Involuntarily, Sean winced. He didn't think too much of helping spread the word of SACGEN. And yes, the Gunhold profile did mention that the students who had discovered the Canadian poet came from the Long Island school that hosted the Department of Energy's pet project.

Raymond, who had been wearing a solemn expression all through the meeting, burst into a wide grin as soon as they were out of the principal's office. "This is it, Delancey!" he exclaimed, and began singing a souped-up "Happy Days Are Here Again."

"What are you babbling about?"

"Theamelpos! It's in the bag! Q-Dave loves us because we made him look good with our poet, so we're *in*, Delancey! *In!* Farewell and *adieu*, Secaucus! It does not grieve Jardine half the nucleus of a carbon atom to see you go!"

"But what about your files? What about all those people you figured were going to go ahead of us?"

"We blew past them! Listen, if there's one thing Q-Dave loves, it's feeling important. Gavin Gunhold is almost as good for him as the windmill. That's how good old Delancey and sweet old Jardine zip past Mr. Cool and his mother on the PTA, cruise ahead of Amelia Vanderhoof and her grade point average, and leave all those other bozos choking in a cloud of our dust. We may even — dare we say it? — inch out Cementhead! We're *there*, Delancey! Nothing can stop us now! We're talking beaches, sun, Miss Stockholm, and her five hundred closest friends, and as soon as we get back, luck, luck, and more luck! And for a little variety, we'll have luck! No more bombs, lightning bolts, rotting garbage, and ten-ton flame balls raining down on Jardine!" He looked up at the ceiling. "What's the matter, boys? Is Jardine getting a little too quick for you? Hah! You can sit up there and *sulk* for all I care!"

Delirious with happiness, he began to waltz around the hall with an imaginary partner, humming *Theamelpos* in three-quarter time. A few students saw him, and stared at Sean in perplexity. Sean only shrugged, but he couldn't help smiling when Mindy appeared at the end of the hall, caught sight of Raymond dancing, and literally ran away.

Raymond was so happy that he wanted to make friends with everyone he'd offended, starting with

Howard Newman. So they headed for the poker game and found to their surprise that the table was gone. A few yards away from the usual spot sat Randy and Chris, leaning against the lockers, writing furiously in their notebooks.

"What happened?" Sean asked. "Don't tell me Howard's still sore at you guys?"

"Naw," said Chris, barely looking up from his work. "Show him a toothpick, and he'll forgive you for setting his hair on fire."

"We're going to lay off poker to work on our entries for the big contest," Randy explained.

"What big contest?" Sean asked.

" 'What SACGEN Means to Me,' " said Randy. "It's a two thousand word essay all about how great the windmill is. Kind of a bummer, but I've just *got* to be one of those six winners."

The glow on Raymond's face faded slightly, to be replaced by a puzzled look. "Did you say *six* winners?"

"Yeah," said Chris. "The top six essays get an all-expenses-paid trip next summer to this great Greek island. It's called — uh — " He began to fumble through some papers.

"Crete?" asked Raymond hopefully.

"No." Chris pulled out a Xeroxed sheet and looked at it. "Here it is. Theamelpos. Eight weeks. Wow!"

"How did you find out about this — contest?" Raymond asked weakly, his face well on its way to making the transition from shining to gray.

"Q-Dave announced it this morning," said Randy. "And everybody got a sheet explaining the details. Practically the whole school's entering."

"Could you excuse me for a moment?" said Raymond politely. He staggered into the nearby washroom.

"What's the matter with him?" asked Chris.

"Something he ate," Sean explained as terrible moaning began to waft out through the washroom door.

"That's right. Don't kick Jardine when he's down. Wait till he starts to get up. It's time for another exciting, fun-filled episode of *Let's Get Jardine*. This week our grand prize goes to the contestant who can burn Jardine out of Theamelpos just when he's got it *in the bag*!"

"What's he doing?" Chris whispered.

Sean walked into the bathroom to keep Raymond from drowning himself. He found his English partner leaning on one of the stall doors as though having to struggle to stay upright. He said, "Raymond, I'm sorry." And for the first time, he really was. Raymond might be the original Captain Obnoxious, but his claim to having no luck was perfectly valid.

Raymond just shook his head. "No need, Delancey," he said quietly. "Jardine is battered and bruised, but he's still kicking. It's almost reassuring that *they* haven't gone soft on him. So now we have to try twenty times as hard as everyone else. We have to butter up the windmill so big that Q-Dave'll fall at our feet."

"Uh-uh," Sean said. "Not me."

"What do you mean, not you? If you don't do an essay, you can't go to Theamelpos. We're in trouble because half the school is going against us now — a nice little touch after the hours of effort

Jardine put into ripping down notices and putting up decoys. But we've still got a slight advantage. If we write real butt-kissing essays, Q-Dave'll recognize our names because of Gavin Gunhold. In other words, this is a disaster, but it isn't quite a catastrophe, and if we really work hard, we can keep it from turning into an apocalypse.''

Sean shook his head. ''I don't go for this big snow-job about how terrific SACGEN is supposed to be. Don't you remember all those articles? 'Oh, the students are childish and rebellious.' Not one word about blackouts and breakdowns. So now Q-Dave's come up with a plan to get a thousand signed statements saying they were right all along and that the windmill works perfectly. I think it stinks.''

''But,'' Raymond argued, ''if you don't enter the contest, he'll still have nine hundred and ninety-nine signed statements, and you'll have to sit on your can all summer thinking, What is there to do today?; the answer, of course, being, Nothing. I've got an uncle in New Jersey who can hook you up with a job, but Jardine wouldn't recommend it. So do the essay.''

''No, Raymond. Don't you see? I'm hit by all this garbage twice as hard as anybody else. I squint through blackouts and flickering lights all day, and after school I go home to Techno-ville. I listen to my mother lecturing about SACGEN and how much she'd love to teach here while my father carts in the latest electronic masterpiece. I've *had it* with technology! Writing that essay is against my principles.''

''Who said anything about principles? This is

getting to Theamelpos! We can work on having principles when we get back. Then we'll be lucky dudes with relaxed attitudes, great tans, and thousands of telephone numbers from the area code of Sweden."

"I don't get it. You said yourself that all you cared about was 'getting Jardine to Theamelpos.' Well, with me out of the picture, that's less competition for you."

"Yeah, before! But it's always been me and you, Delancey. Ever since the poetry assignment. Jardine isn't used to not having you around."

"Well, if you go to Theamelpos, you'd better get used to it," Sean said decisively, "because as of now, I am a nontechnological person. Anything that was invented after the telephone, I don't want. Including and especially SACGEN!"

Randy and Chris were right. The whole school was buzzing about Mr. Hyatt's new contest and the prospect of a vacation on Theamelpos. Sean expected Raymond to be canvassing everyone he knew, to find out exactly how stiff the competition was going to be. In fact, Raymond did him one better, striking up conversations with total strangers just to find out if they intended to enter an essay. The outlook was not good. At least several hundred people planned to go head to head for the trip Raymond had earmarked for himself during the very first week of school. Everyone, from big Ten-Ton Tomlinson to funky Leland Fenster, from lofty Amelia Vanderhoof to Nikki's friends Marilyn and Carita, was planning essays.

Even Ashley showed an interest in the "What

SACGEN Means to Me" contest at lunch, although she was clearly not thrilled by the idea of a two thousand word essay. "Steve said he'll help me with it. If we could both win, that would be fantastic!"

"I'm not doing an essay," said Sean, and Ashley gave him the same you-should-have-your-head-examined look he'd been receiving all day from Raymond.

"Oh, I almost forgot." She reached into her purse and produced a large manila envelope. "More mail for Gavin. *What's Up?* forwards it to my house. And speaking of Gavin, I need a lot more of his time. After that great *New York Times* article, who knows what could come next?"

"Superstardom," said Raymond confidently. He looked at Sean and mouthed the word *Theamelpos*. Sean looked away and regarded the green of Ashley's lunch absently. Miami Beach was a quiet affair that day. The poker game was shut down until further notice due to essay writing, and even tray-surfing action was reduced to nil. Everywhere, students could be seen poring over sheets of paper, dreaming up nice things to say about the machine that hadn't worked properly for more than a few hours at a stretch since the very first day of school.

Ashley was talking so much about Gavin Gunhold that she worked herself into a state of excitement, and couldn't eat her lunch.

"Jardine couldn't eat *her* lunch even if there was no Gavin Gunhold," Raymond commented, as Ashley rushed off to cash five dollars into quarters so she could make the poet's business arrangements from the school pay phones.

"Hi," Danny Eckerman seated himself across from Raymond.

Sean looked around for Mindy, but she was on the other side of Miami Beach, hard at work on what was probably Danny's essay on "What SAC-GEN Means to Me."

Danny beamed at Raymond. "So what's new?"

Raymond kept his eyes on his lunch. "Jardine doesn't have any time for anything to be new, because he spends so much of his time consulting with you on things. I read it in *The Eckerman Report*."

As usual, the president was undaunted. "Christmas is coming up pretty soon, and I'm organizing some social events for the big buildup. But because I'm so busy, I could use some help. Got any ideas?"

Raymond put down his knife and fork and regarded Danny. "As a matter of fact, I'm getting an idea right now. It's for our next hilarious comedy sketch. Check this out: You won't shut up, so I shoot you with a bazooka."

Danny looked thoughtful. "It could work. Do you know where to get a fake bazooka?"

"I'm not going to use a fake bazooka. Do you know where to get an asbestos-coated flak jacket?"

"Well," said Danny, "I was thinking more along the lines of an ongoing activity that could lead up to the Christmas party. I know you'll come up with something, Raymond. It's like I was just telling Mindy: There's room for him on the Eckerman team."

As the president walked off, Raymond leaped to his feet and wound up to bounce a hard-boiled egg off Danny's head. Sean sprang just in time and put an iron grip on Raymond's arm.

"You shouldn't have done that, Delancey," Raymond seethed. "You just ruined another hilarious comedy sketch!"

"What are you going to do?" Sean asked, easing his English partner's arm down until the egg once again rested on the lunch tray. "He expects you to work up some Christmas thing."

"No way," said Raymond grimly. "May Jardine be condemned to the eternal fish fumes of Secaucus if he ever lifts a finger for the greater glory of Danny Eckerman!"

It was another typical evening at the Delancey house. Gramp was upstairs in his room answering fan mail and practicing his yo-yo technique, and Mr. and Mrs. Delancey were experimenting with the argon-neon laser against the side of the Schnitzenbergers' garage. Sean was in front of the TV, which was switched to something other than the Weather Channel for a change, when Nikki entered. "Hi, Sean. How's it going?"

The look of open friendliness on her face instantly put Sean on his guard. "Okay," he said tentatively.

Nikki sat down. "I was just thinking. Raymond and I seem to get along pretty well. And you know about how I think he's cute and all that."

"So?"

"So I was wondering if you could fix it so we could go out together."

"You and Raymond?" Sean sat bolt upright. "Nik,

I told you to stay away from him!"

"But that was way back at the beginning of the year. Now you guys are best friends. Come on, Sean!"

"Best friends?! Are you crazy?" Sean lay back again. "Forget it. Take a walk."

He heard the sound of paper rustling, and looked up to see his sister pulling a folded clipping from her pocket.

"I was looking through last week's Sunday *Times*," she began.

"But we didn't get a paper last Sunday!" Sean protested nervously. This wasn't exactly true. The paper had arrived, but he, knowing it contained the Gavin Gunhold profile, had tossed it down an open manhole.

"This is from Carita's paper. You're in this article, you know, Sean — you, Raymond, and Ashley. How come you didn't tell Mom and Dad?"

Sean was sweating now. "I didn't think they'd be interested."

"Now, this poet guy is fascinating," Nikki went on meaningfully. "He's Gramp's age, and he looks a lot like Gramp. And this yo-yo business — didn't Gramp used to be a yo-yo champion?"

"Nikki, what are you trying to say?" Sean blurted.

Nikki smiled. "Do you think Raymond will be free this weekend?"

Sean leaped to his feet. "You're trying to black-mail me into setting you up with Raymond! Give me that clipping!" He lunged for the paper, but she deftly kept it just beyond his reach.

"This Gavin Gunhold thing is really a coincidence. Do you think Mom and Dad will call it a coincidence?"

"Don't show it to Mom and Dad," Sean pleaded. "Please!"

Nikki folded up the article and popped it into her pocket. "Sure, Sean. Oh, by the way, tell Raymond I'm free Friday and Saturday. Whenever's best for him." She walked out.

" 'Maybe once in a lifetime comes along a technological advancement so utterly amazing that one cannot help opening one's mouth and gaping in admiration. Such inventions were the wheel, the electric light bulb, and the solar/air current generating system. SACGEN is the third most important development in the last hundred thousand years, and to attempt to describe it in a mere two thousand words is like trying to detail all of the great cathedrals of Europe in three lines on a breakfast cereal boxtop. As a DeWitt student, every night before I go to sleep, I spend a good three quarters of an hour just thinking about how lucky I am to be able to go to school with this miracle machine.' " Howard looked up from his paper and smiled with satisfaction. "Well, guys, what do you think?"

"I don't get it," said Sean. "You *hate* the windmill. How can you say all that stuff?"

"I have a dream," said Howard, closing his eyes and tapping his temple gently. "I see myself winning the contest. I see Q-Dave bringing me up in front of the whole school to congratulate me. And just when all the kids are freaking out, thinking

I've gone totally crazy, I hear myself say, 'Q-Dave, you poor dope. This essay is a crock, and the windmill stinks. And as far as your exotic Greek vacation is concerned, you can take it and run it over with your Cadillac, except that I let the air out of your tires.' Then, just as Q-Dave's about to hit me, the windmill goes on the fritz again, and he can't find me in the dark."

There was general laughter.

"Has anybody seen Raymond around?" Sean asked.

"Fortunately, no," said Howard.

In fact, ever since the contest had begun, Raymond had been hitting the books, researching the SACGEN project from all possible angles, planning an essay to knock the principal's socks off. At school he spent every spare moment in the library; at home he was hard at work, his answering machine intercepting all incoming calls. Of the two thousand words in his essay, he promised Sean, "nineteen hundred and fifty of them are going to butter up the windmill. The other fifty are going to be *and* or *the*. I intend to swell Q-Dave's head so much that I wouldn't be surprised if he sold his Cadillac and bought a Lear Jet."

"You have no principles at all," said Sean in disgust.

"If you're expecting me to disagree with you, Delancey, forget it. Because when Jardine sticks his punch card in the time clock of J & J Fish Processing Inc., God forbid, it's going to be with the knowledge that he fought, screamed, lied, cheated, and connived right up until the very end."

The only reason Raymond happened by the poker game at that moment was to circulate an ugly rumor that Theamelpos was experiencing a plague of poisonous snakes. Sean had heard about it before, both from Amelia Vanderhoof and later from Ten-Ton Tomlinson. He had been so sure it was Raymond's doing that he didn't even feel the need to extract a confession from his English partner. The present problem was more immediate. Nikki wanted a date with Raymond, and the poetry assignment, Gavin Gunhold's career, and possibly Sean's life were all riding on it.

"What's the word on the hockey season?" Chris asked Raymond.

"Affirm," put in Leland. "My anticipometer shows big-time vub to get out there and slap black disc, baby!"

"I was on the phone with the league people four times yesterday," replied Raymond glibly. "And I can't find anyone who can give me information. You know what's got me even more worried is this poisonous snake thing. Nobody told me that Theamelpos — "

"Raymond, I need to talk to you." Sean grabbed Raymond and hauled him bodily into the nearby washroom.

"What's the big idea?" said Raymond irritably. "My snake scare is going over great. I'll bet I can cut the number of entries in half — maybe more!"

"Never mind that. We've got trouble." Sean outlined Nikki's threat to expose the Gavin Gunhold deception to her parents if a date with Raymond wasn't pending.

Raymond looked totally bewildered. "I understand the blackmail part, but why does she want to go out with *me*?"

"Raymond — get ready for this — my sister loves you."

"You're kidding!"

Sean shook his head sadly. "She *worships* you. I don't know why. If I was a girl, you'd be the *last* guy I'd look at, but there it is."

Raymond was amazed. "But Jardine doesn't have luck with women!"

"He still doesn't!" Sean snapped. "This is my sister you're talking about!"

"Don't get excited, Delancey. I *hate* your sister. She's the one who introduced Ashley and Cementhead."

"That's better," said Sean. "Just take her to a movie, feed her a hamburger, and shut her up. A necessary move to keep our dead poet afloat — no more. Or the next big blast that hits Jardine will have nothing to do with those mysterious people in the sky!"

Nikki was on cloud nine when Raymond called to ask her out Friday night. She began bragging to Marilyn and Carita, both of whom were now far too jealous to endure her company. Raymond withdrew back into his cocoon of work, emerging only now and then to tell people about the poisonous snakes on Theamelpos.

It was the first time since October that Sean had what he wanted most — to be away from Raymond. But whatever extra time he might have had was taken up. Superagent Ashley Bach was orchestrating Gavin Gunhold's career, and Sean owed it to Gramp to be there every step of the way.

Before Sean's very eyes, Gramp was turning into a star. Life with the poet/personality/yo-yo ace became a blur of TV, radio, magazine, public reading, TV again, and so on. There were rides in limousines every day, and producers and network executives saying, "Mr. Gunhold! Delighted to meet you! You can't believe how much we've been hearing about you!" Each day there was a little more fan mail for Ashley to hand over, and a whole new stack of invitations for Gavin Gunhold to appear.

Sean knew it had all gone too far when, as he, Ashley, and Gramp were walking past a construction site after a spot on *News at Noon*, a hard-hatted worker took one look at Gramp, and dropped an armload of bricks.

"Hey! I know you! You're that guy!"

The three stared at him.

"The guy! From the TV last week! You know. 'The stuffed moose looked at me on registration day.' And you played with a yo-yo. You know — the guy!"

Ashley glowed. "You're right, sir. This is the one and only Gavin Gunhold."

"Wow!" whistled the worker. "Can I have your autograph? It's for my sister."

Readily, Gramp produced a pen. "Certainly, my good man."

"Great!" The man peered over Gramp's shoulder. "Make it to Ernie. Wow!" He turned back to the job site. "Hey, Louie, guess who this is? Gordon Gunfield!"

"Who's that?" a voice called back.

Ernie was indignant. "What are you — an idiot? Everyone knows Gordon Gunfield. You know — 'the registration day moose looked at me.' On television! He's really famous, you moron! If you hurry up, you can get his autograph, too!"

Sean grabbed Gramp and Ashley. "Come on, let's get out of here!" A few blocks down, he bought Gramp a pair of sunglasses from a street vendor, and instructed him never to take them off.

But the sparkle in Gramp's eyes practically showed through the shades, so overjoyed was Patrick Delancey with his newfound fame. Sean had never understood that distant gleam in his grandfather's eyes, not until he'd become Gavin Gunhold, and the gleam had turned into a dance of light.

"I knew it all along" was Raymond's opinion. "The very first time I saw Gramp heave that bagel through the salami at the deli, I said to myself, 'Jardine, this is a totally cool guy.' So what if he's eighty-eight? All he needed was a way to shine, and we gave it to him."

"We got him involved in a plot," Sean amended.

"We took a fantastic old guy who was going out of his mind with boredom and made his life fun again. You may not realize it, Delancey, but we're considerate and loving grandsons to do this for him."

On Friday night, Raymond, under strict instructions laced with death threats from Sean, took Nikki to a movie, Burger King, and then home. On Saturday morning, Nikki telephoned the entire population of the ninth grade to tell them about it.

Raymond himself said, "She's really a pretty nice

girl, Delancey. Jardine had a halfway decent time. She talked all about how her big brother pushes her around too much."

"Hah!" snorted Sean in disgust. "My sister is Genghis Khan in training!"

To avoid Nikki floating around the house on cloud nine, he decided to go upstairs and help Gramp with his fan mail.

"Listen to this. 'Dear Mr. Gunhold. Who do you think you are? Who cares if you can play with a yo-yo? Your poems all stink, and you are an obnoxious crazy old man. Signed Norbert Freeland.' Hmmm." Gramp paused thoughtfully, then began to scribble on the FROM THE DESK OF GAVIN GUNHOLD stationery Ashley had bought for him. *Dear Mr. Freeland, Blow it out your ear. Yours very truly, Gavin Gunhold.*

"You're not going to send that, are you?" Sean asked, sifting through more letters.

"Watch me," said Gramp, sealing and stamping the envelope.

"Here's one," said Sean. " 'My husband and I are your biggest fans. We are an elderly couple, and we greatly admire how you show that older people are quite capable of doing extraordinary things. Thank you, and good luck in your career. Edward and Emma Crabtree.' "

"Good people," said Gramp positively. He looked confused as he examined another letter. " 'Greetings, Mr. Gunhold, baby. Your poetry does radioactivity to my thinkometer, zipping my nut with holographic images. The vub orbs me so positive that I had to fling this communication — "

"Here, Gramp, let me try." Sean scanned the

letter and, sure enough, it was signed Leland Fenster. He shuddered. If even Leland was a Gavin Gunhold fan, the dead Canadian poet could be nothing less than a household word.

Leaving Gramp to his adoring public, he descended to the TV room and switched on the set.

". . . and in 'The Bargain,' Gunhold is commenting on the American consumer," said a prominent NYU professor.

"Very similar to the symbol of the stuffed moose in 'Registration Day,'" agreed a colleague from Yale.

"I disagree," said the third specialist. "Gunhold's poems are nothing more than astute commentary on human foibles. Consider 'Household Security,' where the attack dog — "

Head spinning, Sean switched over to a hockey game. How much longer could he keep all this from his parents? Just yesterday, the family had entertained the argon-neon laser salesman and his wife. Mrs. Argon-Neon had spent the whole evening staring at Gramp, saying she was positive she'd seen him somewhere before.

Even more important, how long could the whole deception go on? Did someone really have the missing obituary from the New York Public Library? If yes, why hadn't he shown himself? And if no, how long would it be before word of poet Gavin Gunhold would travel up to Toronto, and to someone who knew the truth?

Eleven

The poetry assignment, although relegated to the background in all the excitement over Gavin Gunhold's career, was almost finished. Raymond had lost interest ever since "What SACGEN Means to Me," feeling that the project was no longer a factor in getting to Theamelpos. It was Ashley Bach, once described by Raymond as a "death sentence" to the project, who was doing most of the work. Steve Semenski's little sister had agreed to do the typing at $1.25 a page.

There were still only seven Gunhold poems, but this was easily explained. Gunhold's sudden popularity left him little time for original work. The project contained analyses done by all three partners, and included many opinions supposedly belonging to the poet himself. In addition, there was a videocassette of all the Gunhold TV interviews, and copies of all his press clippings. This made up for the fact that the written work came to only sixteen pages instead of twenty-five or thirty, according to Raymond.

"The bottom line is, who cares?" he commented. "My essay on the windmill is coming out great."

Monday was the deadline for "What SACGEN Means to Me," and by the time Sean arrived at school, Raymond had already made his submission, skimmed through some of the competition, and estimated how many potential entrants he had scared away with his poisonous snake rumor. (There were two hundred and seventy-three essays. He figured at least that many had opted out.)

"I put my paper about a third of the way down the pile," he told Sean. "Not at the front, but not so far back that Q-Dave'll be bored when he reads it."

"Oh, there you are." Mindy O'Toole jogged up to them. She was trying to act casual, but was clearly unnerved by Raymond. "Danny wants to know how the plans are coming along for the Christmas activities."

"They aren't coming along," said Raymond.

Mindy frowned. "Danny said you guys are helping him on this."

"No," Raymond insisted. "We're not 'helping' him with anything. Tell him to leave us alone."

"Say that we're really busy, so we don't have

any time to work for him," Sean suggested diplomatically.

Raymond shook his head. "Tell him that we have all the time in the world, and could very easily work for him, but that we don't want to because he's a jerk."

"Don't tell him that," Sean told Mindy.

"Yes. Tell him that."

Mindy looked frightened and ran off.

On Wednesday, Sean found himself on his own for lunch, since Raymond was off helping Miss Ritchie in the library, and Ashley was at Burger King with Steve. As he made his way toward Miami Beach, he was taken completely by surprise when Mr. Hyatt came up to him. The principal was hardly seen at all lately, as he had locked himself in his office to read the "What SACGEN Means to Me" essays.

"Mr. — Delancey, is it?" asked Hyatt.

"Yes, sir," said Sean tentatively.

Mr. Hyatt awarded him a pat on the shoulder. "*Excellent* paper on SACGEN, young man. I'm very impressed."

"Oh, you must be thinking of the other guy — Jardine. Raymond Jardine."

"His was outstanding, too. Both of yours were enlightening, informative, well-researched, and enjoyable to read. I've got my eye on you two."

"What paper?" Sean mused aloud after Mr. Hyatt had walked away. Clearly, something was up, and it was a good bet that Raymond was at the bottom of it.

He found Raymond in the library atop a ladder, struggling with an enormous READING IS FUNDA-MENTAL poster. Every time he succeeded in lining up one corner to the wall, the other three would curl up on him. When he tried tacking the bottom edge first, the top of the sheet rolled up and conked him on the head, causing him to lose his grip. The poster fluttered down to land at Sean's feet.

Sean picked it up and shook it at Raymond accusingly. "I just found out that I handed in a SAC-GEN essay. What's the story here, Raymond? And you'd better make it good!"

From his perch, Raymond shrugged. "What can I say, Delancey? Sure it was me. I realized I couldn't convince you to do an essay, so I got to thinking. All along that tough, cruel road, who was with Jardine every step of the way? So I wrote one for you."

"You had no right to do that!" Sean exclaimed hotly. "You know exactly what I think of that stupid windmill!"

Raymond studied his sneakers. "I'm sorry, Delancey." He sighed. "How'd you figure it out?"

"Because Q-Dave stopped me in the hall to commend me on my paper."

Raymond jumped and almost lost his balance. "He did? Fantastic! That means he liked mine, too, since they were almost exactly the same! Sorry to be so happy while you're chewing me out, but we're back on the road to Theamelpos!" He snapped to attention and gave a rigid salute to the west. "Secaucus, hail and farewell. You put up a heck of a fight. Jardine had to try fifty times as hard as

214

everybody else to avoid your diabolical clutches, but this time you lose."

"Raymond, I'm not finished with you yet!" Sean thundered.

"Don't you see?" said Raymond. "You're more than Jardine's English partner. You're his cohort — his comrade — his fr — "

"Don't say 'friend,' Raymond. Just — don't say it!"

Raymond looked dejected. "Well, the least you can do is climb up here and help me with this poster."

"No way," said Sean, tossing the roll up to his partner's waiting hand. But as Raymond resumed his struggling, Sean could bear it no longer. "Oh, let me show you how to do it before you end up killing yourself!" He scrambled up the ladder and grabbed the rolled-up paper from Raymond.

Suddenly a loud grinding noise roared through the school, and the lights began flickering erratically.

"Attention, students," said Engineer Sopwith through the p.a. system. "It is imperative that you — " his voice was drowned out by static " — immediately. Thank you." Then the power went dead.

"Terrific," groaned Sean into the gloom. "Perfect timing."

"Hey, shove over, Delancey" came Raymond's voice. "You're hogging the ladder."

"I'm on my half, you're on yours. Shut up and hang onto that poster."

"I don't have the poster. *You* have the poster."

"*I* don't have the poster. Where is it?"

"Maybe it's on the wall."

"How could it be on the wall? It was rolled up. Wait — here it is. Raymond, stop shaking the ladder!"

"I'm not shaking the ladder!"

"Well, *somebody's* shaking the ladder! Raymond, we're tipping over! Raymond! *Do something!*"

There was a great crunch as the ladder fell over, sending Raymond and Sean reeling into a magazine display rack, which keeled over on top of them just as the lights came back on.

"That's right. Throw Jardine off a ladder. And hey, while he's down there, so it shouldn't be a total loss, drop a shelf on him. What the heck."

Sean shook off the copy of *Techno-Living* magazine that had landed on his face open to the feature on argon-neon lasers. He wriggled out from under the rack and, with the help of Ten-Ton Tomlinson, set the freestanding shelf back upright. "Just another day in the life of SACGEN, miracle of technology," he said sarcastically. He looked down at Raymond. "Come on. Let's get out of here."

Raymond made no move to get up off the floor. "I can't, Delancey. My ankle is broken."

"Don't be an idiot, Raymond. I'm not in the mood."

"I'm serious, Delancey. My ankle is broken."

On the point of walking out the door, Sean wheeled and regarded his English partner sprawled on the floor. Raymond looked decidedly unhappy, and very pale.

"*His ankle's broken!*" howled Sean in a voice that carried throughout the building. "Don't just stand there! *Do* something! Get a doctor! Get an ambulance! Boil water!"

"I don't want any tea, Delancey, and I'm not having a baby."

Sean didn't stop babbling hysterically even as the ambulance arrived and two uniformed attendants moved Raymond carefully onto a stretcher.

"The windmill did this!" Sean seethed. "I'm going to go into that control room with an axe, and then Q-Dave is *really* going to know what SACGEN means to me!"

"Delancey, shhh!" admonished Raymond, momentarily forgetting his ankle. "If you open your mouth in front of Q-Dave, you'll blow Theamelpos for the two of us!"

But Sean raved on. "Who cares? This is the last straw! I'll say it to the Secretary of Energy himself! The windmill is a piece of — "

"Oh, the pain!" bellowed Raymond suddenly, completely drowning Sean out. *"The a-gon-y!"*

Quickly, the attendants hustled the stretcher into the ambulance. Sean clambered up with them, refusing to leave without a physical struggle.

"You guys brothers?" asked one of the attendants as they pulled out of the school drive.

"Much closer than that!" Sean exclaimed fervently. "And SACGEN will *rue* the day that it did this to Delancey's best friend!"

Raymond's stay in the hospital was a very short one. A few hours after the cast had been put on his leg, his mother and father were able to take him home. Sean was still there, still issuing wild threats against SACGEN. Raymond seemed more upset at having to move temporarily out of his garage apartment than at anything else.

The Jardines dropped Sean off in time for dinner, giving him a whole new audience for his ranting and raving. It broke up the evening meal. Gramp let out a roar of outrage and ran for the telephone to call Raymond and make sure he was all right. Nikki beat him to the phone, however. She could not eat while Raymond was suffering, and had to notify Marilyn and Carita of these ill tidings. This left Sean alone with his parents.

Mrs. Delancey refused to accept that SACGEN could be responsible for the accident.

"What do you mean, Mom? I was *there!* I fell, too!"

"You kids blame SACGEN for everything," she retorted.

"A thirty-three million dollar project can't go that wrong," her husband added reasonably.

"You think I don't know why you're making this up, Sean Delancey?" his mother went on. "You're feeling guilty because you were acting up in the library, and your friend got hurt as a result of it. That's the *real* reason for all this." At that, she and her husband walked out, heading for the den to "eat in peace."

Gramp came back into the kitchen. "I got through. He's okay."

"How'd you get past Nik?" Sean asked.

"I just threatened to melt her Rolling Stones records. You know, Jardine said you made a real spectacle of yourself at school when it happened."

Sean grinned sheepishly. "*He's* taking it a lot

better than I am, I guess. Honest to God, Gramp, the guy's got no luck! None at all! Zero! Zip! Zilch! And does he complain? Well — he does, but he's got a right!" He shook his head. "SACGEN's got to go."

Gramp pushed his dinner away, lit up a Scrulnick's, and chuckled. "You'd better think twice before you take on the whole Department of Energy. But if you do decide to bomb the school, let me know so I can express-mail the argon-neon laser over. No sense wasting all that good dynamite."

"I'm not kidding, Gramp. It may sound crazy, but in the ambulance I swore I'd get SACGEN this time. I don't mean blowing it up, but showing the world what a big lemon the whole business is, and putting an end to it once and for all!"

Sean couldn't get to sleep that night, the day's upsets running riot through his mind. A month ago, he would have been sublimely grateful for anything that would have put Raymond out of commission. Now here he was, foaming at the mouth, ready to do battle over that same Raymond, Raymond the embarrassment, Raymond the pest, Raymond the schemer, Raymond the obnoxious, Raymond the eleventh-grade garbage bag.

Well, at least Raymond was okay. In six or seven weeks, the cast would come off, and everything would be fine — until the next time SACGEN conked out. Then someone could end up with more than a small fracture. Maybe a concussion, or worse. There were no two ways about it. SACGEN was a menace, and the students deserved protection.

Fat chance. All the newspapers and magazines

were positive that SACGEN was the big success of the decade. Everyone was so busy patting everyone else on the back that, when the students tried to give the real story, they were dismissed as spoiled brats making trouble. And because of the cover-up, it was only the DeWitt kids who had seen blackouts and breakdowns. There was truth to be told here, and no one would listen.

Sean sat up in bed, shaking his head to clear it. There was something wrong with a world where no one would listen to twenty-two hundred students whose education and well-being were in danger, while an eighty-eight-year-old poet with a yo-yo had the ear of the entire nation.

Wait a minute! Of course! No one would pay attention to twenty-two hundred teenagers, but what if they had a spokesman? A famous spokesman, like Gavin Gunhold?

Flinging the covers aside, he crept out of bed and padded barefoot out of his room and down the hall to Gramp's door.

Gramp was enjoying a good dream, as his face was blissful in repose. His right middle finger was moving rhythmically, as though attached to an imaginary yo-yo, and he was murmuring, "On registration day at taxidermy school. . . ."

"Gramp — are you asleep?"

Gramp opened one eye. "Buzz off."

"Gramp, it's me — Sean."

Drowsily, the old man sat up, squinting at the clock on his night table. "It's four o'clock in the morning! What are you — crazy?"

"I just had the greatest idea for Gavin Gunhold."

"Oh, him. He's pretty much booked up until May. Call Ashley."

"No, no!" Excitedly, Sean related the idea of having the poet speak for the students of DeWitt and expose SACGEN to the world.

Gramp was unimpressed. "I'll say whatever you like, but there's no reason for anyone to take my opinion of SACGEN seriously. I'm a poet."

Sean shook his head. "All we need you for is to get the people and the media to show up. We organize a special 'Thank You' reading at the school, fill the place, and wait for SACGEN to go on the fritz. When people see it, they'll *have* to believe it."

"But you claim the Department of Energy sends over a busload of engineers every time SACGEN is in the public eye. Surely they'll do it again for us and our reading."

"Yes," said Sean, "but you'll explain exactly what we're doing, so the reporters won't let the Department of Energy pull any cover-up. We'll let Sopwith and Johnson work the windmill, just like it was a normal day at school and, with everyone watching, the other engineers will have to sit tight. Then it's "The Gavin Gunhold Show" until the windmill breaks down."

"And will it?"

"Of course it will. It always does."

Gramp thought it over. Finally, he said, "You know, you're not a robot after all. You'll never end up pledging your life to an argon-neon laser."

Sean grinned. "It's a good plan, huh, Gramp?"

Gramp lay back down. "If it works, I'll be the first one to admit you're a genius. But if something goes wrong, *you're* the one who explains to your mother why we have to move to a new town."

Howard Newman was so impressed by what Sean had to say that he stopped dealing the cards. "No way!"

"Yes," Sean insisted. "We're going to get the windmill once and for all."

Carefully, Howard refunded the five toothpick ante to Randy, Chris, Leland, and Ten-Ton, and shut down the game in order to give Sean his full attention. "Talk to me."

Quietly, Sean explained to them the upcoming Gavin Gunhold presentation and the plan to discredit SACGEN. "Mr. Gunhold has already agreed to do it, and if I can count on a few helpers to make sure the engineers don't try to pull a fast one, it should go off smooth as silk. The windmill will break down in front of witnesses and reporters."

"Yeah, but it'll still be standing," said Howard, vaguely disappointed. "I was hoping for something with a little more violence. But listen, hey, whatever does the job."

"Awesome idea, Sean," Chris approved.

Leland nodded. "The vub resonates, baby."

"Great," said Sean. "One last thing. Raymond will be back at school in a couple of days, and he's really mad at the windmill because of his ankle. Don't tell him about the plan. I want it to be a surprise."

This was something that had occurred to Sean on the way to school. Someone who brought shame and ridicule onto SACGEN, and therefore Q. David Hyatt, would be the last person in the world se-

222

lected to go to Theamelpos. So Raymond could not be told about the plot against SACGEN, because he would do anything and everything to stop it. It was a little sneaky, keeping him in the dark, but it was necessary. SACGEN had to go, for Raymond's and everyone's good.

"Right," agreed Howard. "We don't tell Raymond. It'll be our get-well present to a dear friend."

Ten-Ton looked confused. "Howard, you don't like Raymond, remember?"

"I am big enough to forgive and forget," said Howard piously. "As soon as the windmill did a number on his ankle, I forgave and forgot."

"So I can count on you guys," said Sean. "Great."

The plan was in motion. Ashley had already pledged her full support to the venture, although Sean hadn't mentioned anything about SACGEN. To her, Gavin was appearing as a thank-you gesture to the school that had discovered him. This way, Ashley couldn't leak the news to Raymond.

The two made an appointment to see Mr. Hyatt for permission to go ahead, and naturally, the principal was overjoyed. Here was an opportunity to show off his suit, his car, his SACGEN, and his poet, all on the same night. He praised Ashley and Sean for their initiative, escorted them out of the office, and rushed to phone the Department of Energy with the good news.

The next day, Raymond was back in school, thump-swinging deftly around on his crutches. By the time Sean arrived in the morning, his English partner was being waited upon like some Oriental warlord by Nikki, Marilyn, and Carita. His cast already bore several smart signatures, including that of Leland Fenster, with the dedication *Zunging negatoid, baby. Get positive soon*. The victim was seated on an inactive radiator (from the good old days before SACGEN), balancing on his lap a tray that held an enormous Burger King breakfast, while his fans hovered around, watching his eating with great concern.

"Don't forget about your French toast, Raymond," Nikki counseled wisely. "Here, you can wash that down with some coffee."

"Hey, Delancey," Raymond greeted Sean. "Come on over and grab some hashbrowns."

Sean kept his distance until the girls went off, bearing the empty tray.

"Having a broken ankle isn't too bad," Raymond proclaimed as Sean settled himself on the radiator beside him. "Everyone's treating me like delicate crystal. Miss Ritchie can't hit me up for any garbage jobs, because I'm injured. And the cast comes off in six weeks, add another month to strengthen the ankle, and a nice safe caution period after that, and Jardine will be good as new to zoom off to Theamelpos in July." He chuckled. "Wouldn't want to give Miss Stockholm damaged merchandise."

Sean felt a sudden pang of conscience. The attack on SACGEN was sure to put hopes of Theamelpos in the grave. He grimaced. It was just Raymond's consistently lousy luck that the chance to get a shot at SACGEN had to come up now.

"I've got some news," he began carefully. "Ashley and I are setting up a public appearance for Gavin Gunhold right here at DeWitt on the sixteenth."

Raymond's face broke into a big smile. "You're a real pal, Delancey. This'll be the icing on the cake for Theamelpos. Q-Dave'll die of happiness. But how are you going to fix it so your folks don't show up?"

"They've got a big party in the city that night, so they won't be around."

Raymond nodded in contentment. "Fan-tastic. Before, I was pretty sure we were going to Thea-melpos; now I'm positive. Gramp is the sweetest guy in the world to do this for Jardine. And I'm not going to forget you either, Delancey."

Sean was sure of it.

Danny Eckerman walked up to them, oozing charm. "Well, well, and how are we feeling to-day?"

Raymond scowled. "We *were* feeling fine, but then something real ugly came up."

"I was really shocked to hear about your leg," said Danny in concern. "Do you think it'll interfere with your preparations for the Christmas activities?"

"I'm working just as hard now as I was before," Raymond assured him. "I was doing nothing, and my future plans include a lot of the same. Now beat it."

Danny's smile never wavered. "If you need some help, I can arrange to get you somebody, because the time really is running short."

"Now I know why the doctor gave me two crutches," Raymond informed Sean conversation-ally. "One is to lean on, and the other is to beat off annoying idiots." He raised a crutch threaten-ingly.

"Well, I'd better be going," said Danny pleasantly. "Keep me posted on your progress."

Raymond patted his crutch. "That's another good thing about having a broken ankle."

Ashley did her usual thorough job of publicity, and the Gavin Gunhold reading at DeWitt was assured of a large audience. With her faithful boyfriend, Steve, at her side, she sent out press releases, printed up thousands of fliers, and recruited students from her art class to deliver them door to door. Mr. Hyatt was so excited over the project that the school paid the expenses. For good measure, he sent notices to all parents, urging them to attend. Long Island's *Newsday* published an article on the upcoming reading, and even the New York papers mentioned it. Gavin Gunhold was news.

Gramp was serene during the big buildup, and continued to answer his fan mail and smoke his Scrulnick's as before. There were a few anxious moments when Mrs. Delancey asked who this famous poet was, and how she, an English teacher, had never heard of him. But Sean and Gramp managed to bury the issue under many other subjects. Nikki, fortunately, chose to keep quiet.

Howard was happy but nervous over the upcoming sneak attack on SACGEN. The sheer importance of the plan was taking his mind off cheating at poker, and he began losing thousands of toothpicks. So he postponed the game until after the windmill's demise, and the poker players just sat around their table, chortling over their roles as SACGEN-busters.

Sean himself was completely wired over December sixteenth, a mass of tingling nerve endings, vibrating in a vacuum. There was nothing for him to do except be scared — that, and to appear totally nonchalant in front of Raymond. With everything in motion rolling up to the big event Monday night, he couldn't help reflecting that he didn't even recognize himself. As recently as September, his life had been normal. Sure, he was a basketball star, and a popular guy, but everything had been safe and easy and straightforward; now here he was, embroiled up to his nostrils in a plan to put an end to a thirty-three million dollar project. He had gotten Gramp into it, too, not as himself, but as a long-dead Canadian poet, scheduled to emcee the revolution.

With Raymond and Nikki the only people aware of Gavin Gunhold's true identity, and Howard and his crew the only ones who knew the real purpose of the gathering, Sean felt himself at the center of a web of intrigue and deceit, withholding at least some information from everything else. It was definitely not Sean Delancey. This kind of scheming and conniving would have been a bit much even for Raymond Jardine.

Well, it was all worth it. This was the windmill. All year, he'd been blabbing about how something should be done about it. And now was the time when he would put his money where his mouth was. Sure, he was going to catch a lot of flak for this. He might even get booted off the basketball team. But let it never be said that Sean Delancey wasn't ready to stand up for his principles.

Twelve

Monday, December sixteenth, was a crisp, cold night with a clear, starry sky. Gavin Gunhold was scheduled to appear at eight o'clock and, first thing in the morning, the Department of Energy had sent an extra squadron of twelve engineers to help Sopwith and Johnson. SACGEN had been a model of behavior all day.

Just before seven, the people began arriving, eager to get good seats to see the famous poet. By quarter past, the DeWitt parking lot was full, and even Mr. Hyatt's Cadillac was forced to seek out space on the street. There were a good number of mobile units from radio and TV stations, and the newspapers and magazines were widely represented as well. The gym was filling up rapidly, and it was soon apparent that this was going to be a standing-room-only performance.

Sean peeked out from behind the stage curtain and surveyed the crowd. There were a lot of DeWitt students and their families, but there also seemed to be many faithful Gavin Gunhold fans who had come from far and wide to see their hero in person.

"A full house," he announced to Gramp, who was sitting with Ashley and Steve.

"I'm really excited," said Ashley. "Gavin, you're just going to knock 'em dead!"

"Maybe even better than that," smiled Gramp, winking at Sean.

Sean grimaced. All weekend he had thought about Raymond and the terrible shock his English partner would go through when Gramp revealed the true purpose of the evening. He knew Raymond was in the front row in the VIP seats, and decided he must go out there and do the honorable thing. Raymond had to be warned about what was coming so that the shock would be lessened. And it was only right that he should hear it from Sean's own mouth.

He found Raymond in his seat, sucking up to Mr. Hyatt and senior engineer Quisenberry, who was heading up the task force to keep SACGEN from revealing its weaknesses in front of the biggest crowd of visitors the school had faced thus far.

"It's a wonderful evening," Raymond was saying. "Not only will the community get to hear our poet, but they'll also have a chance to get a good look at SACGEN."

Hyatt was eating it up, while Quisenberry looked disgusted.

"Raymond, can I have a word with you?" Sean put in.

"Not now, Delancey. I'm busy."

"But Raymond, it's important."

"I said not now. We'll have plenty of time to talk on Theamelpos." He turned back to the principal. "You were saying Mr. Hyatt. . . ?"

Sean retreated. Well, if Raymond wouldn't be approached, then it would just have to be a shock.

Randy jogged up. "We're all ready, Sean."

"Good. We'll be starting in a few minutes. It won't be too long after that."

By eight o'clock, all the seats were filled, and the gymnasium was circled by standees. Sean was just about to give the signal for Ashley to introduce Mr. Gunhold when Mindy appeared at the microphone, Danny at her side.

"Good evening, everybody. I'm sure we're all excited about having Mr. Gunhold here. But first let's have a big hand for the person who made all this possible — our student body president, Danny Eckerman."

There was polite applause. As Danny stepped up to the microphone and opened his mouth to speak, a crutch reached out from the front row and slammed down hard on the president's toes.

"*YEEOOW!*" Danny howled right into the microphone as the DeWitt's students broke into laughter and applause.

Mr. Hyatt looked at Raymond in shock.

"Oh, it was planned," said Raymond with a dazzling smile. "We're comedy partners. I didn't really hit him. He just pretended it hurt."

Ashley walked out onto the stage, clapping. "Oh,

thank you, Raymond and Danny, for another hilarious sketch. They are two really funny guys! And now, ladies and gentlemen, the man we've all been waiting for, everybody's favorite poet, *Gavin Gunhold!*"

To thunderous applause from all present, Patrick Delancey ambled onto the stage, flashing the thumbs-up signal to Sean, who was hiding on the sidelines, white-faced and terrified.

"Thank you very much. You're a nice, friendly audience, and I want your full cooperation, especially you fellows from the press. And also parents who have children in this school. We'll get to all that poetry claptrap in a few minutes, but first I want to conduct a little SACGEN test."

Raymond, Hyatt, and Quisenberry suddenly sat bolt upright in the front row. A confused murmur buzzed through the audience. In the crowd, Sean could see Leland Fenster's mother, president of the PTA, frowning in perplexity and, a few rows behind her, Mr. Kerr, looking on with great interest.

"You know," Gramp went on, "it always bugs me that, every time I pick up a newspaper, I read about what a fantastic success SACGEN is, but when I talk to the DeWitt kids, they tell me the blasted thing breaks down every five minutes and doesn't work for beans. So tonight we're going to find out.

"Now, here's something to think about. On a normal school day, SACGEN is handled by two full-time engineers. So you folks from the newspapers — count the number of engineers in that control room tonight. There are thirteen men in there right now, and just in case they can't hack it, their boss is in the front row here, thinking up

231

ways to shut me up before I drag his windmill through the mud."

All at once, the students present began to cheer and, in the groundswell of reaction, Mr. Hyatt leaped to his feet.

"Get out of my school, you old troublemaker!"

Gramp smiled in recognition. "You must be Q-Dave. My friends the students have told me all about you."

Quisenberry stood up. "I'm Senior Engineer Quisenberry of the Department of Energy, and I'm telling you that there is absolutely nothing wrong with this SACGEN unit."

Hoots and catcalls crested over a loud chorus of boos.

Gramp beamed down at Quisenberry. "I was hoping you'd say that. So you won't mind if we simulate a typical day. Sean, give the signal to remove the eleven extra engineers from the control room. And if some of you ladies and gentlemen of the press could do us a big favor and make sure that it's done properly — "

"This is an outrage!" Quisenberry shouted. "We do not have to defend our project — "

"Your project *has* no defense!" Gramp thundered. "Ask the boy sitting next to you how he got his broken leg! During a blackout, that's how!"

"It's only my ankle!" Raymond cried. "It's not that bad! I don't mind! I like it!" But it was too late. Mr. Hyatt was already looking at him with undisguised loathing.

Quisenberry folded his arms across his chest. "I refuse to participate in this madness!"

There was a roar of discontent from the crowd.

232

A portable microphone was thrust under his nose. "What are you afraid of that you refuse to let Gunhold go ahead with this test?" demanded a local news reporter.

"Yeah!" Suddenly two more microphones appeared.

Quisenberry surveyed the situation. He was the center of attention, with cameras, microphones, and faces all turned to him. Pens were poised above notepads, ready to copy down his every word. What could he say? "All right, go ahead. SACGEN has nothing to hide."

"Terrific," said Gramp. "And in the spirit of cooperation, we invite you to sit down and shut up. Okay, Sean. Tell your people to turn on the school. This is a normal day, and Engineers Sopwith and Johnson are manning the windmill."

There was a great cheer of victory. As Howard and his crew raced all through the school halls, flicking light switches and turning on equipment, Ten-Ton Tomlinson led the eleven bewildered extra engineers into the gym, escorted by a contingent of media people. The test was on.

There was a rush for the school pay phones as reporters hurried to alert their superiors as to what was going on at DeWitt.

"Splendid," said Gramp. "Now, would anyone care to hear a little poetry?"

As he began to read and discuss the poems, Ashley found Sean in the wings. "I don't get it," she said. "What's Gavin doing?"

"He was really upset about Raymond's ankle," Sean replied glibly, "and he vowed to get the windmill."

233

Ashley looked confused. "But Raymond just came backstage to tell me how mad he is."

"It's more important than just what one person thinks," said Sean evasively. "Mr. Gunhold's helping us out in our moral fight against being pushed around just because we're teenagers."

"Oh, wow!" said Ashley. She paused to listen to the audience reaction as Gramp read "Fruit Fly." "He's a great man."

"He sure is," said Sean, and had never meant it more in his life. He went to look for Raymond, and found him slumped in Gramp's backstage chair, staring up at the ceiling.

"Raymond. . . ."

Agonizingly slowly, Raymond turned, as though the effort took every ounce of energy in his body. "There he is — the man who killed Jardine. Doesn't it figure that, after all I've been through, all the terrible luck I've endured, all the obstacles I've made it past, the crushing blow is dealt by my best friend!"

"I did it for you," Sean barely whispered. "Your ankle — "

"If you're waiting for me to say thanks, don't hold your breath. If you really wanted to do me a favor, why didn't you just cut my throat? It would have been nicer than to pluck me off a beautiful beach in the Aegean and drop me in Secaucus."

"It won't be that way, Raymond. I'll take the blame. I'll tell Q-Dave it was all my idea."

Raymond shook his head. "I already told him that. He doesn't believe me. This is it, Delancey, *and it's all your fault!* I'm not too thrilled with *your* grandfather, either!"

Onstage, Gramp had finished his poetry, and was

warming up for a little yo-yo demonstration, while chatting engagingly with the audience.

"While we're all here, anybody got any use for some extra engineers? Maybe a little wiring around the house?" It got a big laugh. Quisenberry glared at him.

Howard and his group were standing in front of the control room entrance.

"This is too cool!" Howard crowed gleefully. "The windmill's as good as gone!"

"Orb me radioactive, baby!" Leland agreed.

"I don't know," said Randy nervously. "The lights look perfect. I hope we didn't pick the one night when the windmill's actually going to work."

Sean, too, was paying close attention to the lights, waiting for that first flicker that would indicate a breakdown was on the way. He checked his watch anxiously. The time was dragging.

Gramp had been on for almost forty-five minutes, and there was still no sign of windmill failure. Sean caught a ferocious look from Q. David Hyatt, smoldering in his seat in the front row, and swallowed hard. The only positive sign so far was that Gramp seemed to be ready to go on for hours, and his audience showed no indication of tiring.

Howard came up behind him. "Sean, you want to see something that's going to make you smile?" He led the way to the control room, grabbing a few nearby reporters and counseling them to come along. "There," he said blissfully. "Isn't that just poetry in motion?"

Inside the glassed-in control room, Sopwith and Johnson were racing around like rats in a maze, pressing buttons, flicking switches, and turning dials as red lights appeared all over the numerous monitoring boards.

"What is it?" asked the *Daily News* reporter.

"The beginning of the end," said Howard smugly.

"Two men can't run the windmill," Sean explained. "Every one of those red lights is something going wrong. During a normal school day, they just shut it down for a while, or let it break down, and then fix it. Tonight they've got to keep it going at all costs, because you people are here."

Sean ran to convey this news to Gramp, who interrupted his yo-yo display for the announcement. "You fellows from the press might want to take a look at the SACGEN control room down the hall. I'm told the monitor boards are lit up like a Christmas tree, and there's more running and jumping around in there than in the NBA championship."

Quisenberry squirmed uncomfortably as reporters and camera crews all rushed for the door.

Those who stayed for the rest of the yo-yo action all agreed that this was Gavin Gunhold's classic performance. But the sweat and action on the stage was nothing in comparison to the frantic running around going on in SACGEN Control Central, where Sopwith and Johnson were fighting a losing battle against the red lights on their panels as the press looked on, fascinated. Every now and then, a few sparks would fly from a board, and one of the engineers would be on it, twisting, rigging, and slapping it back into place until the next time.

"I didn't know those two idiots were this good," commented Randy in reluctant admiration. "Look at the mess they've got, and the lights are still perfect."

"It can't last," said Howard confidently. "This is the happiest night of my life."

At last, Engineer Johnson was grudgingly granted permission to go to the bathroom. He took off like a jackal, doubled back, and shot into the auditorium, ending up at the feet of Senior Engineer Quisenberry.

"Sir, we're going to have to shut her down, or let the power flow drop, or something!" he rasped, breathless.

"No way!" Quisenberry whispered back. "Keep it going!"

Johnson shook his head. "We could have a disaster on our hands!"

Quisenberry grimaced. "Just buy us a little more time," he whispered. "We'll figure something out."

Suddenly, Johnson felt an iron grip on his shoulder, and wheeled to find himself staring into the extremely large face of Ten-Ton Tomlinson.

"No cheating," warned the football star, hustling Johnson back to the control room.

Quisenberry and Mr. Hyatt left the gym soon after.

"I guess they just don't appreciate poetry," said Gavin Gunhold, who was winding down the presentation into a friendly question and answer period.

The sparks were flying in the control room, but the lights remained steady as Sopwith and Johnson continued their frantic scramble to keep SACGEN going.

"He's crazy!" exclaimed Sopwith, beating out a small fire with his coat. "He's putting the whole unit in danger!"

Sean was looking at the lights nervously. Sure, the reporters could all see what was going on in the control room, but it would take a real blackout to put the icing on the cake. Come on, SACGEN — quit!

The fire doors at the end of the hall burst open, and in marched Quisenberry, at the head of a long line of uniformed policemen.

"This building is to be cleared in two minutes, by order of the Department of Energy!" shouted the senior engineer.

Microphones appeared from all directions. "Is it true that you're stopping the test because SACGEN is about to break down?" called a reporter.

"SACGEN has passed any test! As of now, you people are all trespassing!"

Quisenberry led the officers down the corridor and into the gym. Sean ran in through the back entrance to try to reach Gramp first. He ran onto the stage just in time to hear his grandfather announce, "Under arrest? Don't you like poetry either?"

Cries of protest went up from the crowd as two policemen jumped onto the stage and grabbed Gramp by each arm.

Nikki, who had been in the wings consoling Raymond, caught a glimpse of Gramp being hustled out of the gym in the arms of the law, followed by a large group of angry spectators. She took off like a shot. Bewildered, Raymond went after her, propelling himself laboriously on his crutches.

"Please, officers!" Sean was saying. "Leave him alone! It's all my fault! Honest! Arrest *me!*"

Howard took one look at Gramp on the way to the door, and shouted, "Hey! You can't leave now! The windmill isn't dead yet!"

Gramp seemed to be enjoying himself immensely. "Do I get one last cigar before the firing squad?"

"Cover-up! Cover-up!" shouted a newsman who was being ejected, camera and all, from the building.

"Yeah! Cover-up! Nuke the windmill!" This from Howard Newman.

The students began to take up the chant. "Nuke the windmill! Nuke the windmill!"

Nikki burst onto the scene, grabbed Gramp's arm, and tried to pull him away from the officers. "Let him go!"

Ashley rushed up, frantic with worry. "Gavin! Gavin, why are they doing this to you?"

Gramp shook his head. "Everybody's a critic!"

Mrs. Fenster grabbed her son. "Leland, I want to know exactly what's going on here, and I want to know now!"

Leland was in a state of emotional upset. "This is a negative vub — "

Mrs. Fenster blew her stack. "Vub! Vub! I'm sick to death of hearing about vub! Speak English!"

The front doors of the school were flung open, and the police ushered everyone — students, guests, and media people alike — out into the cold night air. The last thing Sean saw before a purple-faced Q. David Hyatt slammed and locked the heavy doors was Quisenberry and his eleven extra engineers swarming like ants into the turbulent SACGEN control room.

The driveway was lined with police cars. The two officers flanking Gramp pushed him into the lead car, and Nikki with him, since she refused to let go of his arm. Sean tried to climb in after them, but he was gruffly shoved away and placed in the second car.

"Sean, where do you think you're going?" bellowed Howard. "We're not finished yet!"

"Gavin! Gavin!" Ashley burst onto the scene. *"What have you done with him?"* she bawled, right in the face of the officer in charge. He responded by stuffing her into the car with Sean.

"Ashley!" Steve Semenski barreled heroically forward to protect his girl friend. But unfortunately at that moment, Raymond, thump-swinging at top speed, smashed through the line of spectators. The two met head-on with a resounding crunch, and a flailing crutch bonked the officer in charge right over the head.

"Hey!" Raymond and Steve ended up in the third car, watched over by a very angry policeman.

As the three cruisers pulled away down the driveway, an hysterical Leland Fenster took off after them in a full sprint. "Wait, babies!" He ran right up until the third car turned out into the street. Then he wheeled, and shook his fist in frustration.

"Zung!"

Dan and Tina Delancey couldn't remember having enjoyed a party this much in years. Manhattan people were so up-to-date on technology. The conversation had gone from *Techno-Living* magazine in

240

general to argon-neon lasers in particular when the daughter of the house, a girl of Nikki's age, came running out of her room.

"Mrs. Delancey, come quick! There's a riot in DeWitt! At the high school!"

"Oh, Dan, the children are there!" The Delancey's rushed to the TV set just in time to see Gramp, in the custody of two burly police officers, holding up the two-finger V-for-victory sign to the cameras.

"Oh, my God! It's Pop!"

"Oh, Dan! Look who's with him! Nikki! My little girl is being arrested!"

"The poet, apparently, was conspiring with some students to discredit the SACGEN project," crackled the audio. *"Exactly who besides Gunhold is involved is not clear, but it is believed that this boy"* — there was a close-up on a face looking miserably out the window of another police car — *"had a major role."*

"Sean!" chorused the Delanceys.

In a matter of minutes, they had found their coats, made their excuses, and were on their way back out to Long Island, more specifically, the DeWitt police station, and the three other members of their family.

They weren't jail cells, exactly. They were just three locked rooms where the DeWitt offenders had been placed. Gramp and Nikki were in Room A, Gramp looking smug and self-satisfied, Nikki nervous, but not frantic.

"How about this, Nik?" the old man said, slapping his knee. "Who says older people can't do interesting and exciting things?"

241

"Certainly not you, Gramp," said Nikki. "But we're in jail!"

Gramp shrugged. "A minor detail. Besides, we'll be out of here in no time."

Nikki looked worried. "I hope so."

In Room B, Raymond was collapsed on a small wooden chair, staring up at the ceiling while Steve paced the floor, slapping his fist into his palm.

"Don't worry about a thing, Ray. When they put us in with the criminals, I'll see to it that nothing happens to you. I'll say, 'If anyone does anything to my friend Ray, I'm going to bust his face into a million pieces.' That's what I'll say."

"Oh, shut up, Cementhead."

"Cementhead?" A delighted smile spread over Steve's face. "Oh, I get it. My name is Semenski, and that sounds like Cementhead. What a great nickname! I like it!"

Raymond looked up at the ceiling. "He likes it."

"Knowing you has taught me a lot about friendship," Steve went on philosophically. "When I saw you hobbling on your crutches to rescue Ashley, it brought tears to my eyes."

"Mine, too. But that was because I'd just taken a cement block in the face."

"Seriously, Ray. You and me, we've seen the best together; we've seen the worst. We're going to be friends for life!"

Raymond just groaned.

In Room C, Sean was totally downcast. His great plan, which had exposed Gramp, cost Raymond Theamelpos, and landed family, friends, and himself in jail, had all come to nothing. The windmill had suffered mightily, but had persevered. Sure, the media had seen the control room panic, but that wasn't enough. The breakdown, the sure thing, hadn't come. The one and only time that Sean Delancey made a decision more important than whether to shoot or pass had turned into the biggest mess of all time.

Ashley spoke up. "Well, I sure wish I knew what was going on."

He looked at her, his beautiful Ashley, thrown in the slammer because of his pigheaded stupidity. And then he was spilling his guts, confessing everything, because she had a right to the truth. He told her how the real Gavin Gunhold was dead, and how he and Raymond had been writing the poetry. He told her about Raymond and Theamelpos, and the importance of the poetry assignment. And he told her about Gramp, and how they had planned all along to go after SACGEN tonight.

"So that's the story, Ashley," he concluded, shamefaced. "I don't blame you if you hate me." He turned to face the wall, and waited for her to condemn him as a liar, a conniver, and a fraud.

It didn't happen. Instead, she said, "I could never hate you, Sean."

And from then on, Sean was unclear on the actual order of events, because his memory went a little gray. But somehow, in the seconds that followed, Sean Delancey wound up kissing Ashley Bach, both in custody in this romantic place, jail. He felt like he'd just scored fifty points — he could almost hear the cheering of the crowd.

Suddenly, Ashley looked deeply disturbed. "Oh, Sean, I — but what about Steve? — oh, I'm so confused!"

"Don't be," said Sean in his deepest voice. "You and Steve are great for each other. Really. This was just one of those things." Then he thought about what he'd said, and could have cut his tongue out and eaten it. He'd just given up a chance with the girl of his dreams. He hadn't done anything this stupid since deciding to go head to head with the windmill.

"Sean, you're the most wonderful person in the world," said Ashley honestly. "I'll never forget this."

Oh, well, easy come, easy go. He felt a great rush of elation. Well, Cementhead, that horseshoe's still up there working for you. She's all yours. Sean Delancey has given her to you. Why? Because he's something much more important than just the best player on the varsity basketball team. He did it because he's a *nice guy*. So let's call it even on the Karen Whitehead's underwear thing, okay?

When Raymond found out about this, he'd say, "That's right. Give Jardine a friend with cole slaw for brains." Well, he wouldn't tell Raymond. This was his own private secret.

The Bachs arrived first to pick up their daughter, followed a few minutes later by the Semenskis. The Jardines were out, so when the Delanceys turned up just after midnight, they collected the balance of the prisoners.

Mrs. Delancey didn't even wait until they got out to the car before the lecture began. It was loud and long, easy on Nikki ("the innocent child") and on Raymond ("You're not mine, thank God") but extremely hard on poet Gavin Gunhold. "Pop, I can't believe what you've done! You, who are lucky enough to be in a position to live your golden years in peace with people who love you — to get mixed up in such scandal with your no-good grandson! And as for *him*. . . ." Then the real roast began. Sean soon memorized every single scuff and mark on his sneakers as his mother flayed him alive with words that would have offended an axe-murderer. When his father tried to intercede on his behalf, he was told, "You have nothing to say, Daniel Delancey! This is our fault, too! Ou son has obviously lost direction, and we didn't even notice! Sean, I want you to admit right now, for good and all, that there is *nothing* wrong with the Department of Energy project in your school! *SACGEN works perfectly!*"

An enormous explosion rocked southern Long Island, echoing in all directions. The sky lit up like day as a huge fireball rose above the houses to the north.

"The school!" chorused Raymond, Sean, and Nikki.

With a squeal of the tires, Mr. Delancey wheeled down a side road and headed for DeWitt High.

Cars were converging from all directions, their occupants curious as to the source of the violent eruption. The Delanceys arrived just as the DeWitt Fire Department screeched up the driveway, sirens howling. Sean was the first one onto the scene, Gramp hot on his heels.

The school building was still standing, but the apparatus on the roof was completely gone. In its place, fire blazed. It looked as though SACGEN had been surgically removed and replaced by a wall of flame.

Flaked out on the lawn a safe distance from the building, engineers were scattered like tenpins. Q. David Hyatt was there, too, dancing up and down in the eerie glow of the blaze. The crowd began to gather behind the line of fire fighters, who were training their powerful hoses on the roof. Gingerly, Quisenberry and his thirteen engineers got to their feet.

An ancient Buick with a broken muffler roared up to the curb, and out jumped Howard Newman, shrieking like a banshee. "It's dead! The windmill's dead!" Randy, Chris, Leland, and Ten-Ton were with him, and the five formed a circle and began a joyous dance, exchanging high-fives with one another.

Spying Gramp, Howard broke away from the revelers and sprinted over to embrace the old man. "You did it, Mr. Gunhold! You killed the windmill! You're the greatest poet in history!"

"But what happened?" Nikki asked, stumbling up with a limping Raymond.

Gramp smiled. "All the king's horses and all the king's men couldn't put SACGEN together again."

"They overloaded it keeping everything working during the presentation," Randy explained. "Then even all fourteen of them couldn't save it."

"It was only a matter of time," added Chris breathlessly.

Leland was hysterical. "Positive vub, baby! Quasi-radioactive vub! Super high-powered mega-bang vub! Oh, this is just *great*!"

"*AHA!*" exclaimed Ten-Ton, pointing a big finger at Leland. Leland looked embarrassed, and slunk off into the crowd.

A local reporter approached Mr. Hyatt. "Was there anyone in the building?"

"Only myself and the engineers," replied the principal, totally devastated, "and we got out just in time."

Another ten minutes of activity had the fire under control and, as the smoke cleared, the spectators were able to get a good look at DeWitt High. With the exception of a few windows shattered by the explosion, the school looked perfectly normal, minus the SACGEN superstructure that had been on the roof.

"Gramp," said Sean, "I'm so sorry I made such a mess of things. I'm sorry I got you thrown in jail. I'm sorry I got you involved in the whole Gavin Gunhold thing. I'm just sorry, that's all."

Gramp looked at him as though he had a cabbage for a head. "What are you — crazy? I've lived eighty-eight years, and I've never had such a high time in my life! Kiddo, you make Long Island worthwhile!"

Epilogue

DeWitt High School shut down for two days for a thorough cleanup. There was surprisingly little damage to the school itself, although the SACGEN superstructure had literally disappeared, and the core was completely burned out. The heavy walls built to protect the core unit had actually protected the school. Thus the classrooms and hallways were intact, if one discounted the acrid aroma of a back-yard barbecue in certain areas. To the students, it was sweet perfume.

Howard Newman had found a small, charred gear wheel on the front lawn of a house across the street from the school. He now wore it on a sterling silver chain, and invited everyone to come and touch it for luck. He called it, simply, "Fried Windmill."

The Gavin Gunhold story had come out completely when the media had checked the police report and found the eighty-eight-year-old yo-yo ace registered as Patrick Delancey. Gramp, Sean, Raymond, and Ashley spent most of Tuesday on the phone with reporters. The story of the big deception made all the papers, hand in hand with SACGEN's spectacular demise.

Sean had talked to Raymond by telephone, but his English partner still seemed totally destroyed by the loss of Theamelpos. There was no life to Raymond's voice, and no hope. Gramp had tried to cheer him up with the news that Buffalo was under forty inches of snow, but Raymond remained unresponsive.

Despite his worries over Raymond's morale, and the fact that Gavin Gunhold's career in poetry was over, Gramp's spirits were high, and he was back in front of the Weather Channel, smoking his Scrulnick's, drinking his prune juice, and scanning the national weather map for low pressure systems to cheer on.

The strangest reaction of them all, though, was that of Tina Delancey. She had been deathly quiet after the dying echoes of the SACGEN explosion Monday night, and had woken up Tuesday morning with a purpose.

When Mr. Delancey came home from work that evening, he found the family's entire collection of technology, including his beloved argon-neon laser, piled high at the edge of the curb, awaiting the trash truck. He located his wife, who was sitting cross-legged in the center of the living room, weaving a tapestry. To his unspoken question, she replied, "This family is going back to nature."

By nightfall, he had already organized their first hike.

When Sean arrived at school on Thursday, he could almost feel the familiar electricity of the Long Island Lighting Company flowing through the building. It was most refreshing. There was a festive atmosphere among the students, and Sean was on the receiving end of countless messages of congratulation. It reminded him of the morning after the big game, only this was ten times better.

He found Raymond thump-swinging morosely up to his locker. There was a note taped to the door, summoning *Jardine, R.*, to Mr. Hyatt's office at three-twenty.

"Well, this makes it official," Raymond lamented, rummaging through his locker and producing a thick paperback entitled *2001 Useful Phrases in Modern Swedish*. "Good-bye, Theamelpos." Pivoting on his good leg, he tossed the book with the perfect form of a Sean Delancey, swish! into the garbage can fifteen feet away. A quick check of Sean's locker showed that he, too, was to present himself at the office at three-twenty.

"Q-Dave's going to kill us," Sean predicted mournfully.

Raymond shook his head. "No such luck. We're talking guaranteed Secaucus here. But first we've got Kerr to deal with, remember?"

Sean slapped his forehead. "I forgot! Ashley's got the finished poetry assignment! He'll never accept it! We're going to flunk! I'll be kicked off the team!"

"Nice hindsight, Delancey. Why couldn't you have blown up the windmill a few weeks later, when the semester was over, and the selection for Theamelpos was already made?"

They met Ashley outside English class and entered together, presenting a united front.

"Ah, the Gunhold group." Mr. Kerr wore an enormous smile. "I was wondering if you people had the nerve to show up today. Good. I have a great deal to say to you."

The three approached the desk, and a chair was found for Raymond.

"Before you come up with another outrageous pack of lies, at which you are extremely adept, let me show you this." He reached into his top drawer and produced the old, faded Gavin Gunhold obituary.

"So *you* had it!" Sean blurted.

"Ah, this document is familiar to you. I thought it might be. So, you see, I've known for some weeks now that you were up to something."

"Why did you let us go on with it?" asked Raymond.

The teacher shrugged. "I suppose I rather liked your poetry. And I wanted to see how far you would go. I must admit you surprised even me."

Ashley held out their neatly typed assignment, complete with collected clippings and videocassette. "I guess you don't want to see this anymore, sir."

"Are you kidding?" Mr. Kerr stood up and snatched the material out of her hand. "I've been waiting for this for weeks! Weeks!" He paused. "I'm giving you all C's. Bear in mind that it's strictly for effort."

"Thank you!" said Sean breathlessly, and led the Gunhold group back to their seats.

"And tell your grandfather," Mr. Kerr called, "that, in my professional opinion as an English expert, he throws a mean yo-yo."

"I can't believe he passed us!" breathed Sean. "He's not such a bad guy after all."

Raymond was unimpressed. "Are you kidding? If he'd tried to flunk us, I would have reported him to the New York City Public Library like *that*!" He snapped his fingers. "He stole a clipping! That's research material!"

Sean and Ashley laughed, mostly with relief.

Sean was navigating the halls en route to last period when Mindy O'Toole strode purposefully up to him.

"Danny Eckerman just wants you to know that he had absolutely nothing to do with all the stuff that happened Monday night."

Sean nodded, not surprised, and said nothing.

"Also," Mindy went on, "you and Raymond aren't allowed to continue planning the Christmas activities, or any other social stuff like that. Danny completely denies any connection with you, and — "

"Stop." Sean held out his palm, policeman-style. "I've heard entirely too much about what Danny says. Everyone in the school has heard too much from Danny. I have a question for you, Mindy. Are you a real person, or is Danny a ventriloquist? No one cares what Danny says. What do *you* say?"

Mindy looked thoughtful. "Well, I'm having a party Saturday night. Want to come?"

Sean started. What had happened to their fading relationship? Could it be fading back in again? He said, "Is it personally sponsored by Danny Eckerman?"

"Oh, no. Danny's not invited. He's a drag at parties."

Sean hesitated. Maybe her invitation had come about just because he was the SACGEN hero, the windmill slayer. No, that couldn't be. He'd *always* been a hero — after all, who had the sweetest jump shot on the varsity basketball team? He was no *better* than before — just a little more well-rounded.

"Yeah, thanks, Mindy. I'll be there."

Last period was, in a way, the first computer class of the year, and all systems worked perfectly for the introductory demonstration. The students were delighted to welcome back Mr. Lai. He was not officially reinstated on staff yet, but he felt it was his right to conduct at least one lesson in peace.

When the class was over, Sean found Raymond, and the two presented themselves at the principal's office. Ashley and Steve were already waiting there. Ashley had been summoned as the third member of the Gunhold group; Steve was there since he had hung around just enough to be implicated in the caper. Steve had been so enchanted by Raymond's nickname for him that he was wearing the brand new muscle shirt he'd bought. Across the chest it read in sparkling letters: CEMENTHEAD.

Inside the office, they found Mr. Hyatt and Senior Engineer Quisenberry, their expressions only slightly less friendly than the war frenzy of the ancient Philistines.

As he sat down beside Raymond, Sean resolved that, no matter what happened, his friend would not have to spend his summer gutting fish in New Jersey. Sean would ask his father to pull strings so the two of them could work in his office in the city. Or, if that didn't pan out, they'd find jobs somewhere — anywhere. But he would save Raymond from Secaucus.

Quisenberry conducted the meeting, as Mr. Hyatt seemed beyond speech. The principal had arrived at school that morning by bus. His Cadillac was in the body shop, having been sideswiped by a fire truck Monday night.

"Well, I suppose you people are really proud of yourselves," growled the engineer, pacing in front of them. "I suppose you think you're just the cat's pajamas." He leaned over until his face was an inch and a half from Sean's. "You must think it's just terrific that you managed to destroy a thirty-three-million-dollar installation."

The four culprits were silent. Sean suppressed an urge to point out that the explosion had come from Quisenberry's own stubborn refusal to shut SAC-GEN down. The Gunhold plan had only been to cause a breakdown.

The senior engineer resumed his pacing. "Just in case you think you've accomplished anything, I'm here to tell you that SACGEN is being rebuilt — right here. The blueprint for SACGEN II is already finished. Construction begins in March, and the new unit will be operational for the Fourth of July weekend." His eyes narrowed, and he stopped in his tracks. "It's possible that, on the new opening, the press might decide to dredge up the ghost of Monday night, which, of course, *we've all forgotten*. The Department of Energy wishes you four people to be unavailable for comment in July, to make sure this old story doesn't just *happen* to come up again. Is that clear?"

There were four murmured "Yes, sirs."

Quisenberry stood up and examined a piece of paper on the principal's desk. "Since I don't believe you, I'm going to make absolutely sure that there's no way any of our beloved media can reach you four when the time comes to dedicate SACGEN II. You've each submitted an essay to win a trip to Greece this summer." His face darkened. "Congratulations. You all win. You are going to Theamelpos, Greece, whether you like it or not." And his last sentence was merely a snarl. "Have a nice trip!"

Sean almost broke his neck turning to look at Raymond. His English partner's eyes were glazed over, and great tears were running down his cheeks. His whole body quivered.

Mr. Hyatt blew up at Raymond. "I don't want any argument! I can't believe you! You've been caught outright! Now, take your punishment like a man!"

Raymond nodded vigorously, but the tears kept coming.

The principal stood up. "And don't try to get out of it! The airline reservations have already been made in your names!"

Raymond began to bawl out loud.

"Oh, get out of my office! You're blubbering all over my shag carpeting!"

"Don't worry, Ray," said Steve once they were out in the hall. "It won't be so bad. Honest. Don't cry."

"You're so stupid, Cementhead!" Raymond exploded. "I'm not crying! I'm *crying! Jardine is going to Theamelpos!*" Delirious, he hugged Sean, Steve, Ashley, and a very startled janitor who happened to be passing by.

Steve shook his head. "Ray, you're a great guy, and because of what we've been through together, we're friends for life. But sometimes you can be pretty weird."

Sean's grin was positively idiotic, just from watching Raymond's celebration.

"We're going to the mall to get something to eat," Ashley said. "You guys want to come with us?"

But Raymond was already propelling himself at breakneck speed down the hall.

"Not today, Ashley. See you tomorrow," Sean replied, and took off after Raymond.

He found his friend digging through the garbage can near his locker, head down, hurling refuse in all directions. "I can't believe it!" came his muffled voice. "Some slob threw garbage on my phrase book! Ah! Here it is." He came up with *2001 Useful Phrases in Modern Swedish*, and scraped half a jelly doughnut from the back cover. "*Jag tycker om din simskostym, Jolanda* — 'That's a lovely bathing suit you're wearing, Jolanda.' "

Sean was so happy for Raymond that he couldn't

stop laughing. "All right, Raymond!" he gasped. "You're going to Theamelpos. I want you to promise right now that there isn't going to be another word about how you have no luck! Come on! Say it!"

Raymond's smile would have lit up the eastern seaboard. "Delancey, the way Jardine feels right now, I swear I'll never complain about anything again as long as I live!"

Just then the p.a. system cracked to life. "Your attention, please. This is Coach Stryker. This announcement concerns those students who signed up for the varsity ice hockey team."

The smile on Raymond's face faded to zero. "How'd he find out about that?"

"Would you all please see me in the next few days regarding equipment and uniforms. And make sure you all get a mimeographed copy of our upcoming practice schedule."

"Hah!" grinned Raymond. "Jardine wins again!" He gestured toward his foot. "I can't play! I have a broken ankle, thank God! You, Delancey — *you* have to play as punishment for almost blowing Theamelpos for Jardine! But I'm in a cast until January twenty-sixth!"

Coach Stryker's voice was heard again. "Oh, yes, our first game will be January twenty-seventh."

Raymond checked the calendar on his watch, then looked down at his cast. "So much for not having to play." Then he threw his head back and stared accusingly up at the ceiling.

"That's right. . . ."

About the Author

GORDON KORMAN says the luckless Raymond Jardine is one of his all-time favorite characters. "I used to feel a lot like Raymond," he says, "as if there were a mysterious force in the sky, making sure everything went wrong for me."

One thing went right for Gordon Korman: His first book was published when he was thirteen years old. He has now published twelve books for young readers, among them *This Can't Be Happening at Macdonald Hall!*, *Our Man Weston*, *Don't Care High*, and *Son of Interflux* (a YASD Best Book for Young Adults).

Korman is a native of Ontario, Canada, and was graduated from New York University's School of Dramatic Writing in 1985. He divides his time between Toronto and New York City, and writes full-time.

point®

Other books you will enjoy,
about real kids like you!